The Cats of the Castle

Book One: Quest for the Key

Bart Scott

Theme Park Press
www.ThemeParkPress.com

© 2016 Bart Scott

No part of this publication may be reproduced, distributed, or transmitted in any form or by any means, including photocopying, recording, or other electronic or mechanical methods, without the prior written permission of the publisher, except for brief quotations embodied in critical reviews and certain other noncommercial uses permitted by copyright law.

Although every precaution has been taken to verify the accuracy of the information contained herein, no responsibility is assumed for any errors or omissions, and no liability is assumed for damages that may result from the use of this information.

Theme Park Press is not associated with the Walt Disney Company.

The views expressed in this book are those of the author and do not necessarily reflect the views of Theme Park Press.

Theme Park Press publishes its books in a variety of print and electronic formats. Some content that appears in one format may not appear in another.

Editor: Bob McLain
Layout: Artisanal Text

ISBN 978-1-68390-029-0
Printed in the United States of America

Theme Park Press | www.ThemeParkPress.com
Address queries to bob@themeparkpress.com

For Sean, my son, and for Murphy, the original cat of our castle. There'd be no Oliver without the inspiration of both.

Prologue

Missouri ~ January, 1912

Missouri winters were awful. This was the worst one yet, the boy thought as he pulled his threadbare brown coat closer to his body. Even winter in Chicago hadn't seemed this cold. Surely it wasn't this wet. The blizzard had started around supper time the night before and hadn't stopped since. Snow was well over two feet high on the ground in some places. White drifts shaped like waves on the ocean were collecting against the houses along his route. A thin boy of just barely ten, with a newsboy cap pulled down over his brown hair, he trudged along dutifully in the dark, straining his eyes to make out the numbers of the houses along the street through the falling snow and sleet.

Only a few minutes outside in the wet, heavy snowfall and he was soaked to the bone, which only made the cold feel even worse. His old canvas bag full of newspapers felt like he was lugging a load of bricks. The strap dug into his shoulder, making it ache with each step. He pushed his boots forward through the thick snow, already piled up higher than his shins. This might be a little easier if the sun was up, he silently complained. Of course if the sun were up he'd already be late, and he'd likely get the buckle end of his dad's belt. He just pulled his cap down to his brow and kept moving forward.

The boy carried on along his route, digging through drifts to reach the porches and carefully, quietly slide rolled-up newspapers inside each storm door. After a while, the bag was finally starting to feel a bit lighter, but there were plenty of houses left to reach before dawn. The wind was whipping at his face so hard it burned more than it chilled. Tears streamed backward to his ears where he was certain they were forming icicles on his earlobes. Why hadn't his father just stayed a carpenter, he grumbled, cursing his lot in life. He'd be happy to hold a ladder or a bucket of nails. At least it could wait until after breakfast. Not like this stupid ol' paper route.

There was a gurgle in his stomach. The hollow hunger that makes your head spin and your knees knock. He needed to hurry up. As it was, there'd only be a few minutes to wolf down some of Mother's biscuits with a bit of jam before he'd have to run off to school. Fortunately, this particular morning he had a backup plan. He felt for the lump inside his coat, reassured the little package hadn't fallen out somewhere in the snow. Recently, he'd discovered a new treat and it fast became one of his favorite things in the world. Frankfurters. His oldest brother, Herb, had come around for a visit and taken him to a ball game where the boy learned they were a popular snack. Well, frankfurters and peanuts, in fact.

His brother bought one of those *red hots* for each of them. They came stuffed in a roll with pickle relish and mustard. It was like nothing he'd ever tasted. He remembered the sweet smell of the smoke while they cooked over a fire, and how the skin popped every time he took a bite. They'd never had these funny pink sausages at home. Ever since, when he could get away with it, the boy set a few extra papers aside to sell at the train station on his way to school.

Dad didn't pay him a red cent for his hard work so it was only fair, he reasoned, that he earned a few on his own. Yesterday on his way home he'd stopped by the market in town and bought himself three franks for a nickel. The man thought it a little strange a nine year-old boy buying meat, but he said his mother had sent him. Besides, his money was as good as any adult's, wasn't it? He had ducked around the side of the shop and devoured one right away. It wasn't even cooked, but he didn't care. He came to prefer them that way. The butcher had wrapped them in brown waxy paper so he buried the other two in a drift beneath his bedroom window, packing it down tight over them. He had been grateful that morning when he slipped away to retrieve them that no raccoons had picked up the scent and made off with them in the night.

There were only a few more houses to go. Then, if he hurried he could steal a few minutes in the warm entryway of the apartment house at the end of the street. It had a hissing radiator where he could warm his hands and thaw out a little, before he had to get home. Moreover, he could enjoy his secret snack, which might have to sustain him through the morning, as he'd have to fight off his dad and brother for a biscuit. He crept up the next two porches and gingerly opened the door to slide the papers inside without making a sound. When he finished delivering the last paper he turned to walk down the three wooden steps. Without warning, his boot hit a small patch of ice under the snow. The boy felt his foot slip right out from under him. The leftover papers in his bag threw him off balance and he tumbled sideways into the air. There was no railing to grab on to. Nothing else he could do but fall.

Things went dark. And quiet. It was different from the hush of the early morning street. Suddenly the world fell deathly silent. So quiet, you could almost hear it. He was still alive; at least he was pretty sure he was. Nothing hurt. His eyes fluttered open, but he still couldn't see anything.

His face was pressed against the cold snow. The boy tried to push himself up, but his hands only sank deeper. It only took a second to realize what had happened. The tall drift that had piled up alongside the house had broken his fall, and now he was trapped inside it. He tried to get up on his knees, but that was no use either. He just sank in deeper like custard. Plus, his legs were so cold it hurt to move them very much. The rough, wet fabric of his trousers felt like it was cutting his skin.

For a moment the kid started to panic. Was he about to *drown* in snow? Well, suffocate would probably be the right word, he figured. Still, how long might it be before someone came out of that house and found him? If he was in there too long, he'd catch a bad case of frost bite at the very least. He'd heard of a fellow that had to have the tops of his ears cut off because of it. And that's when he felt something strange. A quick, warm flicking at the top of his ear.

"Hey!" he called out. "What is that? Roy, is that you? Knock it off and help me up!"

Then he heard it. A frantic sniffing sound. He knew at once it was a dog. At least he hoped it was a dog, and not a hungry coyote...or a bear. Not that they'd ever seen bears around the area, but with his current luck anything seemed possible. No, he told himself, it was probably just some stray dog that was wandering around town, looking for someplace warm. Would a dog get hungry enough to eat his ear? Suddenly he felt a similar flicking on his right side. Was there another dog? Did they think he was dead?

"Beat it," he called as loud as he could. His voice was too muffled to be heard.

He dug his forehead into the snow and rolled it side to side, trying to make some space. It wasn't much help, though. He yelled at the dogs again but there they stayed, sniffing wildly at his back. Then suddenly he felt the snow start to shake around him. No, it wasn't shaking. It was falling away, on both sides. These dogs were digging out the snow around him. He felt cold air reach his left arm between his glove and sleeve. He immediately tucked his arm in and with as much effort as he could muster, rolled himself sideways pushing down snow until he was on his back. He found himself looking straight up at the purple sky. That meant in a few minutes the sun would break over the horizon. He'd better get moving.

That's when a long black snout attached to an old white face appeared in his view. Hot breath melted the snow on his eyebrows. Its lopsided pink tongue dangled over his head. It was a Labrador, or some such thing. It was practically grinning at him, he thought. Then something started pushing at his other side, burrowing under his arm. Before he could look over, it was hoisting him up with its head. The black lab did the same, quickly sliding its muzzle under his elbow and lifting up, occasionally pushing its head against his back. In a moment he found himself sitting straight up, staring at two funny-looking dogs who'd somehow come to his rescue. The other was a shaggy yellow mutt, about the same size as the lab.

"Well, thank you," he said, not sure what the appropriate response was in such a situation. After all, he'd never been pulled out of deep snow before, let alone by animals. They weren't growling or baring any teeth. In fact, they both seemed pretty friendly. "I think I'm okay now. I sure do appreciate your help."

Then the lab stuck a paw up on his thigh and patted at it. It gave as light whimper and cocked its head. The yellow mutt started sniffing at his coat again. It gave a little whine of yearning as well.

"Oh," he said, quickly realizing what they wanted. "Smell my little snack, do ya?"

Both animals excitedly sat down, then stood back up, and then sat again expectantly. Though cold and wet, the boy couldn't help but chuckle at these two funny creatures.

"Well, alright," he said with a sigh. "I suppose it is only fair after all. I might have frozen to death stuck in that snow. At the very least I'd have caught the devil of a case of frostbite."

He reached inside his coat and pulled the brown paper package from his pocket. He unwrapped the two raw franks and his own stomach growled painfully. Still, much as it hurt to give up his treat, right was right. He tossed one frank to the black dog who snatched it in mid-air and devoured the pink meat. He held out the other to the yellow dog who took it slightly more politely. Still his teeth made short work of the skinny sausage.

"Who'd have ever thought my life would be saved by a couple of silly critters like you two?" he said with a smile. The boy reached out and scratched each dog behind the ear. They licked his frayed gloves appreciatively. Or, he thought, perhaps some of the grease had soaked into the yarn.

"Especially you," he went on, tapping the black lab's nose while its pink tongue dangled once more out the side of its mouth, "you *goofy* thing!" The dog gave a bark of approval.

"Where on earth did you two come from, anyway?" he asked. "And what are you doing out in this weather? Come to think of it, you might be asking what am I." Both animals just stared at him with their big oafish grins, tongues wagging.

"I know you can't talk. But boy it would sure be swell if you could. I sometimes dream of talking to animals. Wouldn't that be something?"

"Hey, kid," a voice called out in the darkness down the street. It was his brother Roy. "What are you doing over there? Sitting down on the job?"

"You two better go," he said to the dogs, shooing them away. "I don't want him to think I've been fooling around with a couple of strays."

"You alright, kid?" Roy called, closer now.

"I'm alright," he answered, getting to his feet. "The step was slick. I'm fine now." He looked back to where the dogs were sitting in the snow, but they were gone. He quickly looked around to see where they'd gone, but there was no sign. They hadn't even left tracks in the snow.

"I hope you're finished with your route," Roy said, finally reaching his little brother, who was futilely trying to dust snow off his trousers. "Pa will be awful sore if you ain't. You don't want that, and I don't want to hear him tanning your backside again."

"I'm done, I'm done," the boy answered. "Don't you worry about Pa...or my backside."

"Well, let's get home. The sun will be up soon. We've got just enough time to eat a quick breakfast if we're lucky."

Thankfully, Ma had a pot of hot grits and warm biscuits waiting when they got to the small family home. Pa only made a brief comment about them lollygagging. His kid sister, Ruth, made a crack about his clothes being all wet, but he reminded her it had been "snowing like a banshee" so his parents didn't get too upset. The kids inhaled their breakfast, ignoring their mother's admonishing that they'd get indigestion. Soon his belly was full and warm, and he wasn't the slightest bit upset about giving away the treat he'd been hiding. The boy grabbed his books by the door and took off down the road, following in the tracks dug out by the milk truck. The snow had quit falling, so maybe the afternoon route wouldn't be so bad.

That night, he dropped into his bed, exhausted as always from an early start, a long day at school, and then rushing to get the evening edition delivered on time. School was never much interest to the boy. Most days he couldn't say he enjoyed it any more than delivering papers. He liked staring out the window and doodling at his desk; although that day he had enjoyed the special science lesson. They learned about the planets. He was particularly impressed with the tiniest one, far, far away from Earth. It had a funny name. What was it again, he tried to remember? Oh, that's right, Pluto.

Suddenly he became aware of a strange light glowing on the wall across the dark room. He sat right up like a shot. Was it Pa? Was something the matter? There was nobody else in the tiny bedroom but Roy, and Roy was fast asleep. He looked to the window and there it was, just on the other side of the glass. An eerie yellow light bouncing up and down. He slid out of bed and crossed to the window. It almost looked like the light from a lantern, but he couldn't see anyone holding it. As he watched, it reared back slowly and started floating side to side.

The boy rubbed his eyes. This must be a dream. It was like the light was just bobbing along on the air. Like a fallen star that stopped falling a few feet short of the ground. Then it darted away, toward the front of the house. Quietly he crept out of the room and tip-toed through the house toward the front door, hoping not one of the old floorboards would creak. Through the window he could see the light now hanging around outside the front door. Its yellow glow lit up their dark porch. Then, in an instant, it went black. The light disappeared completely. Like a candle snuffed out with wet fingers.

Walt looked around to make sure nobody else was up. Ma and Pa's door was closed. He could hear his old man snoring away down the hall. He squinted hard and carefully turned the handle to the front door, just praying it wouldn't make a sound. Gently, he gave it a tug. The last thing he needed was to be caught out of bed, let alone sneaking outside in the night. Pa would tan his hide for sure. He poked his head into the cold winter air. He knew he'd better not let that door stay open long. If a breeze blew through that small house, his goose would be cooked.

There was nothing. Not a soul in sight. Nor did he see the strange glow. Did he imagine it, he wondered? Could it have been the reflection of some passerby with a light? A lost railroad worker or farmhand heading home late? About to close the door and creep back to bed, the boy happened to glance down at the porch. Now he had to be seeing things! Or else this truly was a strange dream. A few inches from his toes was a little bundle, a dark sachet about the size of an apple, tied at the top with gold string. He bent down and picked it up. It had weight, but was soft, like sugar. There was a tag attached to the string. From the moonlight reflecting off the white snow he could just make out the words written at the top:

For Walter.

"Who could've...?" he whispered, trailing off as he turned the tag over. There was more writing—some kind of poem, or limerick. It turned out he didn't have time to stand there and read it.

"*Walter Elias Disney!*" snapped the harshest whisper he'd ever heard behind him. It was Mother. "What in blazes are you doing out here? Get back in that bed before your father wakes up!"

Instinctively, he hid his hands, and the package, behind his back. He quickly made up a story that he'd thought he'd heard something on the porch, a possum or a raccoon. She apparently bought it, as she just said shut the door. The last thing they needed was some raccoon in the house. Those awful things are mean as snakes and tear up everything, she lectured. He obeyed and quickly scurried past her. Ma watched him with her hands on her hips all the way back to his bedroom, which made it harder to keep the strange package out of sight. He hopped into bed and stuffed the bundle under his pillow. He pulled the blanket over his head and waited until he was sure he heard Ma's door close again.

Young Walt was wide awake now. His imagination had been captured by the strange delivery and there was no way he was going to fall asleep anytime soon. He pulled the little package out from under the pillow. He gave the string a tug and the top came loose. Carefully, he opened it up. Even in the dark, whatever it was inside was glistening a strange shade of blue. It was so bright it didn't require a light to be seen. Walt quickly shut the bag tight again. He whipped the blanket off his head to make sure Roy was still out cold. He took another look. Whatever it was inside the bundle was shining like a million blue stars. He stuck his fingers inside. It felt like sand. A million magical granules of soft, shiny blue sand.

Walt remembered the writing on the other side of the tag. He read it once by the sparkling blue light, and then again. It didn't entirely make sense. It rhymed, but it almost seemed like some sort of instructions. Walt went over the strange words a few more times.

Because of your kindness, your wish has come true. To hear the words of the wild, a small sprinkle will do. One day the world will see kingdoms from you. Keep moving forward, you'll see that it's true.

"Well, I'll be," Walt whispered. "What on earth does that mean?"

Chapter One

It was late. The last waves of guests made their way under the train tracks and out the gates. There was always that last mob that lingered along Main Street, U.S.A., browsing the Emporium on the corner, or just perched on the curbs with an ice cream or a churro. They just weren't quite ready to leave the magic. Many would turn and stare back at the statue of Mr. Disney and Mickey, and the towers of Sleeping Beauty Castle glowing pink, purple, and blue. Beyond the castle, the crooked, snow-covered mountain called the Matterhorn reached into the night sky. They sauntered slowly past the Crystal Arcade or the Main Street Cinema. The guests' eyes twinkled like the white popcorn lights that outlined the shops along Main Street as they stared off at Adventureland to the left of the castle, wishing they could sneak in for another turn on the Jungle Cruise or search for lost treasure in the Temple of the Forbidden Eye. Or else they gazed with wonder at the rockets of Tomorrowland just to the right.

Finally, with the help of friendly, albeit exhausted cast members, the last guests shuffled out. Disneyland was finally quiet. The late-night crews could clean up, balance their tills, check ride vehicles for hats, glasses, or bags accidentally left behind. All attractions would be powered down until morning when they could make magic all over again. When Disneyland closed at night, however, not *all* the magic was turned off.

Sleeping Beauty Castle was a pink structure with blue cones atop her many towers and turrets, with pennants flying from each tip. The base of the castle was a mighty rampart of grayish stone with hints of blues and pinks, surrounded by a moat. A bridge underneath gave guests passage through the open center of the castle into a world of dreams and fairy tales called Fantasyland. From there, they could make their way to the dusty Old West streets of Frontierland.

From the highest narrow window in the center of the castle, a black-and-white cat looked down on Main Street. He was careful to hug the shadowy edge of the frame. Normally, a cat in a window wouldn't raise too many eyebrows, but one wearing a green vest might stand out a bit, even at Disneyland. In a short while, when the park dwindled down to the overnight skeleton crew of security guards, technicians, and custodians, Oliver and his companions would begin their shift as well.

He licked the black side of his paw and smoothed down a tuft of white fur on his cheek. He could see from the corner of his eye that it was sticking up a little crazy. Must've slept on that side, he thought. Not that appearance mattered most nights, as he spent much of his time avoiding being seen, but *Lilli* would be along soon.

"Ready to go, Oliver?" creaked an old voice from behind him.

Startled, the young cat turned quickly to see Thurl, oldest of the Castle Cats, and their leader. Thurl's white face with its long beard and smooshed pink nose was locked in a playful smile. His drooping purple cap which matched his robe sat crooked on his head, bending his already curled ear.

"Or would you like another minute to further beautify yourself?" Thurl continued to tease.

"No, I...um," he stammered. "I just had something in my fur." Oliver leapt down to the floor, slightly embarrassed.

"Of course." The two cats walked down the quiet castle corridor together. Thurl's walking stick click-clacked along the stone tiles of the floor. His staff, as he referred to it, was in fact a silver plastic wand with a clear ball at the top with tiny lights inside that spun wildly when a button on the side was pushed. Down the side in fading sparkly letters was "Disneyland." Once upon a time, many like it were sold on Main Street carts just before the parade and fireworks. Thurl's purple robe swept along behind him as he hobbled along. "So, my boy, what is your plan for tonight? Fantasyland first?"

"Actually, I thought I might take Adventureland and New Orleans Square tonight. I'm, uh, worried that we might not be giving them enough coverage. They are very vulnerable, you know, with all the trees and water."

"Ah, I see," said Thurl, nodding and suppressing a smile. "Not because Lilli mentioned she'd like to take Main Street, and it's likely you might bump into each other somewhere along the hub?"

"Oh, well, I mean, what? Did she say that? I suppose it is a good idea that we all, uh, mix it up. Take turns learning each land, just in case."

"Of course." Thurl smiled, then cleared his throat, seeing his young squire's discomfort, and forced his face to look somber again. "Quite right. Good thinking!" It was too much. Thurl couldn't help but chuckle.

If Oliver's face wasn't covered in black-and-white fur, he might have turned bright red. The older cat continued walking down the stone-lined hallway. Oliver took this as the signal it was time for work. He tightened the belt around his waist and patted the scabbard hanging at his hip. Oliver never left the castle without his trusted sword, even if it was a plastic souvenir from Fantasyland. He knew they weren't truly knights, but they were as close as you might find after hours in Disneyland.

They walked down a narrow stone staircase that wrapped around and around and opened out into a dimly lit parlor. This was a room few humans knew existed, and even fewer had seen. The walls were gray stone, and dark red carpet covered the floor. In the center of the room was a long wooden table surrounded by matching chairs, two on each side and one at each end, upholstered with thick burgundy cushions.

In the center of one wall hung a large, framed map of Disneyland, flanked by ornate medieval tapestries all around the room and black-and-white photos of park attractions. At the end of the room was a wide wooden door. Over it hung a plaque with an expression:

Even dreams require protecting.

No author's name was given, but Thurl knew perfectly well who first spoke those words, and to whom he said them. Below these words, carved right into the door itself, was the crest of their order. An intricate image of a cat holding a shield across which he draped the end of his cloak and crossed his sword. The cat wore a wide-brimmed hat with a plume. Over his hat, carved in English, were the words "Royal Order" and below the shield, in Latin, *Felibus et Castelli*—Cats of the Castle.

There were two other cats already waiting at the table when they stepped off the stairs. One was a stocky tabby with short silver fur lined with black stripes. He wore a black vest with silver buttons. His name was Elias. A tough veteran alley cat who bragged no rat ever escaped his claws. He was leaning back in a chair with his feet up on the table and his paws behind his head. He casually saluted Oliver, but when he noticed Thurl eyeing him, Elias leapt to his feet.

The other cat was long and lean with wild yellow fur, wearing a shabby brown cardigan sweater. Around his waist hung a tool belt with snapped pouches and a coil of rope. He had wild tufts of fur on the sides of his face and round spectacles perched on his nose. Above the thick lenses covering his eyes were multiple others of various sizes, shapes, and even colors he had invented that could be flipped down when necessary. He was holding a wide, heavy manual, flipping pages and reading rapidly, whispering the words out loud. He hadn't even noticed them come in.

"Kimball," said Thurl. The yellow cat shrieked and dropped his book.

"Oh, uh, sorry, Thurl," he stammered. "Just catching up on some light reading I found in the library this morning. History of the Linear Induction Motor. It's really very fascinating."

"Sounds riveting," Elias sneered. "Should be a big help if a possum tries to sneak over the gates with a linear induction motor vehicle."

"I'll have you know that at the Florida property, linear induction motors revolutionized theme parks," Kimball began to lecture. "Not to mention, our own California Screamin' right next door."

"*Guys*," said Oliver stepping forward, "let's not do this tonight. Save the energy for the park."

"Yes, sir," said Elias sarcastically. "I guess I missed the meeting where we elected you king of the castle."

"Knock it off," Oliver said, shooting him a look. "I'm not trying to be king. We have a duty and all you two seem to do is bicker."

"Oliver is right," said Thurl. "I think you should all head off as soon as possible. There's a strange moon in the sky. A nearly full moon, in fact. Those almost always lead to strange events, especially here."

"What, like werewolves and such?" Elias asked skeptically.

"You'd do well to hope not," said Thurl.

"No, he's right," Kimball interjected. "In the human world, hospitals, police departments, all sorts of professions report the full moon as resulting in greater incidents of unusual and unexplained...."

"Kimball," Oliver stopped him. "What do you mean, Thurl?"

"Vermin, gate crashers, malfunctioning machinery," Thurl explained. "Even inexplicable occurrences within the attractions. Strange sounds and voices in the dark. Attractions reported as turned off suddenly operating. Even audio-animatronic characters operating on their own."

"Well, that's creepy," Elias quipped.

"Now Thurl, animatronics just *coming to life*," said Kimball doubtfully. "With all due respect, that doesn't seem scientifically possible."

"I'm simply saying prepare for anything tonight. That would be an extreme example. But I've seen extreme before. Just exercise great caution. I expect you all home safe in the morning."

"Speaking of," said Elias, "Aren't we missing somebody?" He cast a taunting look at Oliver. "Where's Princess Fancy Pants? Did you scare her off, Romeo?"

"I'm sorry," came a female voice from the stairwell, "who is that you're asking about?"

Lilli appeared in the doorway. Lean, tan fur with brown ears and twinkling blue eyes. She wore a long lavender tunic belted at her waist, the hood draped across her shoulders. Oliver felt like he'd swallowed a live butterfly. She raised her paw and with a flick, extended all five claws, staring directly at Elias.

"I don't believe I know any *Princess Fancy Pants*," she said. "I'm sure you must be thinking of someone else."

"Alright, then," Thurl said tapping his staff on the map. "It's time. Elias, you're on Frontierland, Rivers of America, and the outskirts of Critter Country."

"Whatever you say, boss."

"Just remember," Thurl cautioned, looking directly at Elias, "stay away..."

"...*from Splash Mountain*," Elias finished his sentence. "I know. I know."

"It's simply easier to avoid possible confrontation. If there were any problems there, well, they'd be taken care of without our intervention."

"Yeah, well," Elias muttered, cracking the knuckles in his front paws. "It would be nice to have some real action around here sometime, besides just chasing off mice."

"Kimball, I want you to cover Tomorrowland," Thurl said, ignoring Elias. "Don't forget to make regular rounds of the Autopia track."

"Excellent," said Kimball, pushing his glasses up. "From the monorail track I can maintain a bird's-eye view of the entire land."

"Oliver will be patrolling Adventureland and New Orleans Square," the old cat said, sliding his staff across the map.

"Yes, Thurl," said Oliver dutifully, suppressing a smile.

"Yes, sir," Elias whispered mockingly. Oliver shot him a dirty look. Elias had always given Oliver a hard time since he'd joined them a few years before. It seemed to never sit right with Elias that Thurl had seemingly taken an immediate shine to the scrappy black-and-white kitten the day he wandered into the park.

"Finally, Lilli," Thurl said loudly, "Fantasyland and Mickey's Toontown are your domain tonight. Don't forget the Story Land Canal Boats."

"No, of course not," she nodded. "Those model castles along the river would be a good place for small intruders to hide."

"More importantly, it seems a family of moles has made the Storybook Land flower bed their new home. Their tunneling is tearing up the red flowers. It falls on you to convince them to move on."

"Oh, no, *not moles*," Elias joked. "What next, shrews?!"

"Elias," Thurl snapped. "Be grateful our current battles are light. We are fortunate. In my day, the Cats of the Castle encountered some strange and terrible forces, far more dangerous than vermin or trespassing teenagers. Were I you, I would happily chase away moles and rats the rest of my days."

"I'll take care of it, Thurl," Lilli added, watching Elias shrink in his chair like a child who'd been scolded for breaking something in the Emporium.

"Very well, you all have your assignments," Thurl continued. "Remember, keep to the shadows. Hug the edges of the streets and buildings. Stay safe."

The four younger cats nodded and lined up dutifully in front of the large wooden door. Thurl reached up with his staff and pushed back on a wall sconce. There was a muffled *clank* inside the wall and the heavy door swung softly out into the night. The cool night air filled the room. Below, the castle moat lay still, the fountains all turned off. There was a familiar bubbling under the water and five wide, flat stones rose up above the surface.

"Oh, and one more thing," Thurl said, lowering his staff in front of the group to keep them from exiting, "Oliver, Lilli, it wouldn't hurt for each of you to take a quick stroll up and down Main Street periodically. The night watchmen usually have it covered, but then again, we are here to see what they don't."

"Oh, um, sure," said Oliver. He looked at Lilli who shrugged and nodded. "Good idea."

Thurl winked at him and lowered his staff.

"Excuse me, Thurl," Kimball interjected. "I'll be in Tomorrowland so really checking out Main Street would be no prob…"

"Kimball," Thurl said, "your concern is that Autopia track. It's a lot of ground to cover."

"Yeah, don't worry, Kimball," Oliver said. "We can handle it."

The Castle Cats leapt down and each quickly made their way across the stones and into the park, heading off toward their assigned lands. The stones slowly sunk back below the dark water and the heavy door swung closed without a sound. The spot where it opened once again appeared as part of the solid wall around the castle.

Thurl remained behind. His days of running around the park at night were long behind him. Thurl was very old—unusually old for a cat. He often joked he was in the autumn of his ninth life. But then, like the others, Thurl was no ordinary feline. He shuffled across the room to where his favorite picture hung. It was a black-and-white photograph of the castle from the outside. Emerging from the center archway on the backside, as if heading for a stroll through Fantasyland, was none other than Walt Disney. It had been taken early one morning, before the park gates had opened. The street below his feet was still wet, and an empty Main Street and the Disneyland Railroad station were just a blur in the background. Walt wore a cardigan and a striped shirt, instead of his usual suit. It was a famous shot that had since been used on everything from postcards to coffee mugs. That morning he'd been taking a stroll through the park—*inspecting*, most people assumed.

The truth, however, was only revealed in this particular photo hanging in the cats' secret castle chamber. This was not just another print, but the original, untouched photo. It had been altered in every public print; but in this version, just as the photographer had seen when he snapped the candid shot, Walt was not alone. Bounding alongside his shin was a lean, black cat with a white face. He had a funny strip of black fur along the white of his chin. The cat looked up at him, mouth open. Any humans who saw it might assume it was a stray begging for food. In truth, they were deep in conversation. That cat's name was Mr. Lincoln, the very first Cat of the Castle.

Walt named him that. He'd been discovered sleeping inside a crate of extra suits and spare parts for an Abraham Lincoln animatronic. The box had been shipped back to California from the New York World's Fair where the figure had premiered in 1964. One of Walt's Imagineers, the name he gave the men who helped him create all the wonderful attractions at

Disneyland, had tried to shoo the stray away with his jacket. Walt ordered him to stop. He was tickled by the cat's "strap beard."

"Just like Mr. Lincoln himself," Walt said with a grin, scratching the purring cat behind the ear.

The cat gave him an idea. He remembered his days of touring two-bit amusement parks around the country years ago, as he was dreaming up a grand theme park of his own. One thing he could never stand was seeing rats and roaches in a park. They'd scurry between guests' ankles or hang around the garbage cans scavenging for food. Nasty, disease-carrying critters, Walt used to snarl with one eyebrow raised. No respect for what was a properly designated bathroom, and what wasn't. There were many aspects of a theme park he could control, but pests he wasn't sure about. Until that day he met Mr. Lincoln.

The poor stowaway cat was weak and hungry from the journey. It couldn't even muster the strength to run off. Walt scooped him up and placed him in a box lined with packing blankets.

"Say, somebody fetch some water and a shallow saucer," Walt called out. "And a can of tuna. This poor fella's starving. Imagine being cooped up in that crate all the way from New York."

The Imagineers scratched their heads, but Walt was the boss so somebody did run off to the commissary and returned with the order. The cat lapped up the water, and as soon as a small plate with a lump of tuna was presented, ravenously devoured it. Pleased, Walt put the box in the back seat of his car and drove off without so much as a goodbye. He wasn't headed home where some thought he might be planning to surprise his wife with the cat. Instead, he drove to Disneyland. He carried Mr. Lincoln's box from his private parking spot and through a backstage area, taking one of the many secret paths he designed when Disneyland was built. This one wound its way around and through the Jungle Cruise, crossing stepping stones and hidden footpaths before ending up at the back stairs to his secret apartment above the firehouse. Once inside, Walt set the box down on a red couch in the living room. The cat popped its head up over the side, looking around curiously. Walt took a seat in an adjacent chair with pale blue cushions.

"There you are, Mr. Lincoln," he said. "Hope you don't mind my naming you. I'm sure you have some name of your own, but of course I don't speak cat any more than you speak human. Figured I ought to have some sort of a name to call you by. Seems rude to just call you *cat*. Why, I can't stand to be called Mister, and I suppose that's about the same thing."

The cat sat there staring at him. Its green eyes seemed to be studying this strange human in the chair across from him. Walt chuckled at the animal's perplexed expression. The creature was surely all mixed-up after a rough journey from New York in a crate to this apartment suite. And now here was some crazy human talking at it. Walt put his hands behind his head and laced his fingers together.

"You know," he said, "we ought to do more with cats. We haven't been too kind to your species, now have we? We did ol' Pete, and he wasn't too nice of a fellow. Then of course there were those two awful Siamese cats in *Lady*. And that Cheshire fellow, although he's not actually mine. Had to license him from the Carroll estate. I should have my boys work up something new. Some kind of picture that shows cats in a more likeable light. What do you think?"

Mr. Lincoln sneezed and shook his head, as if he had a fly in his ear.

"You haven't got the foggiest idea what I'm saying," Walt chuckled. Then his eyebrow went up, as an idea sparked in his brain. "There is something we could do about that. If you don't mind, of course."

Walt crossed the room to a small desk with a locked roll-top. He fumbled with a ring of keys until he found the right one and opened up the desk. Inside were some framed photos of Walt's daughters, as well as some awards and a little statue of Mickey. He pushed one of the frames aside. From behind it he removed a wooden box, which had been smoothed and varnished. Atop the lid was a carving of Tinker Bell, the magical fairy from *Peter Pan*. There was a lock on the box as well. He found another key, this one quite tiny and made of brass, and turned it inside the little lock.

Walt looked back at the cat. It was now sitting on the couch, watching him intently. No doubt its imagination had been captured at the sound of all those jingling keys.

"I was thinking maybe we might have a conversation," Walt said. "A *real* conversation."

From out of the box he gently removed a purple pouch, tied at the top with a gold string. The faded tag hanging from the ribbon still read *For Walter*. He slid his thumb and finger inside quickly then tightened the top again and placed the bag back in the box. Walt crossed back over to the couch where the cat was waiting.

"Now I promise this won't hurt at all," he said. "Taffy, err, that's my dog—she said it feels like a tickle." He slowly raised his hand out flat. Then he blew hard like blowing out a candle on a birthday cake. As he did a cloud of sparkly blue dust billowed up into the cat's face. Annoyed, Mr. Lincoln shook his head angrily and twitched his ears, giving multiple irritated sneezes.

"Oh, now, I know it's a little strange," Walt said with a smile, "but just give it a moment. See, I promised it wouldn't hurt."

"*What was that stuff?*" the cat suddenly demanded. Its green eyes went wide and it reared back as if being sprayed with a hose. He clapped a paw over his muzzle. Walt erupted with laughter.

"Did...?" Mr. Lincoln spoke again. "Did I...did you? Can you understand me?!?"

"I certainly can," Walt smiled. "It's quite something isn't it? Pixie dust—blue pixie dust to be precise. Enables humans and animals, well, and fairies, to communicate."

Mr. Lincoln felt his legs straightening out and he sat up straight on the couch, his head lifted squarely between his shoulders.

"I should mention it also imbues animals like yourself with more human characteristics. Anthropomorphizes is the word, I'm told, like we do in our cartoons. But don't worry; you won't become one of us nasty humans. You get to keep your more innocent animal sensibilities. It's perfectly safe!"

"Why did you give it to me?" the cat asked. "Come to think of it, how do you even have something like that? Are you one of these...picks...picks-sees?"

Walt bellowed again. "No, not at all! Just a man like you. Well, you know what I mean. It's a long story, but suffices to say it was gifted to me a long time ago. It's very special. There's only that one bag so I have to use it sparingly."

"I don't understand this," the cat said, examining his arms and paws which had formed stubby little fingers.

"If you don't like it, there are ways to turn you back," said Walt. "You can just be a regular old cat again in no time."

"No, it's alright," said Mr. Lincoln. He shook his legs. "I'm just wondering, why use it on me?"

"Well, now, about that," Walt began. "I was just thinking, you need a home here in California. I've got this big park with plenty of room. You'd have to stay out from under the guests' feet during the day, but by night you'd have the run of the place. There's just one thing I need, and you might just be the cat who can help."

That evening Walt Disney explained that the only thing he feared could ruin his beautiful new park was the one threat his human watchmen couldn't see. Vermin. Scavengers. All the little night creatures that gnawed and scratched and left messes everywhere. The sort that a cat was naturally inclined to deal with properly.

"You want me to catch the mice?" Mr. Lincoln asked.

"Oh, no, not mice," Walt specified, raising his hand. "They won't be a problem. I've made a special arrangement with the mice. Built them their own wonderful little city on some property I own. You really ought to see it, an entire miniature community with modern technology just for mice. Sort of an experimental mouse city of tomorrow. Need a better name for it. I just felt this place was built by a mouse. Not accommodating them just seemed, oh, I don't know, hypocritical."

Mr. Lincoln accepted Walt's offer to patrol the park at night. However it was indeed a gargantuan place for one cat to cover. It didn't take long for him to recruit a few other strays that'd been poking around the fences of Disneyland. He brought them to Walt, who approved of the idea. He sprinkled each with a pinch of pixie dust and called them the Disneyland cats. Still, he thought, one cat was fine, but Mrs. Disney wouldn't be in favor of four cats living in the family apartment. He set about designing a special home for them within Sleeping Beauty Castle. The builders asked what the secret rooms were for, but he just said that he was the boss and he wanted them. When the chambers were finished, Walt furnished them himself and gathered the cats under the castle.

"This is your new home," he smiled with a flourish of his arm. He held out a plastic toy sword and gently tapped each cat on the ear. "I now dub thee, the Royal Order of Cats of the Castle."

Walt only alerted a few of his closest Imagineers as to the cats' presence or why he was making strange requests, like tiny doors and tunnels here or there. The Imagineers, who had come to expect the unexpected from this magical man, didn't even question. They designed the meeting parlor, a library, and the hidden exit within the castle. The cats were not only great at keeping rats out of the park, but also at finding late night trespassers. It was a common occurrence for some bold youngster (and not always so young) to want to see what happened inside the walls after hours, or try to steal a free ride on an E ticket attraction, the most popular rides in the park. Not only was it dangerous, but their clumsiness and lack of knowledge about the complex ride systems could lead to serious damage, both to themselves and the attractions. The cats were good at sniffing them out, and Walt had secret knee-level triggers installed in clandestine locations throughout the park. They could be easily activated by paw or nose with little pressure and would sound alarms in the security office. The guards would arrive shortly, assuming the intruder had triggered the alarm.

Walt had warned that it was best they stay out of sight as much as possible, particularly while the park was open. On occasion one might be spotted, so the cats adopted the practice of quickly dropping to all fours, trying to appear like normal cats, and disappear as quickly as possible. The cats would prowl through the park at night, and sleep most of the day, as cats tend to do. It was just safer if they stayed inside the castle walls, leaving the daytime protection of the park to the humans. It worked well, most of the time.

Thurl leaned on his staff, needing its support more these days. He'd lived an unusually long life, no doubt due to that magical, mysterious blue glitter that made them as they were. But lately, with each passing day, he felt himself growing weary. His days leading the Cats of the Castle were winding down and he understood it. He only wanted to be sure the order would carry on without him.

"Oh, Walt," he sighed. "I am tired. Soon I will have to pass my leadership on to another cat. I am putting my hopes in that youngster, Oliver. What do you think?"

The photograph remained unchanged. In it, Mr. Disney was looking off at something to his right. Mr. Lincoln continued to look-up. Thurl never had asked what they were discussing. He wished he knew. He also wished he were a younger cat again. He quietly yearned to be back out on patrol with his fellow felines. Tasting the night air, leaping between walls and rails, ducking under tracks. Feeling the thrill of chasing down some red-eyed scavenger. Some nights the dangers were greater than others. Even now, something felt different tonight. Something strange. Slowly, Thurl climbed the stone staircase, returning to his room inside one of the castle's towers.

"Stop worrying, old cat," he mumbled softly. "They'll be fine. Just the coming full moon, I'm sure."

Chapter Two

Two hours later Oliver decided things were quiet enough in Adventureland and New Orleans Square, and that he should make a quick loop around Main Street, the entryway to all the magic and wonder of Disneyland. As Thurl had once explained it, this was Walt's ideal version of a small American town square, patterned after the town where he was raised—some place called Marceline. The entire thoroughfare was lined with wonderful shops and restaurants and attractions, all brightly lit, colorfully decorated, and exciting to the eye. It was a straight street up the center of the park from the train station ending at a circular boulevard, in the center of which stood the Partners statue. There was never really a need to assign one cat to the territory. Not to mention it could also be dicey for a cat to spend too much time on Main Street, even at night, as it was well-lit and there weren't many places to hide from human eyes.

Oliver had few memories of his days as a kitten, before he followed his hungry belly and squeezed under a fence along Harbor Boulevard, picking up some sweet smell on the air. The only bits of the human world he remembered were dark, asphalt and concrete lots and buildings that stretched to the sky. Lots of cars speeding down streets, belching smoke and fumes. It was nothing like the beautiful world he lived in now. Maybe it was those dark, fuzzy memories that made him take his job here so seriously. Oliver never cared to see the human world beyond Main Street, U.S.A. again.

Oliver crept from Adventureland, leaving palm leaves and soft rhythmic jungle drums behind, past the Partners statue of Walt and the main mouse and followed the curve to the street. To his left he could see the blue-and-gold torpedo-shaped rockets of the Astro Orbiter, the attraction that welcomed guests at the gates of Tomorrowland. They were docked along the bottom, under a revolving collection of planets and moons and stars, waiting to fly again tomorrow. Somewhere in there, Kimball was no doubt loving life, as he always did patrolling his beloved flashy, futuristic environment. Kimball was obsessed with human technology as well as fantasy—Tomorrowland was the perfect combination of both.

Oliver looked in every direction, making sure there weren't any humans in sight. He darted across the street quickly until he reached a building on the corner with a cone-shaped roof and long pink awning leading to the front door. An iron archway held a pink sign that read Plaza Inn. Oliver stealthily crossed under the sign, slipped past numerous outdoor tables with pink umbrellas. This would be a prime location for rats to go sniffing around. Lots of food scraps, uneaten corners of sandwiches, and plenty of dropped chicken fingers (the very idea turned Oliver's stomach—he couldn't even imagine what the poor chickens looked like before the fingers were cut off). There were ends of ice cream cones, bits of macaroni and cheese, and runaway grapes that rolled off children's' plates. In fact, any given day at the Plaza could be a scavenger's jackpot as some exhausted parent in search of a table might trip and lose an entire tray of food. The temptation of scattered French fries would be more than any rodent could resist.

Oliver quickly made for the window and stretched as high on his back paws as he could reach. It was dark inside. Only the lights of Main Street shined inside. Oliver's green eyes darted this way and that. All looked in order. No hint of movement in the shadows, nor under the tables, or around the counters. The Plaza looked clear.

The cat shrugged. Maybe Thurl's weird feeling about tonight was wrong. Maybe this would be just another quiet night in the park. He followed the sidewalk until he reached a courtyard. Oliver walked around the horseshoe-shaped alley. In the center was a cart full of flower arrangements. Thurl had been right about one thing tonight, he thought. The truth was, the only movement Oliver hoped to catch sight of wasn't that of rats. Oliver had hoped he might *accidentally* bump into Lilli. Sadly, there had been no sign of her, either.

"What would I say, anyway?" Oliver wondered aloud. *"Hi Lilli, want to share a churro?"*

Oliver was about to pop back out onto Main Street when he heard voices. Just as he turned his head he saw two men walking in his direction. They were wearing black hats, just like policemen, and blue short-sleeved shirts with shiny badges over the left side. On the right, each wore a white, oval name tag like all Disneyland cast members. These were Disneyland security officers. One was tall and broad with black sideburns peeking out under his hat and five o'clock shadow on his cheeks. Oliver had seen him many times. His name was Pete.

The other officer was one Oliver hadn't seen before. He was not so tall. In fact, he was nearly a full cat shorter than his partner. His body more closely resembled one of the pickle barrels at the snack stand in Adventureland. His slick red hair was stringy and plastered against his head with sweat. Even the thin, fuzzy mustache across his lip looked sweaty. Panic stricken, Oliver ducked behind the flower cart. Hopefully they'd pass by.

Unfortunately for Oliver, right at the entrance to the courtyard was the Market House coffee shop and bakery. It looked like a three-story

Victorian house with a flat green front and long brown walls along the sides. Outside it stood a handful of metal tables. The place had grown more popular in recent months, ever since they'd added a tiny green-and-white picture of a mermaid on the wall. The cats thought perhaps she was a patron saint of coffee. Market House would also be a primo target for pests. Lots of sweets—sticky buns and donuts and such. At that particular moment, it appeared to be a popular spot for Disneyland security, as well. Oliver heard metal legs scraping across bricks as they each pulled out a chair. The two men were taking a break right at the mouth of the courtyard. He was stuck.

"Great," Oliver whispered, slapping a paw over his face. "Now what?"

"What a crazy night already," Pete, the tall guard, said with a chuckle. He dropped his heavy flash light onto the metal table with a resounding *clang*.

"I'll say," said the shorter, barrel-shaped guard. "I caught three of the biggest rats I ever saw diggin' through a trash can. Well, I didn't *catch* them. I ran after 'em, but they got away. What are you gonna do? They're rats. They have four legs. I've got two."

"And a few more pounds to carry," the tall guard joked.

"Hey, that's not cool Pete. I'm just stocky."

"Alright, Louie, take it easy," said Pete, patting his own belly which was far from firm. "I'm just giving you a hard time. You'll walk those extra pounds off in no time around here."

"Anyway I chased them all the way to New Orleans Square, but then I lost sight of 'em at the Haunted Mansion."

"Yeah, well, if they got into the mansion, we'd never find them anyway," said Pete. He looked at his wristwatch. "Eh, it should be locked up tight by now. They ain't getting in there."

"I should still notify operations," said Louie. "They'll want to send an exterminator through just in case. I'm telling you, Pete, I've seen some rats in my day, but these were huge. I swear, one of 'em winked at me as they ran off."

"I wouldn't worry about rats. We've got contingencies in place."

"What do you mean?"

"Eh, it's complicated." Pete waved him off. His eyes locked on something off in the distance, across Main Street. "Technical stuff. This place thinks of everything. Been like that ever since Walt built it. But you know, I'm thinking maybe you better make a call to the Department of Wildlife."

"For rats?" Louie asked, confused.

"Nope," Pete said, scooping up his flashlight again. "For that big raccoon clawing its way up the side of the Emporium. Come on!"

He stood up quick, pointing down Main Street. Louie followed just in time to see a thick bushy-striped tail vanish around the corner of the massive souvenir store. Pete was already in pursuit, shining his flashlight across the building.

"So, no break then?" Louie asked, as he huffed and puffed trying to catch up.

Relieved, Oliver appeared from around the crates of flowers. *Rats*, he thought. Better head back toward New Orleans Square. That was his territory. He could let the humans deal with the raccoon. He was off to the Haunted Mansion.

A few minutes later, Oliver slinked his way through New Orleans Square, keeping close to the shadows. It wasn't hard, as New Orleans Square tended to be rather dark at night, with the winding narrow street surrounded on both sides by tall Colonial buildings. He could barely make out the writing on the signs hanging over the shops. Oliver ran through quickly.

At the end of New Orleans Square stood two brick pedestals on which hung bronze plaques reading "The Haunted Mansion." These held up the black iron gates of the entrance, and just beyond them a concrete walk with an inlaid pattern of red brick led past a white funeral carriage whose reins hung around a phantom horse. Oliver followed the path toward the tall house with its four white columns and green iron arches. As he approached the tall square antebellum house, Oliver could just see Splash Mountain glowing an eerie orange in the distance between the tall pines. He thought of Thurl's nightly warning to stay away from that place. As an empty log plummeted down the falls, it gave Oliver a shiver even more than the one he had approaching this haunted manor.

In a garden just to the left of the mansion was a cemetery. Many graying stone monuments stood among the moss and shrubs in honor of departed animals. There was a pig, a skunk, even a fat toad on a pedestal. Apparently, the family that lived in the mansion had a wide array of pets. Of course there was a dog; some tall, lean canine with floppy ears—probably a hunting breed, Oliver imagined. It was carved sitting in eternal obedience with a basket of flowers clenched in its teeth. Oliver's lip curled and he couldn't stop a hiss from escaping at the sight of the mutt. He slipped under the guardrail and sat down in the grass before what all Castle Cats referred to simply as *the shrine*.

It was a white statue of a fluffy cat sitting stoically on a pedestal. It was encircled by five small statues of birds looking up respectfully, as they should. Oliver did not know this feline's story, nor did any living Cat of the Castle as far as he was aware. Even Thurl said he did not know the truth behind this monument, and perhaps only the Oracle knew for sure. Whoever this cat had been, he or she was important enough to memorialize here so visiting humans might pay their respects. Oliver hoped his visitation would garner some feline favor as he entered the Haunted Mansion.

Oliver stood again, and made his way to the door. He was surprised to discover it had been left slightly ajar. Very unusual for this time of night. Maybe the cleaning crew was still inside. Oliver poked his head in but saw no one inside the dark vestibule. Dim candles flickered on the walls and a large chandelier alternated between bright and dim. Still, not a single soul was to be found. No people. No rats.

Oliver slipped inside the dark entryway. Slow, haunting organ music was being piped into the air. Oliver shivered. Why would there still be music playing? That's when Oliver noticed a strange opening in the wall. Two heavy wooden doors hadn't quite been slid together. He crossed the red carpet and peered into the narrow space. He could see more flickering candlelight inside a circular room; candles held by grotesque bronze gargoyles. Oliver put his shoulder against the edge of one door and pushed with all his might, digging his back claws into the floor and using his tail for leverage. With a grunt, he felt it slide another inch or two. It was enough, at least for a cat. He took a deep breath, sucking in his stomach and slid through the opening.

This unusual antechamber had eight individual walls. Paintings of humans hung all around him. It was the weirdest art Oliver had ever seen. The details were hard to make out in the dim orange glow. There was a grandmotherly woman with a faint smile, clutching a rose. She was sitting on what looked like one of the pedestals from the garden outside; a gray rectangular affair, but with a man's head sculpted at the bottom. Something was stuck to his head. A strange hat, Oliver thought, with an axe handle? There was a portrait of a gentleman in a suit coat and striped shorts standing atop a barrel. A candle had been painted in front of him, which Oliver thought seemed dangerously close to burning a piece of string hanging near it. There was a name on the barrel but the candle obscured part of it. All Oliver could see was DYNA...someone.

In another painting, a young lady in a lovely lavender-and-white dress holding a pink parasol stood poised on a fraying rope. Apparently she was as agile as Lilli, too. He scratched at his whiskers. The rest of the painting was bothersome. Again, it was hard to tell as he was only a third as tall as most humans, and the walls in this room were pretty high—in fact, they almost seemed to have been stretched, but there appeared to be the tip of some animal's nose under her feet. It seemed long and rounded, with sharp teeth. Probably another awful dog, Oliver figured, although in this light the snout looked almost green. Some people just didn't have good taste when choosing a pet, he shrugged. There was no more time for studying artwork. Oliver had to search for those rodents.

The room had no doors. Not even a window. There had to be a secret panel somewhere. Oliver was sure of it. After all, the Haunted Mansion was a ride. There had to be some way to get guests to the load area to board the vehicles. Oliver turned around in circles, eyeing every space of wall. Then just over his shoulder he caught a glimmer of passing light. There it was—a fracture of space between two of the panels—although after close examination, even calling it a sliver might be kind. This was going to be difficult, even for a cat. Fortunately, Oliver carried a sword. He pulled the toy saber from his belt. Elias often teased him, saying it was useless. It might be a toy, Oliver thought, but it came in quite handy from time to time, especially in dealing with surly possums and other critters. Plus, he just felt cool wearing it. They were after all a Royal Order, just like knights of old. Mr. Disney had said so himself.

The plastic blade was wide and flat, but thin enough that Oliver was able to slide it right between the wall panels. With no small effort, he pushed it like a lever until he was certain he felt the wall start to slide. That's it, he thought. Just one more. He pushed hard and felt the handle smack against the wall.

"That must've done it," Oliver said. Then he examined the panel, which hadn't moved an inch. It hadn't been the wall he felt giving way; it was his sword. It wasn't made to be used as a door lever. The plastic was completely bent. He twisted his sword out of the space. It was ruined.

"Aw, hairballs," he whispered. "Seriously?"

Oliver threw the newly L-shaped sword aside and started working his paws into the tiny gap. Just as before, he wedged his shoulder against the panel and pushed with everything he had. Slowly, the panel did start to inch sideways, little by little. It took a few minutes of Oliver digging his toe claws into the carpet and grunting and moaning, but he finally managed to slide it open enough to fit his shoulder through. Now he was pushing with his whole body until, *pop*, he slipped through into another room. Oliver followed the long narrow chamber. To his left, curtained windows showed flashes of lightning. To his right hung a series of portraits. There was a ship at sea, an old-time military man atop a horse, all of which changed to reveal a new ghastly incarnation of the picture with each lightning flash. His favorite was a woman with long dark hair lying on a chaise lounge. When the lightning struck, she transformed into a giant cat. Who could she be, Oliver wondered? Was she the mysterious cat memorialized in stone outside? Kimball once hypothesized she was some mythical goddess that might one day unite cat and man as the two dominant species on Earth. Once humans caught up, of course.

Oliver chuckled at the ropes that were strung between random poles in the floor. It was like some sort of maze, except it just went back and forth. Seemed like the species that created this wondrous park and all these attractions could have come up with a better maze.

Oliver's thoughts were interrupted by the realization that unlike the other rooms, this one wasn't quiet. There was a constant hum and the floor was vibrating. He ran to the edge of a short wall that ran the length of the ropes. At the end, it revealed a moving floor. This was the loading room. Black carriages with high rounded backs called Doom Buggies carried guests deep into the mansion's hidden world of mischievous ghosts and unsettled spirits. The problem was, they weren't supposed to be running at this time of night.

Someone had turned them on. Or, Oliver wondered, was it the moon magic Thurl had implied? Oliver shook his head, remembering the open front door. The parlor doors left slightly apart. Clearly someone was inside the attraction. On the other paw, maintenance workers would leave the doors wide open to make their presence known, Oliver reasoned, and turn on lights so they could see what they were doing. They certainly wouldn't be shimmying through tiny cracks in the wall. Plus, as Kimball had often explained, maintenance almost always locked ride control panels when they were working to avoid accidents. Regardless, someone, or something, was in there now. If it was maintenance or a cleaning crew, Oliver would simply slip out again undetected. If it wasn't, Oliver thought, reaching for the scabbard at his hip. His heart sank, remembering his sword was destroyed.

"Claws will have to do," he mumbled. Gingerly, Oliver stepped onto the moving floor. It was a weird feeling, momentarily throwing him off balance. Once he found his footing, he waited for the next approaching Doom Buggy and leapt into the opening where humans would normally step right in.

Oliver popped up onto the seat and slid back, making sure he was shrouded in the shadows of the vehicle. He was fortunate that his coloring tended to help camouflage him in the dark, though sometimes he had to keep his chin down and his arms folded across his white chest. Oliver sat up straight, his eyes peeled for anything unusual, although that might be hard on a ride full of unusual sights. His mission was to look for rodent intruders, but he relished the chance to ride one of the park's most famous attractions. The opportunity happened so rarely.

"Do not pull down on the safety bar," came a haunting voice over his head. Oliver jumped to all fours, his back bristling. It was just the safety recording, he realized, as his fur slowly fell back into place.

"I will do it for you," the narrator went on. The phantom voice explained that 999 ghosts called the Haunted Mansion home. Oliver was once again glad that Mr. Disney had chosen the castle for the cats to call home. As much as he was certain these spirits were probably harmless, he wouldn't want to find one hovering over his bed in the middle of the night. Not to mention, it just rolled off the tongue. Cats of the Castle was much easier than Cats of the Haunted Mansion. The ride rolled on past a coffin from which a hand pushed against the lid. The occupant desperately wanted out to see who was disturbing his or her slumber. A black raven with glowing red eyes cawed out a greeting, or a warning. Oliver wasn't sure which.

The Doom Buggy soon turned, carrying him backwards through a narrow hallway lined with doors. Invisible forces pushed against them from the other side, trying to escape. Hinges creaked and spirits moaned. Other doors knocked by invisible hands. In a moment, the car swiveled around a corner and turned to face the center of a dark chamber. Musical instruments floated around the room, as if played by a phantom orchestra. It was the *séance* room, where the disembodied head of a fortune teller named Madame Leota lived on, communicating with the spirit world from inside a floating crystal ball. The orb levitated over a table, behind which another cawing raven perched on a high-backed chair. Leota's green face glowed and her eyes opened wide as she called forth spirits from beyond. Oliver wondered if outside the park there were other humans who separated their heads from their bodies and continued living inside a fishbowl. He shook his head, assuming probably not.

Thurl had once explained to young Oliver that the ghosts and frights inside the Haunted Mansion posed no threat. It was all in good fun. So far, he had to admit that despite a few creepy moments, he was really enjoying himself. Then he caught sight of something directly across the circular room that made the smile on his face fade. It was something shocking, but not part of the ride. One of the empty Doom Buggies wasn't empty at all!

It was a human. A man, specifically. Older looking, with a sharp pointed nose on the bridge of which sat a pair of very wide, round eyeglasses. Green and blue lights from the attraction effects reflected off his thick lenses, making it look as if he had laser eyes. The man wore a long gray coat, belted at the middle, and a red scarf wrapped around his neck, which also seemed out of place on such a warm evening. What truly made him look odd was his choppy gray hair which he'd combed up on each side, creating two points on his head, which looked very much like horns. The stranger had a wide, foolish grin plastered across his face.

Who was he, Oliver wondered? A new maintenance worker? Surely not, dressed like that. An Imagineer, maybe? Some of them could be real characters, Oliver had heard. It might explain his unusual sense of style. Still, even they were required to wear name tags in the park. There was nothing pinned to this man's jacket. For whatever reason, perhaps his slack-jawed expression of wonder, Oliver had a feeling the man was seeing the ride for the first time. He seemed too enthralled in the attraction to notice the cat watching him from across the room. The man must have managed to get over (or through) the park fences and walls, or he'd bought a ticket earlier in the day and hidden someplace until the park had closed. Either way, he probably didn't belong there.

Oliver quickly decided the best thing to do was trigger an alarm and get park security to the mansion. They could sort out whether this stranger was meant to be there or not. The problem was, Oliver wasn't aware of any triggers inside the attraction. There was one just outside the Mansion gates, but the key word was *outside*. That would be the tricky part, getting past the man without being noticed. It occurred to Oliver that maybe he could somehow blend in, as a black cat would fit right in with the attraction. However, not a black-and-white one wearing a vest.

Oliver leaned forward, peering over the front of his Doom Buggy trying to figure out his next move. He looked up ahead again and saw the stranger's smile melt away. His nose was twitching and his mouth formed a strange "O" shape. A moment later he let out a screeching sneeze the likes of which Oliver had never heard from human or cat. It even carried over the din of the attraction. It sounded like *ah-ah-ahkershoosh*!

The lenses of his spectacles glimmered as his head began to dart side to side, as if looking for something. Then his face stopped. While his eyes were hidden, his brows arched in surprise. He was looking right at Oliver's Doom Buggy. Oliver's chest tightened. He'd been spotted. The man sneered and pulled the red scarf up over his nose and mouth. In the eerie dim blue lighting with half his face now covered and his wide circle eyes and hair horns, Oliver couldn't help but think he looked like a great owl. He pointed a long finger covered by a shiny black glove at Oliver. The man's head was moving as if he was saying something, but Oliver couldn't hear. Then the Doom Buggy slipped around the corner and out of sight.

He was getting away, Oliver thought. He had to move now if he was going to trigger that alarm before the intruder exited the ride. As the car in front of him turned to roll out of the room, its side opening faced him. Oliver climbed onto the lip of his car, balancing for a second before he leaped forward, landing perfectly on the floor of the buggy. He watched the next vehicle turn almost flush with his. It was an easy jump across, especially for a cat. Oliver dug his back claws into the floor, waiting to make his next jump. At the right moment, he sprang forward when...*WHAM*...something crashed into him in midair, sending him crashing into a shiny cymbal hanging in the air.

Oliver and the instrument created a chain reaction of enchanted instruments crashing into each other, which crescendoed in a horrible cacophony of sound as they hit the ground. It sounded like an orchestra composed of musicians that had just picked up their instruments for the very first time. Good thing there were no guests on the ride. The horrible sound was louder than the soundtrack of the ride. Oliver staggered to his feet, paws on his head, trying to shake off the hit.

That's when he spied it, getting to its feet just a few inches away. A fat brown rat. A big one, too, just like that guard Louie had described. More than half as tall as Oliver. It caught his eyes and grinned. Was that what had hit him, he wondered? It felt like it had been fired out of a cannon. Then Oliver realized the rat was wearing what looked like crudely stitched green pants.

"Clothes?" Oliver whispered.

"Sorry, cat," it sneered. "Doc don't like cats."

Oliver was taken aback. Did that rat just speak? That didn't usually happen. He and the other four Castle Cats were the only animals in the park that spoke, let alone wore clothes. Oliver's feral instincts kicked in. He hissed and sprang at the rodent. They tumbled dangerously close to the track where Doom Buggies were rolling by. Before the rat knew what was happening, Oliver had its arms pinned to floor. The wheels of the ride vehicles squeaked past, rolling dangerously close to their heads.

"Sorry, rat," said Oliver, "but you picked the wrong night to come sniffing around *my* park! Ordinarily, I'd kick you around like a soccer ball awhile then leave you in a cage by the gates, but I don't have time. Just get out. Go pick through Magic Mountain's garbage."

"*Ernf*," the rat struggled in his grip, "you dumb cat! This ain't about garbage! We're on a mission here. And trust me, when he's focused there's no stoppin' the Doc!"

"The Doc?" Oliver repeated. That was the second time the rat said that. "What do you mean? Are you *with* that human?"

"Get stuffed, cat," the rat hissed. "I ain't tellin' you nothin'!"

"A rat who won't talk," said Oliver, tightening his grip. "That's a new one."

The rat opened its snout and bit down on Oliver's paw. With a yelp, the cat instinctively hurled the rodent, whose portly brown body slammed into the back of a passing Doom Buggy with a *crack*, like a baseball hitting the side of a house. The rodent slid down the side and rolled underneath. Its head came to a rest on the edge of the ride track. Oliver got a little queasy, imagining the scene when the next car came rolling through. It wouldn't be pretty. Oliver snatched the rat by the tail just before an oncoming wheel made him resemble Madame Leota.

"I can't believe I just saved a rat's life," Oliver grumbled. He could just hear what Elias would say. Oliver waived his throbbing paw in the air. "If you've got rabies, I'll tie you back to that track myself!"

An oversized, talking rat, somehow connected to a trespassing human. Something strange was going on. Oliver needed to tell Thurl and the others. But first, he needed to set off the alarm. He grabbed a fallen drum, threw the dazed rat under it and turned it back over, trapping him inside.

"If you were smart, you'd stay under here," Oliver said. "A custodial crew will probably be along sooner than later. They wouldn't be happy to see a dirty rat in their attraction. Might not be as kind as I am."

Oliver waited for the right moment and leapt up into the next passing Doom Buggy. He knew the gate-crasher would be nearly through the ride by now. The rat had referred to him as the Doc. Was he really a doctor? He should be called Doctor Owl, Oliver thought with a snicker. But why would a doctor sneak into Disneyland?

The vehicle turned a corner and he was up on a landing overlooking a majestic ballroom. Down below, luminescent dancing spirits disappeared and reappeared on the floor. Other spectral party guests materialized around a long table enjoying a celebratory feast as a ghostly woman with her hair piled up in a bun blew out the candles on her birthday cake. Or was it a *deathday* party, Oliver wondered? He rubbed his side where the rat had cannonballed him. It was already sore. If he wasn't covered in fur, he'd probably be sporting a nasty bruise in the morning.

The car rolled on, passing over the ballroom and into a creepy attic. It looked like a place where the residents stored all their old forgotten furniture and belongings. There were dusty mirrors and candlesticks covered in cobwebs. A filthy old birdcage hung without a feathered occupant—unless it was a ghost bird, Oliver thought. An eerie thumping heartbeat echoed around the dank room. There were also portraits of married couples. Actually, as Oliver looked closer, the bride was always the same. Only the husbands changed, and changed severely, as each man's head would disappear. Just before exiting the attic, Oliver nearly shrieked when his buggy came face-to-face with the ghoulish bride herself.

The speed of the Doom Buggy picked up as he whisked past her. Oliver was relieved to find himself outside the main house. White apparitions were flying through the night sky right before his eyes. Loud music clanged in the darkness. Oliver had a feeling they were nearing the end of the ride, which meant the stranger would be close to the unloading area. Wrestling with the rat had cost precious time. Just as he thought this, the Doom Buggy took another unexpected turn, swiveling around so that it was rolling backward, and began to descend a hill. Oliver found himself staring up at stars against a black sky. Nightmarish trees loomed over the track on both sides.

"Okay," Oliver whispered with a sigh, "this is interesting." He stood up and climbed onto the front of the car. Pushing his feet against the safety bar he peered over the roof of the vehicle, watching the other black cars rolling down toward the ground. Oliver needed to get out of the Doom Buggy. He could navigate the attraction faster on foot. Before he could move, the vehicle began to tip upright again. Oliver found himself grabbing for the roof which was short and smooth. He dug his claws in and scurried up on top of it. Quickly he rolled over and clung to the lip of the roof, letting his body dangle down the sloping back of the Doom Buggy. "Who designed these things?" he hissed.

The car rolled by a terrified animatronic groundskeeper holding a lantern and peering into the graveyard. The old-timer would occasionally turn to look over at the Doom Buggies with a surprised look of complete terror. A scrawny brown dog trembled and whimpered at his side; a sight most cats would have relished. Tonight, Oliver was too distracted to appreciate it.

Turning the corner, Oliver found himself facing a cemetery. A ghoulish head sprang up from behind a gravestone, giving Oliver such a scare he momentarily pulled his paws away and almost slipped off the roof again. All around him ghosts were singing, playing games, and showing off for the vehicles. With a grunt, Oliver pulled himself forward over the roof's edge and clumsily dropped onto the hard seat with a thud.

Oliver stood up on the seat, leaning against the car wall, straining to see through all the action. It shouldn't be tough to spot one pink human with wings for hair. *Bingo!* Oliver spotted the shiny black gloves gripping the safety bar of a Doom Buggy far in front of him. He was drumming along to the music of the grim, grinning ghosts and occasionally wagging one of his fingers as if conducting a symphony. What kind of doctor was this guy, Oliver wondered?

The Doom Buggies were rolling along at a quick clip now, swiveling this way and that as the graveyard party was in full swing. Oliver watched the movement of the empty vehicle in front of him. He was only going to get one chance. Otherwise he was likely to go splat on the tracks beneath it. He had no desire to be the next disembodied soul moving in.

Oliver climbed up on the front of his buggy and braced himself, hind legs on the lip of the car, tail balanced against the safety bar, like he was surfing an invisible wave. When the right moment came, or as right as he could guess, he propelled himself forward. His judgment was only slightly off. He banged into the side of the opening, and tumbled painfully into the car. For a moment Oliver lay on the floor not sure which way was up, his head spinning, his elbow throbbing.

Real smooth, Oliver told himself. No time for licking wounds. He sluggishly found his feet and turned around to climb onto the seat, as he'd have to do it all over again. Surprisingly, he discovered there wasn't going to be room for him. Standing on the seat of this particular Doom Buggy were two more rats, also taller and thicker than any rats Oliver had seen, prior to a few minutes before anyway. They were also standing on their hind legs. It seemed like a safe bet they'd come with the portly brown fellow he'd met in the séance room. The two rats glared at him with smiles on their snouts.

"Well, would you look at this," the taller, lean, gray rat in red shorts with a shock of wild hair on his head clicked through jagged incisors. "I thought those stories about cats in this place was just rumors. What do they call 'em Freddie?"

"What," his accomplice, Freddie, a stocky black rat with a pink nose, asked. He pulled up on the waist of his frayed blue jeans. "You mean cats? They call 'em *cats*."

"No idiot, the stories," the gray rat rolled its eyes. "Those stories people tell, that don't really seem true."

"Um, are you thinking of urban legends?" Oliver interjected.

"That's it!" The gray rat snapped his pink fingers. "Urban legends! I thought the cats in Disneyland were just urban legends."

"Oh, yeah," said Freddie, and chuckled. He was holding a length of rope tightly in his grubby claws. "I guess the big mouse does hire cats after all."

"Gee, fellas," said Oliver putting his hands out in front him trying to seem as non-confrontational as possible. "I hate to break up what appears to be a private party, but extra-magic hours are over. You guys and your, uh, human friend can't be in here."

"Is that right?" the gray one said, raising an eyebrow and scratching at his droopy pink nose. "Looks like Murray ran his big mouth again. I'm telling you, Freddie, the only time he can keep a secret is when he's eatin'! Well, it turns out I got some bad news for you, cat. Things are about to change around your little fun park, starting with rats get to ride anything we want, any time we want!"

"Yeah," the black rat added, "but don't you worry. You won't be here to see it. The cats around here will be the first ones to go. No cats allowed, boss said so. He can't stand your kind. You make him itchy and snotty."

"Alright, Freddie," said the gray one, wincing. "We don't need the details. I'm already a little queasy from these rides."

"Sorry, Mac."

"Boss?" Oliver asked. "So Doctor Owl in the next car is really your boss? Come, on boys. Mac and Freddy, is it? You're with red-scarf guy?"

"Doctor Owl," Freddie laughed. "That's funny. Cause he's got those points, and his big round glasses."

"Shut it, Freddie," Mac snapped. "Who do you think showed him how to get in? We rats have a natural instinct for finding weaknesses in human security. Once we found a weak spot in the fences, he told us to distract any nosey security guards."

"Which we did," the black rat butted in. "Left a chubby one chasing his own shadow 'til he was out of breath in Adventureland."

"And the one that body slammed me back in the séance room," Oliver said, " He's a friend of yours too?"

"That would be Murray," the gray one said. His eyes narrowed. "He's with us. What did you do with him, cat? Eat him?"

"Gross," said Oliver, gagging at the thought. "No! I eat just fine around here—don't need to resort to junk food with tails. He's fine, more or less. But if I were you I'd collect him and get out before the cleaning crew finds him."

"Even Murray can get away from a vacuum cleaner," said Mac.

"Listen, I'm just trying to be helpful. Some humans aren't quite as, uh, *humane* as I am."

"Murray knew the risks," said Mac. "Code of the sewers. A rat falls behind, he's on his own. Right, Freddie?"

"That's right. We got a code. Each rat for himself. Save your own tail, or lose it."

"That's not very noble," said Oliver backing up against the front of the Doom Buggy. He was keeping both eyes on the rats. There wasn't much time left. He couldn't let that human exit the ride before him. Getting past these two rogue rodents was posing a real problem.

"Noble ain't exactly our concern," said Mac. "Survive. That's what rats do."

"Survive and thrive," Freddie added with a grin and stretched out his rope. "That's the code of the rat!"

"Unfortunately for you, Mr. Whiskers," Mac started, "we have a different code for cats. One-on-one—turn tail and run. Two of us and one of you...."

"You're days are through," Freddie chuckled. "See, it rhymes!"

"Oh, come on, Freddie," Mac spat, rolling his eyes and flicking the black rat's pink ear. "You were supposed to attack after you said *through*!"

"Hey, watch the ear!" Freddie shook his head. "Ding-dang, you're right! Okay, say it again."

"Just get him!" Mac shouted.

The black rat nodded and charged at Oliver, holding his rope stretched tight like he was about to snare it around the cat's neck. Without a moment's thought Oliver swiped his sharp claws and snapped the rope in four different segments. The bulky black rat fell forward, colliding snout-first with the front of the car. Oliver reared back and booted the rat into the air like he was kicking a field goal. Freddie sailed out the side of the vehicle just as another ghastly ghoul sprang up from behind a nearby gravestone. The rat squealed as his head lodged inside the spooky spirit's open mouth. Freddie was stuck up to his shoulders in its twisted, grimacing lips. The hydraulic corpse slid back down behind the stone.

Oliver turned back to the other rat, Mac, who was already backing up against the seat of the vehicle. A nervous smile stretched across his snout. Oliver waved his claws just inches from the rat's whiskers.

"Now listen, friend," the rat pleaded, his spindly pink fingers outstretched, "no need to get crazy or nothin'!"

"I'm in a hurry," said Oliver. "Call this a 'get out of Disneyland free' card. Jump off the ride and don't stop running until you scurry under the gates and across Harbor Boulevard."

Mac forced a nervous chuckle. He climbed up onto the side of the Doom Buggy. Looked over the edge of the moving, swerving vehicle and then back to the cat looming over him with ten sharp claws on display.

"You win for now, cat," he said. But the Doc won't give up easy!" With a mock salute, he jumped over the side of the vehicle. Oliver hated letting a rat run loose in an attraction, let alone the park, but the human in the next carriage was a bigger concern right now.

The line of Doom Buggies swiveled to face a row of mirrors down a long passageway. Realizing his reflection could be seen by the other cars, Oliver dropped to the floor. He strained to peer up at the reflection of the buggy next to him. He could see the sleeve of the man's gray coat resting on the edge. Oliver heard him laugh—a shrill cackle. In the mirrors, Oliver saw a cartoonish ghost in a top hat sitting next to the doctor. It pulled off his head and switched it with its own, which made the intruder appear even stranger, with his scarf and thick glasses resting on the glowing ghost body. Oliver peeked up at his own car's reflection to see an impish, bearded ghost perched on the roof above him. Startled, Oliver wheeled around to look up, but no blue toes hung over his ears. He felt his Doom Buggy shifting around again, as they returned to a straight line. The attraction was over. Somewhere above he heard a woman's voice calling, "hurrrry baaack!"

This was it, Oliver thought. He might not get out unnoticed by the creep, but on four legs he could sure as *litter* get past him. After all, he wasn't bound by the dreaded safety bar. The Doom Buggy slowly approached another moving walkway. Oliver bolted out of his vehicle. He sped right up the side of the cars as the man's safety bar lifted and his shiny black shoe began to slide out. Oliver rammed the man's foot with his shoulder as he sprinted by. The intruder tumbled backward, not even seeing the black-and-white blur shoot under his feet. Immediately, sneezes echoed from the Doom Buggy, but Oliver didn't look back. He just kept running down the corridor and out the exit toward dim street lamps.

Oliver slid to a stop. He began frantically checking the concrete for the alarm sensor. The Imagineers had a habit of hiding things "in plain sight" as they liked to say. In the dim, eerie mood lighting around the Haunted Mansion at night, Oliver was having a hard time spotting anything. As if he'd wished it to happen, a cloud must have shifted and the blue light of the moon glinted off something. There it was, sunk into the concrete. The softly illuminated shape of a wedding ring. By day it was completely invisible. Only in the moonlight did it become activated and even then still difficult to spot if you didn't know where to look. Oliver had heard that in Florida the Imagineers sunk a real ring into the sidewalk. He wasn't sure if that one was also a trigger. Oliver pushed his paw down hard in the middle of the circle. He felt the concrete inside sink slightly and then pop back up.

The timing couldn't be more perfect. In the shadowy exit appeared a tall, lanky silhouette of a man with pointy tufts at the sides of his head like a great horned owl. The moonlight hitting his glasses created two eerie glowing orbs where his eyes should be. The scarf around his nose and mouth puffed in and out in anger. At the man's shins, two more sets of eyes appeared, these gleaming red. The rats, Oliver thought. They stepped out into the light and he could see it was Mac the gray rat, and the brown one Oliver met in the séance room, called Murray.

"There," Doctor Owl hissed in his raspy voice, pointing directly at Oliver. "Get that cat! And this time, don't screw up!"

"You got it boss," said Murray. "We'll get him. Bet he knows where the key is hidden!"

Key, Oliver wondered? The two big rats headed straight for him. Hopefully security was just around the corner, Oliver thought. No time for a scuffle. Oliver turned tail and made to run away. The night mist made the stone beneath his paws slick. His sharp claws clicked across the surface, unable to find traction. He could hear smaller claws *clacking* across the concrete, growing too close for his comfort. Oliver pictured their sharp, rabies infested teeth snapping at his tail. He wished he had his sword. Where was security, anyway?

"Stop right there," a voice yelled out in the night as if Oliver had asked a Genie. "Disneyland security!"

Not thinking (and a bit startled) Oliver stopped abruptly, as ordered, and his body fell flat on the ground. It was the two security officers from Main Street, flashlight beams bearing down on the man standing in the mansion exit. Thank goodness, Oliver thought with a surge of relief. He had done his job. Of course, the rats would probably make a break for it into the park, but they could be caught tomorrow, if they didn't run into one of the other Cats of the Castle tonight. For the time being, Oliver just needed to disappear. He rolled over and scrambled into the thick green hedge.

"Don't move," the tall officer, Pete, called out. "The Anaheim police are already on their way."

Oliver looked back to see Doctor Owl backed against a wall beside the exit. In fact, it seemed safe to say he was trapped like a rat. The man was pulling his scarf up to the middle of his glasses, hoping to conceal his identity. His head darted back and forth. Without warning, he ran for it, leaping over the short metal rail and sprinting across the grass, lifting his bony knees high as he ran. His long coat billowed out behind him like a cape. The two rats followed suit, running just a few feet behind him. The doctor cut right through the outdoor graveyard, raising one long leg and stepping up onto a memorial to a skunk called Lilac and over a brick wall disappearing between some trees. The two guards tried to chase after him, yelling at him to stop, but they were in no shape to keep up. For an older man, he was very agile.

"We lost him," Oliver heard Pete huff and puff into his radio. "He ran for it. He's somewhere behind the Haunted Mansion. He'll probably try to make his way out somewhere between New Orleans Square and Critter Country where he came in."

"Roger that," a voice squawked back. "We've got patrols heading that way. They'll check out the fences, too."

When the coast was clear, Oliver emerged from his own hiding place. Knowing most, if not all the humans in the park would be pre-occupied around Critter Country, he took a little less care heading home. He trotted right down the middle of the street on all fours, around the Rivers of America and through Frontierland. He cut through Fantasy Faire with its striped tents where young girls met princesses by day, and around the west side of the castle.

At the edge of the moat, he located a familiar bush with one flower just slightly unlike the others growing around it. Passing guests would probably never notice, but this one was made of plastic. Oliver pushed down on the branch with his paw. A moment later, the water gurgled as the secret stepping stones rose from the murky water. The hidden door quietly spun around and Oliver scampered across to the safety of the castle walls. He needed to find Thurl.

Chapter Three

Oliver found Thurl curled up in the brown leather chair with the high back that sat in the corner of the gathering room. The chair had been a favorite of Walt's, and it was where he would sit when the first Cats of the Castle met. Now it held a place of honor, under a dim, warm light in the corner. It was understood only Thurl would sit, or at times such as now, doze off in it.

"Thurl!" Oliver blurted out. He immediately felt bad, fearing he might startle the elder feline.

"Huh, what, where is the dragon?" Thurl sputtered, quickly snapping to attention. His white beard and whiskers were plastered up over his pink nose. Sensing his own disheveled look he quickly licked a paw and smoothed himself out.

"Thurl, it's me," Oliver said. "Sorry to wake you up. Something strange happened tonight. Wait, did you just say *dragon*?"

"What, dragon?" Thurl said, confused for a moment. "Oh, well, I may have. Er, just a silly dream, of course. What is it, my boy? What's the matter? What's happened?"

"You were right," said Oliver, dismissing the dragon comment. "This was not a typical night after all."

Oliver went on to recount the night's events. He told Thurl about overhearing the guards on Main Street and sneaking into the Haunted Mansion to look for rats. Then he told how he spotted the strange man he'd nicknamed Doctor Owl in the Doom Buggy. Oliver told him how he'd been attacked by the oversized rats, and how they'd chased him out near the exit with the doctor giving them orders.

"They understood him," Oliver said. "The same way we understand humans here in the park. And they speak and walk on two legs. They called him their boss. Thurl, I didn't think any animals could speak with humans, except us."

"They can't. Not usually anyway."

"I thought so," said Oliver, shrugging his shoulders. "But then, how?"

"I suppose there may be other ways, but the only one I'm aware of requires blue pixie dust. And ours is safely locked away. There's no way anyone could have gotten to it without my knowledge." Thurl slid down from the chair and began to pace the room, his staff clicking along the stone floor.

"This is certainly cause for concern," he went on. "Who is the human doctor? And how do these rats come to be in league with him. In my experience, humans despise rats as much as we do. Maybe more. It's what's kept us Castle Cats employed these six decades."

"There's something else," Oliver said. "One of the rats said they were looking for something. He said if they caught me, they thought I could tell them where to find a key."

"A key?" Thurl stopped. He thought for a moment, then his green eyes widened. "You're sure they said a key?"

"Yes. *The* key, in fact. He specifically said he'd find where *the* key was hidden. We don't keep keys. We don't even need them."

"No, not us." Thurl was quiet a moment, staring up at Walt and Mr. Lincoln's picture. "I wonder...but how could it be? How could they know?"

"What is it?" Oliver asked.

Just then the door swung open. Kimball and Elias came bounding in, seemingly in the middle of another argument. Elias was going on how he'd seen a monstrous cat beast skulking around Tom Sawyer Island. Kimball was trying to explain the unlikeliness of that.

"A big coyote, maybe," Kimball said, pushing his glasses up on his nose. "How would a monster get to the island? Is it a swimming monster? Did it paddle a canoe?"

"Maybe it did," Elias growled. "You don't know. Ever heard of Loch Ness. That's a swimming monster."

"Nessie was likely a dinosaur. A plesiosaur to be exact, and that's beside the point because she doesn't exist! How would a lone reptile, or any monster, survive all this time in a cold lake in Scotland?"

"I don't care about Nessie," Elias growled. "How about I paddle you over there? You'll be begging me to save you when this thing's got you up a tree."

"Boys, please," Thurl said firmly. He gestured to the other chairs around the table. "Save your argument and sit. Where is Lilli? Has anyone seen her?"

"Nope," said Elias dropping into a chair.

"Not in a couple hours," Kimball answered, looking at the pocket watch he kept in his sweater.

"Should I go find her?" Oliver asked.

"*Should I go find her, sir*," Elias repeated in a shrill, sing-song voice.

"Do we have a problem?" Oliver said, stepping toward Elias' chair.

"If we did, I'd solve it," said Elias, eyeing him back menacingly. He flicked out one claw and began picking at his teeth.

"Boys!" Thurl raised his voice.

"Not again," came Lilli's voice as she appeared in the doorway. "It's getting so a girl can't leave the castle without you two getting into some kind of quarrel like two-month old kittens! In fact, I'd say you're both behaving like *dogs*."

"Ah, Lilli," said Thurl with a sigh. "Please, have a seat. I'd like Oliver to enlighten all of you about his adventure inside the Haunted Mansion."

"You were in the Mansion?," Lilli whispered to Oliver. He nodded back with a smile, then caught Thurl's disapproving glance and straightened up.

"Oliver ran into some unusual trespassers this evening," Thurl said. "Three rats. Rats that spoke and stood upright."

"Come again," said Elias, raising his eyebrow.

"That might not be the worst of it," said Thurl. "They seem to be in league with a human. They spoke, and it seems followed his orders."

"He's a real character," said Oliver. "They said he's some sort of doctor. I called him Doctor Owl. If you see him, you'll understand."

"Wait, did you say they *spoke*?," Kimball choked. "But Thurl, that's not possible. Not without the blue...."

"Blue fairy dust," Thurl finished his sentence. "Yes, I know. I've already thought the same thing. Nonetheless, Oliver saw them—he spoke with them. Ultimately had a close, and dare I say dangerous, encounter with the trio and their human master."

"Luckily, I found the Bride's Ring," Oliver added. "Security showed up just in time. They chased them into the trees between the mansion and Critter Country."

"I knew it was there," Kimball whispered.

"We must assume now that they are aware of the intrusion, park security will increase their patrols," Thurl said. "Best you all remain inside the rest of the night while we let the humans do their jobs."

"Yeah, that usually works out," Elias mumbled.

"Nevertheless," said Thurl, shooting him a look. The tough cat quickly shut his mouth. "This is a new concern for us. Until we know more, we must exercise extreme caution."

"But Thurl," said Oliver, "we've all faced thousands of rats."

"Not like these. You said so yourself, my boy. You've only chased the standard variety of scavenging rodent. Not since the great war of my youth have we encountered rats such as you describe."

"The great invasion of '89," Lilli said softly.

"You know about this?" both Oliver and Elias asked at once.

"They appeared on a summer night," Thurl spoke softly, distantly. "A great horde of them. Some standing as tall as me, and I barely out of kitten hood. These rats were savages. They came ready for a fight." Thurl paused, staring absently at a glowing lamp on the wall. His lip quivered as the memories flooded back to him. "While we did not know anything about them, somehow they were well aware of the Order. Thankfully, there were more of us in those days. A terrible battle ensued. Injuries were great, on both sides, as were casualties."

"Casualties?" Oliver repeated.

Thurl nodded. "It was a dark day. The Cats of the Castle prevailed and the rats were defeated, but it is hard to say we won. The leader of my order, Fulton, a short but stalwart gray Himalayan, determined there must be other pixie dust out there, somewhere, beyond the borders of Disneyland. We couldn't think of any other explanation. That was the first time we realized the thing that made us what we are could also be used against us. I must say the Order never entirely recovered. It was after that battle that Baxter...." His words trailed off.

The elder cat looked around the table at his four noble young cats, their eyes glued to him. He straightened his shoulders and tugged at his beard with a smile. "Well," he started "let's simply say where once we were many, there were soon extra chairs at this table. However, since the four of you assembled, my hopes are renewed that one day the Order will be complete again."

"What about the key?" Oliver asked. "Is that what they came for that night?"

"The key?" Thurl asked, as though he'd nearly forgotten. "No. Their motivations were simpler. They sought a new home with plenty of food. Their own kingdom, as it were. If these rats are looking for the key, they are a different breed altogether."

"What is the deal with this key?" Lilli asked in frustration, looking at Oliver. "Key to what? The front gates? An attraction?"

"I don't know. One of the rats just said they were looking for some key."

"Not just some key," said Thurl. "If it is the one I've heard tales about, it's *the* key."

"I know every door and lock in this park," said Kimball. "What one key would be worth this owlish character risking arrest?"

"I haven't heard it mentioned for many, many years," Thurl said. "There is a story of a special key, made of solid gold, and roughly seven inches in length." He held up two stubby white fingers, roughly guessing the length. "The handle was shaped like a D, and precious gems were laid into the gold. It belonged to Walt himself. He was known to keep it in his breast pocket at all times. At night, he locked it in a box inside his apartment, which was in turn locked in a desk."

"What did the key unlock?" Elias asked, drumming his gray fingers on the table impatiently.

"Or lock?" Lilli added.

"I can't exactly say. This was a *different* sort of key. The Disneyland key was said to be enchanted. My elder Fulton only said if that key fell into the wrong hands, Disneyland would be doomed."

The cats all looked up.

"How could one key doom the entire park?" Elias finally spoke up.

"It's a valid question," Kimball nodded. "I don't see how a simple key could destroy Disneyland."

"There's nothing simple about magic. That said, I do not know the answer. The elder cats said Mr. Disney used this key to open the park. I thought perhaps they meant it was symbolic. Now, I think perhaps not."

"Well, whatever it does, if this Doctor Owl and his rats are after it, we need to stop them," said Lilli.

"Forget them," said Elias, slamming a paw on the table. He pushed his chair back and stood. "Where is the key? Let's just go get it and bring it here where it's safe. They step foot in this castle, I shred 'em. Case closed."

"I agree with him," said Oliver, standing as well. Both he and Elias looked at each other with surprise. It was rare the two cats stood in agreement.

"I admit I'm happy to see your shared enthusiasm," Thurl said, tapping his stick on the floor. "Unfortunately, I'm afraid I can't say where it is. The Cats of the Castle have never been told where it is hidden. Another reason some of us came to believe it was just another Disneyland myth. Walt and the park have both, over the years, become enshrouded in myths and legends."

"He's right," said Kimball, with a grin. "You should hear the one they tell about the wild cats that run around Disneyland at night."

"As I was saying," Thurl continued with a deep tired sigh, "even if we did know where the key was yesterday, there is no guarantee it would be there today. When Walt became ill, he instructed his brother Roy to continually move the key around the park, making it harder for someone to steal. Since then, every few years, one Imagineer has been entrusted to hide it again. Only two souls ever know the location of the key at any given time. The last person to hide it, and the next. It's an additional safety measure."

"Then what do we do?" Oliver asked, voicing what they were all thinking. "Just sit here and hope park security catches this thief and his rats?"

"Or assume they're the only humans on the outside that know about the thing?" added Elias.

"No, you are right. Action must be taken," said Thurl. "We must protect this park. We must retrieve the key."

"But as you said," Kimball started, "we don't know where it is."

"And we can't exactly go ask Imagineering," added Elias.

"Both true," said Thurl, "but there is someone who might know. The Oracle."

"*The Oracle.*" Kimball's green eyes went wide over the rims of his glasses. His voiced cracked as if it were difficult just to push the word out. "But Thurl, no one has spoken to the Oracle in years. Not even you."

"It's is our only hope. The Oracle has been in the park since before opening day. The Oracle knows every story, every detail, every myth."

"Thurl," said Lilli. "I've heard the Oracle is not fond of cats."

"Yes, I am aware."

"Then perhaps I should go. Sending any one of these three into an unfriendly environment could be, well, you know, counter-productive."

"To say the least," Thurl nodded with a light grin. "You will go, to accompany Oliver."

The black-and-white cat suddenly went rigid. He wished he could rewind what he just heard. Was he just assigned a mission with Lilli?

"Excellent." Lilli looked over at Oliver who was too excited and nervous to make eye contact. She flipped her hood up over her ears. "A mission. You think you can handle it?"

"What? Who? Me?. Of course. It's for the good of the park. It's my duty. Just let me swing by a gift shop and find a new sword."

"You're not be going tonight," said Thurl. Oliver and Lilli both looked back at him, confused.

"But Thurl," said Oliver, "it's too risky to wait any longer. Those rats—Doctor Owl—they could be out there right now. We should act tonight."

"Oliver, they don't know where the key is. At least not yet. Everyone needs rest. You and Lilli will go see the Oracle in the morning."

"In the morning!?" all four younger cats exclaimed.

"Uh, as in *daylight*?" Elias asked. "Isn't that kind of against *everything* you've ever taught us?"

"I know," said Thurl, tapping his walking stick loudly to quiet them. "We rarely work while the sun shines. This is an extreme circumstance. You will slip out of the castle early in the morning, long before the park opens. Much of your journey will be well concealed. Trust me."

"I don't even know where to find the Oracle," said Oliver. "Where are we going?"

"Don't worry, you won't have far to go. Only to the mouth of Adventureland."

"Oh, good," Elias smirked. "Grab me a Dole Whip on your way back."

"There will be no treats this time," said Thurl, gently rapping Elias on the back of his gray head with his walking stick. When he did, the colored lights flashed. "Besides, you're going with them."

"Oh, I'm...huh?" Elias stammered. "But you said Oliver and Lilli."

"You and Kimball will escort them as far as Adventureland. "Then you will stand guard until they return. As I said, we must take extreme precautions."

"Thurl, it's not that far," Oliver said. "We can make the run from the castle to Adventureland without being spotted. The fewer of us there are, the better."

"Tomorrow you travel a different route, my boy. One that none of you has ever seen. And until we know that key is safe and your Owl friend is gone, the four of you don't go anywhere *except* as a team. Now off to bed, all of you. Kimball, set your watch. We rise with the sun."

Chapter Four

The next morning all four cats woke early, mostly due to Thurl roaming the halls of the castle, loudly banging his staff on their chamber doors, calling out, "Rise and shine, little kittens!"

They all emerged yawning and stretching from their small rooms which were hidden throughout Sleeping Beauty Castle, down secret halls and through hidden corridors the average cast member never saw. Each cat had a private room with dark stone walls and a comfortable overstuffed cat bed. Decorations were for the most part sparse. Of course, Kimball's room had stacks of books so tall they could easily be mistaken for pillars holding up the ceiling. Plans, blueprints, and ride operating manuals littered his floor, and a work bench was littered with wires, screws, and mechanical odds and ends maintenance had thrown out.

The floor in Elias's room was covered with the remains of scratching posts he'd made short work of, along with empty plastic popcorn buckets, turkey leg bones, and soda bottles. Raiding the popcorn carts for a late-night snack was his favorite activity, after tormenting rodents. Oliver's room, on the other hand, was always quite neat. There was nothing on the floor, aside from his round maroon bed. On his wall, however, was plastered a colorful paper map of the entire park. He often sat up when he should have been sleeping just staring at it by the glow of a dim lantern, reading the descriptions of each attraction over and over. Oliver felt a very strange but special connection to this place.

No one knew what the inside of Lilli's room looked like. She was a lady, and it would be ungentlemanly of the three boy cats to go peeping around her chamber. Not to mention she might tear the fur off their tails if they tried. Thurl's room was in one of the castle's turrets, but he was always up before them and went to bed after, so they never went there, either.

Once they'd assembled in the hall, Thurl bid them to follow as he shuffled down the corridor. They wouldn't be exiting the castle through the secret side door. The castle, just like all of Disneyland, had been fitted with many "quick escapes" over the years. Big ones like their secret castle door, and small ones, such as trap doors and hidden slides. Some had been created by Imagineers in the know, and some by past cats with an inclination for mechanics, not unlike Kimball. The problem was that over the last sixty years no one had kept a proper list. So while there were many that all the cats knew, there were still some false walls and zip lines whose locations were lost to history. Thurl often cautioned that at any time it was possible they might stumble upon, or *through*, one long forgotten escape.

That morning he led them down a dark hall that came to an abrupt end at a solid castle wall. Five square stone stiles ran along the bottom of the wall, unlike anywhere else inside the castle. Most human eyes (and even many cat eyes) would never even notice how they stood out, but again, human eyes never came this way. Thurl took his staff and tapped three of the tiles, in a deliberate order.

"When...you...wish," he sang softly as he hit each tile. Then he swung back to the first and tapped it two more times. "Upon...a...hmm." He turned to the cats. "Oliver, will you assist me, dear boy?"

"Of course," said Oliver, slightly confused but stepping forward.

"The last tile," said Thurl, pointing with his staff. "That one there. Give it a good push, will you?"

Oliver pressed his foot against it and pushed as he was told. With a click, it gave way and slid forward. The outline of a square doorway sprang forward from the wall just above the tiles with a puff of dust. All the cats jumped back, except the oldest, who stood chuckling.

"Star!," said Thurl, waving the cloud away. "There we are then. My dear, it has been awhile. Now, Elias, just give it a push back, if you don't mind."

Elias shrugged and pushed on the newly appeared door. It slid with little effort at all. In fact, it rolled backward, making a sound like marbles rolling across a kitchen floor, until it was recessed a good three feet and stopped, locking into place with a loud *ka-chunk*. Elias poked his head through. There was a narrow shaft leading down with a metal ladder bolted to the side of the wall. He turned around to look up and saw two metal arms with tiny wheels on either side of the opening, holding the door panel in the air.

"This is the safest way to exit the castle by day," said Thurl. "I suppose I've never mentioned it because, thankfully, we've never needed it. Remember, be quick. Be discreet. Discretion is the word of the day. Now, off you go."

"But wait," Oliver said. "Where does this lead?"

"Down, of course. Once you reach the bottom, there's a tunnel. From there it should be perfectly clear. Trust me. And if you should somehow manage to get turned around, Kimball should be able to suss out the way. Every exit is marked. Remember, you're looking for Adventureland."

"Adventureland," Lilli repeated, thoughtfully.

"Wait a minute," said Elias. "You're telling us there are tunnels under the park that lead to the different lands?"

"Of course," said Thurl. "Well, only the front half. There wasn't time to finish the others. They were meant for use in emergencies."

"This must be where the idea for the Utilidors in Florida came from," Kimball marveled, staring down the shaft. "Only there, they made them big enough for vehicles, storage, and all their operational needs."

"But how can this lead to Adventureland?" asked Oliver. "We're surrounded by the moat."

"That you are," Thurl said, with a wink. "Which reminds me, I recommend you walk quickly. The tunnel runs under the water. Well, *through* it, actually. Those walls are sixty years old. I'm sure they're quite solid, but just the same, don't dawdle."

"So where are we supposed to go when we get to Adventureland?" Elias asked.

"You and Kimball will find a good vantage point to hide and wait for Lilli and Oliver to return. Oliver, you and Lilli are headed to Walt's most *enchanted* creation. The place where birds sing words."

"Where birds sing?," Lilli said, then gave a knowing smile. "Ah, I got it. Come on, boys, that sun's not slowing down for us." Without waiting for the rest of them to respond, Lilli climbed over the opening, put her paw on the first rung, and started down. Oliver followed, and then Elias a moment after him. Kimball hung his head over the edge into the darkness. Below he could see a faint yellow glow.

"Disney's most enchanted...," he began to say. Kimball stopped, listening to the echo of his words falling down the shaft. "Oh, Enchanted! I get it. But, *really?*"

"All will be revealed," said Thurl, giving him a push. "Now go. The others are leaving without you."

The four Castle Cats took their turns shimmying down the narrow ladder, the three boys racing to catch up to Lilli. The shaft was so narrow that their tails brushed the opposite wall and occasionally each other's heads more than a few times. How a human could have ever fit down this passage was the true mystery. People must have been much skinnier in the 1950s, Kimball offered. They seemed to be climbing down for a few minutes with no indication how deep they'd travelled.

"I think I'm at the bottom," Lilli called up finally. She had lowered her back paw but found no more rungs. She took a deep breath and let go, dropping to the ground. She landed squarely on three of four paws, the fourth (and her tail) raised for balance. It's good to be a cat, she thought. "Watch your paws, boys. The end sneaks up on you."

Oliver lowered his paw for the next rung and it just swung in the air. They had indeed finally reached the bottom. He craned his neck around to look below. In the dim yellow light he could see the concrete floor just a few tails below. He saw Lilli looking up at him, her arms folded and her tail twitching. He wanted to drop swiftly to his feet like a silent ninja, but when he let go of the ladder and his back paws hit concrete, he couldn't slow himself. Oliver stumbled forward, nearly knocking Lilli over in the process. She ducked out of the way and grabbed him by the vest before he smacked face-first into the tunnel wall.

"Thanks," Oliver said, feeling foolish, and patting down his whiskers.

"No worries," she said with a giggle. "It's a bigger drop than it appears. You should've seen my landing. A total horror show. I'm lucky I didn't smash my face in."

"Really?" He couldn't tell if she was being honest, or simply trying to make him feel better. He didn't care. Either way, it helped.

Elias dropped down with a grunt. He stood up quickly with an annoyed look on his muzzle, and straightened his black vest. He was followed closely by the awkward Kimball who landed on his own tail with a yowl. The tunnel only led one way from here—straight on. Dim yellow bulbs lined the walls every six feet or so, giving it an eerie artificial light. The word "Hub" had been scrawled in fading paint with an arrow pointing the way. The four of them all nodded silently, unsure exactly of what they were doing, and headed down the tunnel.

Thankfully, while it was built low, the tunnel was wide, even by cat standards. Oliver led the way with Lilli and Kimball close behind. Kimball was fascinated, whispering gibberish to himself as they walked, trying to deduce exactly where they were, how far they'd walked from the castle, how close to Main Street, etc. Elias coolly followed the group at his own pace. His mind was focused on his growling stomach, and finding a strip or two of freshly cooked bacon once they made it street side. He wasn't used to being up, let alone active, this early in the day.

"We're definitely under the moat," Oliver said. He pointed at the ground just ahead. There was a long puddle of water. As they all looked, another droplet fell from above and splashed down, causing a tiny ripple.

"Well, that's reassuring," Lilli whispered sarcastically.

"Guys, if that's the worst leak that occurred in sixty years, we'll be okay today," Oliver said, trying to sound reassuring. "Right, Kimball?"

The scientific feline looked up at the hairline crack running along the top of the tunnel as another droplet formed. "Um, yeah, sure," he said without much confidence. "Just the same, why don't we pick up the pace a bit?"

They all nodded, took a deep breath, and walked briskly. Kimball took a piece of blue chalk from his belt and began marking the walls as they walked. Once they were past the long puddle and the ceiling of the tunnel was completely dry, Kimball ran ahead a few paces and scribbled "compass," with an arrow pointing up. Kimball determined they were right below the large compass rose, just like the one found on a treasure map, that was inlaid within the brick just before the castle moat.

"Always a good idea to update," he mumbled, seeing the other cats staring at him. "In case we have to use these again."

They traveled farther down the tunnel until they reached a dead end. The tunnel broke off to the left and right. Another ladder ran straight up the center of the wall to a circle in the ceiling.

"We must be under Main Street," Elias announced.

"I don't know," said Lilli. "Seems like we should have gone a little farther. This must be the hub."

"Correct, " said Kimball, still doing quiet calculations with a fuzzy finger in the air. "If I'm right, we should be just under the Partners statue. But then where would this ladder lead?"

"No time to worry about it right now," said Oliver. "Come on. The sooner we get to the Oracle, the sooner we can go home."

"Somebody's nervous to meet the Oracle," said Elias.

"Don't start," Oliver sneered.

"Hey, I don't blame you," said Elias. "However weird we are, I hear even weirder things happen around the Oracle. Been here since the beginning, knows all, sees all. And possibly hates cats. I wouldn't want to go strutting into his yard, either."

"Shut up Elias," Lilli snapped. "You still sleep with a stuffed mouse."

"Hey, it's a stress doll," said Elias. "I've got anger issues."

"Just shut up," Oliver snapped. "We have to get moving. The park opens sooner than later, and then we'll have to dodge thousands of guests in broad daylight. Adventureland's gotta be this way."

"Whatever you say," Elias saluted. "Lead the way, Captain."

The cats marched down the passage to the right until they reached another ladder bolted into the concrete wall. Lilli pointed at the wall beside it where someone had painted "Adv Lnd."

"If my guess is correct," she said reaching up and grabbing a rung before pausing and whispering some very Kimball-like gibberish of her own, "yes, I think we should actually be right near the Tiki Room."

"Shouldn't I go first," Oliver said, as she started to scale the ladder. "Just in case."

"I'm sorry, have I given you any indication that I need your protection?" she snapped. "I'm no withering damsel in distress, Oliver. I'll go first."

Lilli climbed the ladder until she was just below the street. It was dark and shadowy above the dim lights of the tunnel. Above her head Lilli could just make out the curve of a round metal disc, like a manhole cover. She reached up and pushed her paw against it. It didn't budge. Irritated, she moved up another rung and pushed her shoulder against the side of the circle. Nothing. Not even the hopeful sound of metal scraping concrete.

"Fine!" she yelled back down. "I might need a paw."

Oliver quickly scurried up the ladder and slid around beside her. "What seems to be the problem, ma'am?"

"It's locked. Or rusted shut or something. Anyone would need help."

"Totally understandable," he said, wiping the grin off his whiskers. "Strength in numbers. Good idea."

"Hey, lovebirds," Elias shouted up, "you're not sittin' in a tree. Can you move things along?"

"I'd like to stuff a lovebird down his throat," Oliver said, shaking his head and sighing. "Sorry about his big mouth. I never said we were…"

"Ignore him. That's what I do. If you respond, it just fuels him. Besides, he's just jealous I didn't ask *him* for help."

That makes sense, Oliver thought. Wait, what? What did that mean? Had Lilli asked him to help on purpose? If so, was it just because he'd been closest to the ladder? Then again, there was no question the stocky Elias was the stronger of the two of them.

"Hey, you with me?" Lilli snapped. "Let's push together. Maybe if you try from the middle."

Oliver reached up to place his paws against the center of the cover. There was something round, a metal ring—like a donut built into the cover.

"Um, I may have found something," he said. He wrapped his paw around the ring and twisted. It was stubborn, having not been turned in decades, but the ring squeaked and squealed until it finally gave away. With one full turn, they both heard a click echo above them.

"That's it! You got it Ollie!"

"Alright, now let's push."

They both gave a good shove and the lid lifted. They were momentarily blinded by a sliver of bright morning sunlight. Oliver squinted until his green eyes adjusted, then cautiously peaked out to see if the coast was clear. Lilli had guessed they must be close to the Enchanted Tiki Room. They were close, alright. Just across the beige stone street, in fact. He looked up and saw a jagged stone tile was affixed to the top of the hatch. He was peeking right out of the street. In peak hours, thousands of guests walked right over this passage without ever having a clue.

Oliver could see the long oval sign reading "Walt Disney's Enchanted Tiki Room" so clearly that he could make out every flower carved around the red letters on the yellow background. He could see the triangular thatched roofs of the Tiki Room theater poking into the sky above the courtyard where guests would wait to enter. Soon there would be cast members serving pineapple ice cream swirls to those waiting in the hot sun. Suddenly, a pair of brown leather shoes and tan-colored pant legs appeared about six inches from his nose. Oliver reared back in surprise.

"What is it?" Lilli asked.

"A human," he whispered back to her. "Right outside."

"Should we get out of here?"

Oliver just shrugged and poked his head back up.

"What in the world is *that*?" they heard the human say in a deep, booming growl.

Oh, no, Oliver thought. We're busted! We better run for it.

"The California Commission for the Control of Infectious Feral Species?" the voice questioned loudly. "Again I ask, what is that? I've never heard of it."

The man wasn't referring to a pair of cat eyes peering out of an opening in the street. Relieved, Oliver pushed up the lid a bit further. He could see a tall, black-haired man in a blue shirt and yellow tie, speaking into a cell phone. He had a white cast member tag on his chest. His eyes weren't looking anywhere near the ground.

"Well, I don't care if he is a doctor," the man went on. "We're trying to get the park opened. He should have called first. There are proper channels for these things, even for government inspectors. Tell him he'll have to wait. I'm busy right now...what in the world?"

The shoes suddenly turned. They were pointing straight at Oliver's peeking eyes.

"Uh, nothing. You know what? Just bring him here and I'll talk to him," the man's voice said, much more quietly. "I have to go." One foot took a step toward the partially open lid.

Oh, no, Oliver thought. He looked over at Lilli and mouthed the word *go*!

"What?" she asked?

"Go! We have to get out of here!"

Without another question, Lilli quickly climbed back down the ladder. When she was clear, Oliver let the lid drop back down and he loosened his grip on the ladder. He slid all the way down like a circus clown.

"Run!" he called out, trotting toward the confused threesome. They all turned tail and ran back down the tunnel the way they had come. They stopped at the fork in the tunnels near the ladder that led to the hub, attempting to regroup. Oliver was watching the tunnel nervously. He expected to see a human come jogging at them from Adventureland any second. Fortunately, it didn't happen. Maybe the man thought his eyes had been playing tricks on him.

"OK," Elias said, "you want to explain what just happened?"

Lilli stepped forward. "There was a human. Right outside the hatch, blocking any chance of reaching the Tiki Room."

"What do you suggest now?" Elias grunted at Oliver.

"Not to alarm anyone," Kimball said, "but the park opens soon. We better think of something quickly, or else go back to the castle and formulate a Plan B."

"No," said Oliver. "There's no going back without seeing the Oracle. Thurl would be disappointed in me."

"In all of us," Lilli added. "Come on Kimball, you're the smart one. What do we do?"

"Well, let me see." He looked down the tunnel behind him, and his eyes rolled around behind his glasses as he thought. "Given our current circumstance, we only have two options. We go that way toward Tomorrowland, where even if we can get to the street unnoticed, we'd have to circle back around the entire park to get to Adventureland."

"Not a great option," Oliver said, shaking his head.

"What's your second idea?" Lilli asked.

Kimball looked at the ladder. He nervously pushed his glasses up on the bridge of his nose. "We go up."

"Fine, stand aside," said Elias. He pushed past the rest of them and grabbed the ladder, stepping up onto the first rung. "I'm going first this time."

"Be my guest," said Oliver with a mock bow.

"It was only a thought," Kimball said, concerned. "It's a longer run to the Tiki Room from here."

"At least it's action," said Elias. "I'm tired of sitting around this sewer pipe." He quickly shimmied up the ladder until he found himself surrounded by darkness. He reached another metal lid just as the others had before. Elias reached up and pushed hard, expecting it to open right up. They could hear him grunting as he pushed against it vain.

"Aren't you going to tell him?" Lilli asked, looking at Oliver with her eyebrow raised.

"Tell him what?" he winked.

"Oliver!"

"Oh, fine." Oliver looked up and cupped his paws around his mouth. "There's a wheel in the middle. You have to turn it." There was silence for a moment.

"I knew that," Elias finally growled back. He felt around in the shadows until he found the metal ring. He turned it as instructed until the click of the lock rang through the tunnel. Elias gave it a push and the round door opened right up.

"Go slow," Oliver whispered up the ladder.

Elias rolled his eyes and pushed the cover open just a few inches and peered out. He couldn't believe the view. He was looking right down the middle of Main Street, U.S.A. The wet, empty streets glistened in the sun. He had an unobstructed view of the train station. No guests. Only a few oblivious park cast members way down at the other end. It was just an empty, impeccably clean, small-town street, lined with colorful shops quietly waiting for a new day of controlled chaos to begin.

"It's Main Street," he called back down, loudly. "Looks like the coast is clear. Elias pushed the round cover all the way up until it locked into an upright position, allowing him to climb out. He hoisted himself up and put his paws down, to find them sinking into soft soil. He was surrounded by pink, yellow, and purple flowers. He quickly craned his head around and he was staring at a concrete pedestal and an engraved plaque that read "Partners." Elias didn't even need to look up. This portal opened up in the base of the iconic statue of Walt Disney and Mickey Mouse in the center of the hub. The lid to the tunnel was camouflaged with matching turf and flowers. No guest would ever notice a difference when the hatch was in place.

"Hurry up," he called back down into the tunnel. "You guys are not going to believe this."

Elias rolled out into the flowers. The other three cats quickly emerged from the tunnel one after another. Each had the same dumbfounded expression when they stepped down on soft grass and spotted the spring flowers all around. Kimball quickly climbed up onto the pedestal, wrapping an arm and his frizzy yellow tail around Mr. Disney's leg. He flipped his binocular lenses down over his regular glasses. He was peering off toward Adventureland, shielding his vision from the morning sun. There was no sign of any human on a telephone. All Oliver and Lilli had to do was get across unnoticed.

"All clear," he called down. "I'd say now is the time. You can run right in the front entrance unnoticed."

"Well," Lilli said, looking to Oliver with a slight smile and a shrug, "you heard the cat. Now is the time."

He smiled and nodded. "Now is the best time."

"Then get going," Elias said with a sigh, rolling his eyes at them both. "They never even used that song here. Sheesh!"

"Alright," Oliver said. "You two stay here. Keep low and guard this tunnel entrance. It's our quickest way back home."

"And we'll be cutting it close," said Lilli. "We're looking at less than an hour before the park opens. Who knows how long it's going to take to find this Oracle, let alone talk to him, or her,...or it, I guess. We could find ourselves diving through that hole just as a herd of sneakers and flip-flops comes marching up Main Street."

"Let's not be dramatic," said Elias. He gestured to Sleeping Beauty Castle just over the drawbridge from their position. "If you really get in a pinch, the castle is right there. Just run for it."

"You heard Thurl," said Oliver. "We cannot be seen. We take the tunnel back. It's the safest way. Just stay here, will you?"

"Don't worry, Oliver," Kimball interjected. "We will keep this access point secure. Just get in and back as quickly as you can."

"He's right," said Lilli, whacking Oliver on the arm. She skipped right past him, cutting through the flowers and pulling her lavender hood up over her brown ears. Lilli slipped between the bars of the circular rail around the statue and took off running for Adventureland. "Let's go, Ollie!"

"You better go," said Elias, with a chuckle. "Your girlfriend's halfway to the Jungle Cruise, *Ollie*."

Oliver balled his fist and tried to think of a comeback. Or better yet, he thought about knocking Elias off the pedestal. Instead he just glared and shook his head, before turning and jumping down without a word. It took no time to reach the entrance to Adventureland. Oliver found Lilli with her back pressed against a trash can near the Tiki Room entrance.

"What took you so long?" she teased.

"Traffic."

Not to be outdone, he bolted off toward the entrance to the attraction. It was an archway made of gnarled dark wood with a yellow oval sign like a surfboard that read "Walt Disney's Enchanted Tiki Room" in red. Two torches jutted out in front of it to light the sign at night. Once through the arch, guests entered a tropical courtyard where they waited for the showroom to open. It was lined with high walls and lush greenery. Orange and white tapestries hung overhead featuring Tiki masks and tribal lizards along with other exotic designs.

Oliver was just about to enter when he heard human voices. He nearly tripped tail-over-whiskers when he saw three men standing just inside, only a few feet away. Lilli, not noticing, plowed right into his back, knocking him in farther. It only took her a second to shake off the collision and see why Oliver hit the brakes so abruptly. She quickly grabbed him by the vest and pulled him out of view. They ducked into the bougainvillea plants and palm fronds underneath the Enchanted Tiki Room sign.

"Great," Lilli whispered. They were safely out of view, but they also could see only one of the men. "I can barely see. Who are these guys? And what are they doing in here?"

"Well, that guy there..." Oliver huffed, catching his breath after being plowed into and pointing, "is the man who was...talking outside the tunnel opening. I recognize his shoes. The other one is wearing a security uniform. I didn't get a good look at the third guy."

It was true. The third man was almost completely obscured from their view.

"As I told your security man," they heard the hidden man speak in a shrill, gravelly voice, "I represent the California Commission for the Control of Infectious Species."

There was something familiar about his voice, Oliver thought. They could see his long bony fingers handing the small white rectangle to the park employee. It was a business card. Oliver had seen park executives hand them out. It was a way humans identified themselves to others. Apparently it showed how important they were, or at least how important they thought they were. It was a weird custom, he thought—although he imagined it was better than a silver tag on a tight collar around the neck.

"The CCCIS?" the park manager chuckled, his deep voice sounding both annoyed and bemused. "I'm sorry, sir, but I've been a manager here for many years and I've never heard of your office. And we're very busy. There are necessary procedures in place to control this sort of thing."

"It's *doctor*, if you please," the man hissed. "My name is Doctor Sorrel Powers. Perhaps you'd prefer I return in an hour or two with an entire inspection team garbed in lovely bright yellow hazardous material suits and a search warrant from the governor of California himself!"

"Listen," the manager started, "Mister...."

"Doctor!" the man spat. "Doctor Sorrell Powers!"

"Right, uh, Doctor," the manager went on, "I'm not trying to be a problem. I'm just a little confused. What exactly is it you want from me? I'm trying to get my park open for the day."

"This is ridiculous," Lilli grumbled. "I need a better view." She looked around at the foliage above them and extended her claws. She quickly climbed up a thin tree and shimmied her body out onto a branch. She was well shielded by leaves but did have a better view. She couldn't see the man's face, but had a good look at his body.

"Seems a little warm to be wearing a long, heavy coat," said Lilli.

"What?" Oliver whispered up at her.

"This Powers guy is wearing a long gray overcoat."

Gray overcoat, he thought? The man took a few steps over. He was talking and waving his hands.

"What is your name, sir?" the man asked.

The manager pulled his tag out a little further off his shirt for the doctor to inspect. "Patrick," he answered flatly. "It's all right here on my name tag. I'm Patrick, from Paterson, New Jersey. My favorite character is Kronk."

"It is my duty to alert you to a major problem inside your park," the doctor said. "You have an infestation here. As much as I'd hate to do it, I am not afraid to report you personally, *Patrick*, if you are turning a blind eye to a serious health risk. And worse, as I suspect, perhaps even encouraging it."

"Infestation?" Patrick said. "Encouraging it? What are you talking about? What infestation? Disneyland is not only the happiest place on the planet, it's the cleanest!"

"Bah! Your park is a breeding ground! I can smell it. This entire property is overrun with mite-infested, disease-spreading, allergy inciting, feral *felis silvestris*!"

"I'm sorry, Doc, but are you even speaking English?" the manager asked, shaking his head.

"Cats! Your park is full of dangerous stray cats!" At this Powers turned and stepped forward, wildly gesturing all around.

Oliver finally got a good look at the face of this Doctor Powers. He knew it in an instant, even if he'd only seen it once before, and just for a moment at that. The unusual *horns* of feathery gray hair, which today he had attempted to comb down, without much success. The thick round glasses perched on the pointy nose; it was all exactly as he'd seen it the night before. The only thing missing was the man's telltale red scarf.

Today around his neck was a spotted bowtie. Until, that is, Oliver squinted and was able to see the familiar red material draped around the back of his neck and hanging loosely inside his coat. Oliver had thought the man was rather thin last night, but there was a hefty paunch in his midsection like a pot-belly emerging from under his coat. Still, there was no question, this was indeed Doctor Owl he'd seen riding the Haunted Mansion a few hours before. The trespasser who sicked his attack rats on Oliver—the same rats who spoke of the mysterious key.

"Lilli," Oliver whispered, "that's him. That's the man I saw last night."

"That's Doctor Owl?" She did a double take, squinting hard to get a good look at him. "Powers? He was the guy on the Haunted Mansion? The rat guy? Are you sure?"

"Absolutely positive. He's the one looking for the key. I can't believe he actually walked right into the park today."

"Guess you ruined his original plan. Desperate times call for desperate measures, as Thurl says."

"Is that what this is about?" they heard Patrick say with a laugh. "The mythical cats of Disneyland? Come on Doctor Powers, you didn't really come down here for that, did you? I assure you, the cats are just another fanboy legend made up to add a little more excitement and intrigue to the park. We are not some secret *haven* for the feral cats of Anaheim. Sure, occasionally one may sneak in, but our maintenance crews shoo them away immediately."

"No!" Powers shouted. "You're wrong sir! They are here. I personally saw one just last...!"

The manager's eyes went wide and he cocked his head. Powers shut his mouth immediately, realizing he shouldn't finish that statement.

"I mean, that is to say, I can sense when there's a cat nearby," he quickly spat. "I'm terribly allergic to cats. Sometimes just thinking of a cat makes me break into a sneezing fit! I know beyond a shadow of a doubt there are cats in this vicinity. Not one—*cats*, plural!"

"I think you're overreacting Doc," said Patrick, taking a handkerchief out of his back pocket and dabbing sweat from his forehead. "You can't believe everything you read. Disneyland is not a wild cat refuge."

"Then why, may I ask," the doctor began, then paused and made a sniffling sound, "do I already feel an irritating tickle in my right nostril? Even now the back of my throat tightens. I've heard these cats only come out at night, but if I didn't know better I'd say there's one within a few feet."

"Guess what, Doc," the manager said, "my wife has a cat. It sleeps on my clothes that I put out the night before. Had I known you were coming, I promise I'd have picked a different shirt. That's the kind of guest service I believe in. Now please, I've really got to get to work and it's already getting warm out here. If there's nothing else, I'd be happy to offer you a card for a free hot dog at Refreshment Corner. It's just around the corner from here on your way out. But I need to get on with my day."

"Get those infernal felines out of here," Doctor Powers warned sternly. "Every single one. From Toon Town to the promenade."

"Listen, Doctor," the manager snapped, momentarily raising his voice, then pausing and forcing a calm smile. He wanted to remain professional and courteous, but hoped it was clear he'd had enough. "If there were such cats in the park, how in the world would I get them out? Do you realize how many people, not to mention how much time that would take?"

"Ah, well, I am glad you asked," said the doctor. "Perhaps, as I am trained in these matters, I can be of assistance myself, if I were granted access to the entire park, merely to inspect for traces of the cats. It's very likely the bulk of them reside in some concentrated area, an agreed-upon hiding place. Allow me unlimited access to your so-called backstage areas. Give me permission to dig around the nooks and crannies of your attractions. I certainly won't be a nuisance to your guests in my search. I am sure I could come up with an agreeable solution to alleviate your cat problem that will not upset your daily routine."

"I'm sorry," said the manager, narrowing his eyes. He pointed at the oval-shaped name tag on his shirt. "Nobody gets that kind of access that doesn't wear one of these babies." Just then his phone rang. He held up a finger to the doctor, signifying he should wait for a moment.

"Yello, Patrick here," he answered. "Yes, Doctor Powers. I'm looking at his business card right now. No, he's right here. In front of The Tiki Room, why? A *what*? You're kidding me! When was that? By who? No way!" Patrick's eyes widened as he listened to the caller. Slowly his head turned to glare at Powers. Whatever he was hearing, it wasn't making him happy. "Nope, I'll handle it."

Oliver and Lilli could see Powers begin to shift nervously and wipe his forehead with his sleeve. He began to nervously fumble with a pocket watch he'd removed from his coat pocket.

"Excuse me, um, Patrick," he croaked, suddenly seeming to have trouble finding his voice. "I just now noticed the time. I'm afraid I've forgotten another appointment. We will have to continue this discussion at another date. I will call ahead next time, as you suggest." He began walking backwards toward the exit.

"Just one second *Doctor* Powers," Patrick growled. His tone had completely shifted from the generally pleasant, helpful demeanor of a Disneyland cast member to an aggravated, even menacing voice. He pushed the end button on his phone and stuck it in his pocket. "Turns out there is something I can do for you. I will be happy to escort you to the front gate. I think we can even arrange a ride for you. A very special ride."

"Th-th-that's quite alright," Powers stuttered. "I can manage on my own. He quickly shuffled off, about to make a break for it.

"Oh, no," Patrick said, quickly darting in front of him, blocking the exit. "I insist."

"Wonder what that call was about?" Lilli said.

"I don't know," Oliver answered, "but it sure took some of the thunder out of Doctor Owl's voice."

As the two men made to leave, Powers turned and stumbled against a planter. He slumped over it and began to fan himself with his hand.

"What's the matter now?" Patrick asked, officially out of patience with this odd man.

"Oh, nothing, I'll be fine," the doctor said, nervously, "just the, uh, the heat. It's nearly unbearable."

"Oh, come on, it's not that bad," said Patrick, who could not see what Oliver and Lilli had a clear view of. Powers opened the side of his overcoat. Something brown and hairy spilled out into the dense plant arrangement. It was followed by something black and then something gray. In an instant, Powers had lost all that extra weight around his middle.

"The rats," Oliver said.

"I don't believe it," Lilli gasped. "His little rat friends were hiding in his coat the whole time!"

"And now that he just released them into those plants they'll have the run of the park," said Oliver. "We have to go after them."

"Not yet," Lilli cautioned. "The last thing we need is to add any fuel to this fire. If Doctor Owl sees us in front of that cast member, he might get the clearance he's looking for, after all. That would be bad. By the way, I can't believe you've got me calling him that, too!"

"Heat?" said Patrick. "It's beautiful out here. Always a beautiful day at Disneyland. Now let's go, Doctor *Mintz*. I'm willing to let you go on your own this time, but come back again and I'll have an air-conditioned car waiting for you, courtesy of the Anaheim Police Department."

"What did he call him?" Lilli asked. "Mints?"

"That's what it sounded like. What happened to Powers?"

"So you've discovered my true identity," the doctor huffed. He straightened up and adjusted his coat, dusting off his sleeves and straightening the collar.

"Yeah, that's right," Patrick answered, matter-of-factly. "My office ran a search for a "Doctor Powers," and your CC...whatever. There's no such person or thing. But they did find a pharmacist in Yorba Linda named Doctor Sorrell Mintz. When we ran that name, guess what else we found out."

"My compliments to your records department," Mintz answered. "I had hoped that unfortunate incident from my youth had long been forgotten; even erased from history. It appears you people do a thorough job, even after so many years."

"If that's the issue, you should've just gone to Guest Relations" said Patrick. "It's been a long time. They could sort this out, and it would've saved you a lot of trouble. Not to mention saved me this wasted time."

"It matters not," said Mintz, turning away. "I will finish what I came here for."

"Maybe so," said Patrick, frowning and gesturing forward. Two park security officers were approaching. "Not today. These gentlemen will see you to the front gates. You've wasted enough of my time already."

Doctor Mintz began walking again, right past the two security men who he refused to acknowledge.

"Happiest place on earth," he muttered. "Not for much longer."

"Make sure he gets out of here," Patrick instructed the officers. "What a kook! No wonder he's been banned since the 60s."

"This is far from over!" Mintz yelled, still walking.

Chapter Five

"Alright," said Oliver leaping out from their hiding place when Patrick was far out of view, "now we go after the rats!"

"No," said Lilli crawling out after him. "We don't. You need to go see the Oracle, remember? That's what we came for."

"But they're running loose in the park right now!"

"And we know what they're looking for. If the Oracle can tell you where it is, we can find it first. Or at least head them off at the pass. Once this key is safe, we can take care of a couple of rats. Right now they're not the priority."

Oliver took a deep breath. She was right. Thurl had given them a task. He needed to complete it before he went chasing rats.

"You're right," he said. Oliver walked to the center of the courtyard and looked all around them. "So, here we are, at the Tiki Room. Where do we find the Oracle?"

They were surrounded by carvings of ancient Polynesian Tiki gods, each set among thick tropical foliage; palm fronds, bright hibiscus flowers, and trees. They had wide, crazy faces painted in blue and white and purple and red. Some showed rows of teeth, others like one called Rongo (who Oliver thought looked like a monkey with a fruit bowl on his head) had their tongues hanging out.

"Maybe one of these guys can tell us," Lilli joked, pulling her hood back. "Who are they, anyway?"

"Ancient Polynesian gods. And goddesses. See that one there with her hands on her hips and the volcano-shaped hat? That's Pele. She's the Goddess of Fire."

"What about that silly fellow?" Lilli asked, pointing to one who was standing on his head, his legs straight up in the air. He had yellow stripes running down his face that looked like bananas. "I can't read his sign. Or is he a she?"

"That's Ngnedei. He's the earth balancer. When Pele blows her top and sets off a volcano, he keeps the world together."

"They seem like a fun bunch." The words had barely left her lips when things took a strange turn—stranger than usual. From someplace unseen, drums began to beat. Ancient drums, pounding out a syncopated rhythm, building louder and louder. A breeze began to blow through their whiskers that quickly built into a strong wind, causing the tapestries overhead to flap and fill with air like sails. Dark clouds rolled in above the Tiki Room courtyard. Flashes of blue lightning zipped through the black shadows.

"Did they turn on the attraction?" Lilli asked. "Is this part of the show?"

"I don't think so," said Oliver, reading the plaque beside a towering, skinny idol with her hands folded on her chest called Tangaroa-Ru. "Look at this." Where before he was certain the Tiki's eyes were carved closed, now they appeared to be glowing green. Atop her head was perched a parrot idol whose wings began to spin wildly like pinwheels. "Goddess of the East Wind. Do you think she could be causing this?"

"Oliver," Lilli whispered, tugging at his elbow, "look over there." She was pointing at Koro, a god with a flat head and jagged teeth. The Tiki idol was swaying side to side and there was no question his eyes were glowing bright green. The drumming was coming from his direction. As they looked around, the two cats realized now that all the Tikis' eyes were glowing brightly. "Do these idols normally have light-up eyes!"

Ngendi, the balancer, began to rock back and forth as though the very ground was shaking below his feet. A tall god with circular eyes like two tiny donuts began to spit water from his mouth into a bamboo tube. The hands of a clock began to tick around his face.

Suddenly a burst of orange fire, so powerful they could feel the heat engulfing them, erupted behind their backs. Both cats spun around in horror. A pillar of fire was blasting from the volcano goddess, Pele's wooden head, as well as from her ears, nose, and mouth, yet none of her was burnt. Finally, the flames relented and her eyes glowed red.

"Who has come to see the Oracle?" Pele demanded. Her booming voice echoed so loudly they were certain it must be audible all the way to California Adventure.

"Um, that would be me," Oliver squeaked.

"Identify yourself to Pele, Goddess of Volcanoes."

"I—I am Oliver. This is Lilli. We are Cats of the Castle."

There was rumbling among all the gods and their eyes flashed brightly. "Tell me, Cats of the Castle, "how do you know of the Oracle?"

"Oh, uh, well…our great elder, Thurl," Oliver answered hoping this might click with the goddess. "Maybe you've heard of him? He sent us. We need to ask the Oracle a question."

"Do you come with pure hearts and noble intentions? For any that dare to enter this sacred circle with hopes of selfish gain, or worse, to dishonor this park will suffer my fire!" A great plume of flame burst from her mountain-shaped crown. The startled cats grabbed each other's arms.

"Please, great goddess Pele," Lilli said. "The park may be in great danger. We only come so that we might protect it. And all who live here."

"Danger? What danger do you speak of?"

"Outsiders," said Oliver. "A human."

"A human? What does Pele care about a human. This park is full of humans."

"This one is very bad," Oliver said. "We believe he's serious trouble. He brought three rats with him and they're loose in the park right now."

"Rats in the park!?" Smoke escaped her ears. "Pele despises rats."

"I'm beginning to myself," said Oliver. "They are searching for something special. A, uh, a sacred artifact that belonged to Mr. Disney. The rats plan to steal it for this human they serve."

"These intruders wish to steal from Mr. Disney!" Pele growled, her eyes lighting up like flares. More fire blasting from her cap. "They shall be cursed!"

"Please, benevolent Pele," added Lilli, "we will stop them. But we are already losing time."

Pele's eyes dimmed and the flame again died down to that of a candle. She was silent a moment, then spoke thoughtfully. "You cats would protect this park, at all costs?"

"Yes," Oliver said. "It is our duty. This is our home."

"Very well," said Pele. Her eyes lit up brighter than ever. All at once, the lightning vanished, the drumming faded as if someone turned down the volume on a radio, and the black clouds dissipated. In a moment the sky over the courtyard was again bright and blue. At the top of a small set of stairs lined with bamboo rails, the doors to the Tiki Room theater slowly swung open.

"Enter, and see the Oracle. Protect the park."

"We will," said Oliver with an appreciative nod.

"Yes," said Lilli, "thank you, great Pele."

The eyes of the Tiki idols slowly dimmed until they were just painted wood again. Oliver and Lilli made their way up the stairs. Oliver took a deep breath and stepped inside the darkened showroom. The sun did its best to illuminate the open theater but much of it remained in shadow. They could make out long rows of benches to their left and right. There were strange shapes and outlines all along the walls and things hanging from above, but it was too dark to see much detail. Lilli was certain she was seeing faces looking down and maybe even creatures crouched in corners and near the ceiling. In the shadows it appeared as if almost everything in there had a face. They stepped in farther. Then the door slammed shut behind them.

Oliver and Lilli were engulfed in darkness. They reached for each other's paws.

"Can't say I like this," Lilli whispered.

"Me neither. I wish I had my sword."

"It was plastic. That's why we have claws."

Cats of the Castle 53

"It was still helpful," he shot back. "At least it made me feel better."

"Yeah well, I'd feel better if you carried a flashlight. They sell them in every gift shop, you know."

A round spotlight appeared on the bamboo ceiling. Both cats felt their ears flatten against their heads as they looked up. Something was slowly being lowered into the light. It was a ring of some kind...with claws. No, Oliver realized, they were gray bird's feet. The ring was a perch. There was a bird in the middle. A parrot, to be exact, with bright green feathers on its head and back, and a white belly surrounded by a yellow tuft below its orange-and-red beak. Its wings were blue, yellow, and brilliant emerald green. The bird cocked its head and turned its beak in a fashion that almost looked as though it were smiling at them.

"Well, well, well," the parrot spoke with a chipper Irish brogue. "Top o' the morning, my feline friends! Fancy seeing the likes of you two here!"

"Sorry to intrude," said Oliver. "We've come to...."

"Intrude?" the parrot laughed. "Not at all! This room was built for guests. It's just been some time since we've had guests covered in fur. I take it you'd be Castle Cats, then? Sure an' I've never seen any of ye, but I've heard tales. Tales of your tails, you might say. My name is Michael."

"Um, nice to meet you, Michael," Lilli said. "Any chance you could point my friend here to the Oracle?"

"Ah, the Oracle. So that's why you've come, then? Well, sure I can show you to the Oracle. It's just that, well, I can't do it alone. I'll need to wake up my feathered brethren. Eh, you two may want to cover your ears."

Confused, they did as was suggested. They clasped their paws over their pointy ears. Michael opened his beak and let out a whistle so loud and shrill, it nearly split their eardrums even while muffled. Both cats winced.

"Jose!" Michael called out. "Fritz! Pierre! Fine hosts, the lot of ye' be! We have visitors in need. Show yerselves!"

Three more spotlights appeared on the ceiling, though from what source Oliver could not tell. From each circle of white light lowered a new perch on which sat a colorful parrot. They were all similar to Michael, except with varying hues and patterns in their plumage.

"Zut alors, mon ami," a French speaking parrot moaned, "what is it? Zee first show doesn't start for anozer 'alf an hour!"

"Yah," seconded another parrot with a German accent. That must be Fritz, Oliver assumed.

"Talk about my siestas getting shorter and shorter," the last bird yawned. That was Jose, the parrot who always started the show. He was possibly the most famous attraction host in the park. Apparently the sleepiest as well. "This is getting ridiculous!"

"Gentleman," said Michael. "I'm sorry to disturb your slumber but some young friends have come in need of help. This is Oliver and Miss Lilli. They have come to see the Oracle."

"Ooh la la," whistled Pierre. "It is a pleasure, mademoiselle. I would be 'appy to escort you myself."

"Watch it, Frenchy," Lilli muttered, clicking her claws together loud enough to be heard on the ceiling. "I bet you'd be just as good as a turkey leg."

"Settle down, Herr Pierre," said Fritz. "Show ze fraulein ze proper respect, yah? Willkommen, mein schatz!"

"Enough of this coddin around lads!" shouted Michael. "The Oracle, remember?"

"Were they cleared by the Tiki gods?" Jose asked. "Senora Pele can be one spicy habanero toward trespassers!"

"Zey don't look like ze burnt bratwurst to me," said Fritz.

"Yes," said Michael. "They were allowed entrance by Pele herself."

"Very well," said Pierre. He cleared his throat and opened his beak. His eyes rolled back into his head. "I will start."

Both cats felt their whiskers go rigid expecting another shrill whistle. Instead, the French bird began to sing, sort of. He let out one solid, perfectly tuned, sustained note. As he did, Fritz opened his beak and began a lower, baritone note in harmony. Michael joined in, a perfect Irish tenor. Lastly, Jose joined the tune. The four birds each emitted their own prolonged, harmonized note. The sound they made was beautiful, almost hypnotic. Oliver and Lilli exchanged looks. What was happening? It certainly sounded wonderful, but they'd come to see the Oracle. Not hear a concert.

The room began to hum with energy. All the lights began to brighten and fade with the sound. Other birds around the ceiling joined in, each singing their own singular note. The carved faces on the tiki poles along the walls opened their mouths and began emitting deep bass tones. The Tiki Room was filled with a cacophony of sound. Suddenly the ceiling above the four parrots made a *thunking* noise and a large square platform began to lower. The four hosts slowly came down with it.

As this strange secret stage rolled closer to them, Oliver and Lilli could see it was lined with small stone statues. Oliver recognized them right away as Hawaiian menehune; small mythical creatures that lived in the islands. Lilli quickly counted the little creatures.

"Seven," she whispered to Oliver. They looked like children, or elves, with pot bellies, big round eyes, and happy faces. These particular menehune looked strangely familiar. Six wore pointed caps and had bushy stone beards. The seventh had neither, but slightly larger ears and a blissful smile.

In the middle of the figures, as if lording over the tiny menehune, surrounded by palm leaves and hibiscus flowers, was yet another wooden Tiki god, not unlike the others outside. This idol had a flat face like a shield.

One carved eyebrow was locked in a triangular lift while the other was straight, almost scowling. Its mouth was shaped in an eternal grimace as though it was angry or in pain. Perhaps the strangest detail Oliver noticed was the two thin strips of wood carved onto the upper lip. It looked like a thin mustache.

The idol's arms were folded across its chest. There was no sign indicating which Polynesian god or goddess it was meant to represent. The stage came to a halt as the perches of the four parrots below just grazed the floor. Bamboo torches on either side of the statue blazed to life with orange flames. All singing stopped. The Tiki Room fell instantly silent save for the haunting drums beating softly in the darkness.

"Now what?" Lilli whispered.

"I don't know," said Oliver. "Is this the...?"

"Silence!" a voice boomed. The eyes of the Tiki glowed with a bright red light. "Behold, I am the Oracle! Who has summoned me in search of wisdom?!?"

"Tha—that would be me," said Oliver, sheepishly stepping forward.

"Identify yourself interloper...oh, it's *you*?" the Oracle said, his voice, while still loud and echoing, switched from angry and foreboding to calm, and even befuddled. "No, no, it can't be you. How could it be? You'd be nearly as old as I am."

"Um, great Oracle, I am Oliver," said the nervous cat, looking at Lilli for guidance. She only shrugged and urged him to go on. "I, uh, that is, *we* are Cats of the Castle. We have been sent by our elder, Thurl. We are the guardians of the...."

"I know who you are," the Oracle said quickly. "I know all that goes on inside this park. I have been here since before the gates opened. And I will be here for many years to come. You happen to resemble someone else. Well, go on then. State your question."

"Right," said Oliver. "Well, there are intruders in the park. A very bad human working with a group of rats. Last night they snuck inside the Haunted Mansion."

"I am aware. Your efforts to capture the rodents were valiant."

"Oh," said Oliver, surprised. "Well, thank you."

"But you failed!" the Oracle snapped, his eyes flashing.

"Yes, I, well, that's true," Oliver said, embarrassed. He began to hope the Oracle wasn't going to interrupt him every time he spoke. "I heard them say they are here looking for something—some kind of key."

"A key?"

"Yes," said Oliver, impressed he'd managed to surprise the Oracle. "The human who brought them is looking for a key. Thurl believes it might be a special key Mr. Disney kept hidden."

"Yes, your master is wise. The one and only Disneyland key was created for Walt Disney himself. It was a gift, forged by fairies, to give Disneyland the power of true magic."

"Fairy magic," said Lilli. "Like us."

"Indeed," said the Oracle. "A turn of this golden key ignited all the magic within this park. It powers every attraction, every note of music, even the rivers and waterfalls that flow throughout."

"One key does all that?" asked Oliver. "What about electricity?"

"Human engineering keeps the basic functions running," said the Oracle. "But you should know by now there is a greater power that flows through this place. Creating Disneyland would not have been possible with human engineering alone. Not in Walt's day. Not even now. Disney knew the secret to harnessing magic, wonder, imagination—the building blocks he needed for this place.

"Mr. Disney knew many secrets. Magic is a wondrous thing, but its secrets must never be revealed to the wrong people. It is best kept hidden. Look at yourselves. That is why Mr. Disney insisted you cats live in secret, avoiding the eyes of the guests. It is why I live here among these birds. And it is for that same reason he kept the key securely hidden. If the wrong person discovered the secret of the key, it could be a disaster.

"What kind of disaster can one little key cause?" Oliver asked.

"More than you can believe. A single turn in the right direction would shut off all the magic in the park."

"Shut it off?" Lilli repeated. "For how long?"

"As long as they chose," the Oracle said gravely. "Were someone to shut it off and throw away the key, our magic supply would be turned off forever. The streets would crack. Animatronic figures would decay. Rides would never run again. My birds would never sing again. Even I would cease to exist."

The two cats had worried looks on their faces. "Do you think Doctor Owl wants the key to turn off Disneyland?" Lilli asked.

"I guess," Oliver answered, "but why? Why would anyone want to shut off Disneyland?"

"Doctor Owl" the Oracle repeated. "Why do you say this, Doctor Owl?"

"The man who wants to steal the key," said Oliver. "He was here again this morning. I called him Doctor Owl because he has this crazy...well anyway, we heard him say his real name is Mintz. Sorrell Mintz."

"Sorrell Mintz." The idol was silent for a moment. "Sorrell Mintz is not allowed inside this park."

"Yeah, no kidding," said Oliver. "He's bad news. We just watched security escort him out."

"No. Sorrell Mintz was banned from Disneyland almost fifty years ago."

"He was *what*?" Lilli asked.

"When Disneyland was built," the Oracle said, "Walt Disney's family kept an apartment above the firehouse. Walt loved spending the night here in his park. After he passed away, it sat dormant, as his brother and the rest of the family decided what to do with it. A few years later, in December of 1968, a twelve-year-old boy from Garden Grove snuck up the back stairs and broke the lock on the door with a hammer. He was apprehended by a security guard who'd seen him creeping around the back of the firehouse. That boy's name was Sorrell Mintz."

"The same Mintz as Doctor Owl?" Oliver wondered.

"It would appear so," said the Oracle. "Young Sorrell was a stubborn child who refused to apologize or tell if he'd taken anything from the apartment. The security man said when he'd burst in, Sorrell was rifling through Walt's things, looking for some kind of special, more likely valuable souvenir. He claimed he was only trying to use the bathroom, yet every other toilet in Disneyland was in fine working order that day, and none required hammers to enter.

"The boy's parents were called but could not be reached. Not sure what else to do, park management told young Sorrell until he returned with one of his parents to confess what he'd done and apologize, he was banned from the park. They hoped it would teach him a lesson. Once he said he was sorry, the punishment would be lifted. But Sorrell never returned. He was eventually forgotten, but the ban remained on the books. In time everyone involved forgot the incident. Everyone except Sorrell Mintz, it would seem."

"So that's what happened this morning," Lilli said to Oliver. "Remember how that manager Patrick got that strange phone call? That's when they made him leave."

"That's right. Mintz got very nervous and tried to hightail it out of the park before security showed up."

"Once security found out his real name, they must have found a record showing he'd been banned.

"The young lady is wise," said the Oracle. If her face wasn't covered in fur, Lilli might have blushed.

"So Mintz got kicked out of Disneyland, and now he wants to shut down the park," said Oliver. "You'd have to be really evil to go through so much trouble, and be willing hurt so many people, just to get revenge for a childhood incident."

"Maybe not evil, Ollie," said Lilli. "Just heartbroken."

"I say again," started the Oracle, "the young lady is wise beyond her years. A lifetime so close to this magical place, but not able to experience the joy that exists inside. So much pain and sadness without admission to the place that heals such woes. That will build up quite a callous on one's soul."

Oliver began biting at his claw as he thought for a moment. "You said he wouldn't admit whether he'd taken anything from the apartment. Was something missing?"

"The guard caught him with a hand inside a wooden box," the Oracle said. "It had been inside a desk where Walt kept some of his more precious keepsakes, according to the family. They did not elaborate, of course. His daughter did say the box had Tinker Bell carved on the lid. Strange for a boy to be interested in such a thing, don't you think?"

"Not really," Oliver answered after a moment. "She was a loyal friend and protector to Pan. I could have used a friend like that as a kitten."

"Yes," said the Oracle. "Well said. Well said indeed. Tell me more about these rats."

"Oh, sure. "Mintz is working with three strange rats."

"Strange?" the Oracle asked.

"I'm not really sure how else to describe them," said Oliver, "but they're not normal. That's for sure."

"You don't say."

"They're nastier than regular rats. They're not afraid of cats. They're willing to fight. They walk upright, and they can talk, just like us. How can this be?"

"Mintz," the Oracle said thoughtfully. "Now it is clear. The box he had when the security guard found him, the one with Tinker Bell on the lid. I happen to know that inside it, Walt kept a certain velvet purple pouch. I think you might be familiar with such a thing?"

"The pixie dust?" Lilli blurted out in disbelief. Both cats had seen that pouch in their youth. Thurl kept it hidden away in the castle, in a location he'd shared with no one.

"That's the one," the Oracle answered.

"It makes sense," said Lilli. "There's no other way those rats could be talking. It has to be the blue pixie dust, right?"

"It would seem more than likely," said the Oracle. "That could be very bad. Particularly if he used it on any other creatures. Walt was very careful on which animals he used it. Despite what some humans would say, there are no inherently bad species or breeds. However, like humans, in the animal kingdom there are good individuals, and bad ones.

"Let me tell the two of you a brief story. Once upon a time, the studio was filming a movie on a tropical island that featured a live tiger. Walt visited the set and when the crew was on a break he snuck over to the tiger's cage. Walt was fascinated with the beast. He found the combination of beauty and raw strength awe-inspiring. Since he'd been assured the big cat was older and quite tame, he took a chance and stroked its side. The tiger did nothing. Deciding it was safe, Walt opened the cage. After all, he owned it. Walt removed a small pouch from his breast pocket and sprinkled just a pinch of blue pixie dust on the tiger's head.

"Shortly after, without consulting the director or the producers, Walt shut down production on the film for the day. He told the whole cast and crew they'd be paid for the day but they were all to go home at once. It was very mysterious, and uncharacteristic of him. Walt instructed the production caterer to send over a dozen raw steaks for the big cat (and a bowl of chili and beans for himself, with a side of salted crackers). Once everyone had gone, Walt and the tiger had a pleasant lunch by a beach. The tiger told Walt he'd been born in a circus and much preferred life in the movie business. The food was better, and nobody cracked a whip or made him do asinine tricks like balancing on a stool. He'd grown fond of the actor's life, and even enjoyed playing at being wild again.

"Walt confided in the gentle beast, explaining how he had a jungle river attraction at Disneyland, and it didn't look too different from the set where they dined together. He told the tiger how he'd always wanted to have real animals living along his river for guests to see and learn about. His Imagineers had convinced him to use mechanical animals instead, and arranged them along the river in humorous scenes.

"The Jungle Cruise was a popular ride from the very beginning, and everyone got a good laugh when they took the cruise. Still, Walt had wanted to do something with real animals. Even then he still kicked around the idea of replacing the mechanical beasts with living creatures, sprinkled with the transformative pixie dust. That way he could assure them they'd be well fed and cared for without ever having to hunt again, and all they had to do was play along."

"In other words," Oliver interrupted, "show off for the guests, and not eat anybody?"

"Very good. The tiger being older and wiser had thought for a moment, then said to Walt, 'I fear you consider a dangerous proposal. I for one would be happy to spend the rest of my days lazing by your pretend river with my meals served to me on a platter. However, other wild animals might not feel the same. You say you would place a live anaconda in a tree just a few feet from boatloads of young humans each day? My human friend, all the negotiation in the world would likely not be enough to prevent nature's eventuality. A snake, even one that talks, is still after all a snake.'

"Walt raised an eyebrow, not used to being disagreed with. He liked it. Finally, he sighed and conceded, understanding the tiger's point. Millions of years of evolution and instinct would probably be too much temptation for some animals to overcome.

"'Say,' Walt had smiled, 'you're pretty insightful for a tiger. I have this idea for an animated picture that takes place in the jungle. It's based on a book...those are collections of paper where we keep our stories. Anyway, this particular book is about a human child who grows up in the jungle, see, and there's this bear that sort of shows him the ropes, and an orangutan and other creatures. There's a pretty good role for a tiger as well....'"

"Do you think Mintz has more pixie dust?" Lilli asked when the story was over.

"For now, it does not matter," said the Oracle. "What does matter is that neither he, nor those rodents, or any other creature finds the Disneyland key."

"Agreed," said Oliver. "Please, Oracle, tell us where the key is hidden. We will go get it and keep it safe inside the castle while security deals with this Mintz problem."

"That would be a wise plan, but unfortunately, I can't say for certain. Even I do not know the exact location."

"Oh it's...wait, *you* don't know?" Oliver said, shocked. "But I thought, that is...well, you know everything!"

"Not the location of the Disneyland key. I choose not to know. It is safer that way. As I'm sure Thurl told you, the key has never remained in the same place for longer than a year or two. Only one person ever knows where it's currently hidden, and only two know where it was hidden last."

"Some system," Lilli said.

"It has worked well enough. Thus far."

"It doesn't matter," said Oliver. "I will find the key wherever they put it last."

"Oliver, that key could be anywhere in the world now," said Lilli.

"No," the Oracle said. "Only anywhere within the park. It can never be removed from Disneyland. It is still nearby. I can feel its power. Do you feel the hum that flows through all of us—the indescribable feeling of happiness in the air that only exists in this place?" The Oracle was quiet. His red eyes dimmed for a moment. "Yes, it is here."

"Well, at least that narrows it down," said Oliver, "sort of."

"I can tell you this, the hiding place will be difficult to reach, yet easy to see. The key is often hidden in plain sight. Look over the whole park. You must find it, my young friends. You are the Cats of the Castle. Your duty is to protect this park from *all* threats, not just rats."

"We will," Oliver and Lilli both said aloud. They looked at each other and shared a nervous smile.

"One more thing, young Oliver. You said this park is your home. You may not understand how right you are. You are part of the legacy. It is a heavy burden, but Thurl has chosen you to be the next leader of the Order. It is in your blood. You are a descendant of the first Cat of the Castle, the one Walt called Mr. Lincoln."

What had the Oracle just said? Oliver was silent as the words sunk in—more like washed over him, making his fur stand up. He was related to the first Cat of the Castle?

"I am?"

"He is?" added Lilli.

"It took me a minute, but it's obvious," the Oracle said with a laugh. "You are his spitting image. You were led here to save the park. It is your destiny. Disneyland is your land."

The Oracle's eyes went dark. The flames of the Tiki torches were snuffed out as though by an invisible breath. The platform began to rise back into the ceiling. Within a few moments it docked into place, leaving a seamless ceiling to the unknowing eye. The four parrots hung silently on their perches.

"Wait," Oliver begged. "You can't just go dark on me! What do you mean I'm the descendant? What's he talking about, my *destiny*?"

"Well, amigo," said Jose. "I'm afraid that's what they call the whole enchilada. When the Oracle says you're done, *you're done.*"

"I fear he's right, son," said Michael. "Perhaps you can ask the Oracle more questions another time. But for now, you heard the man. GO!"

The other three birds nodded to them as they slowly ascended back into their hiding places within the ceiling to wait for the first show to begin. The lights went dark. The Tiki Room doors opened back up to the outside. Morning sunlight flooded the theater.

The cats ran out of the Tiki Room and through the courtyard. They stopped at the road leading back toward the hub and the tunnel passage. Oliver stopped and put a paw out, cautioning Lilli to wait. His head darted around, looking in all directions to be sure the coast was clear. To his left he saw the arching sign that read "Adventureland." Beyond, spread out between the dense jungle foliage and exotic sights and sounds, were attractions like Temple of the Forbidden Eye, Tarzan's Treehouse, and of course Walt's Jungle Cruise. He began to think about the Oracle's words. The key will be hard to reach but easy to see, if they looked over the whole park. That last part struck him in an unusual way. Look *over* the whole park.

"Oliver, what is it? We need to get back to the castle. Thurl will want to hear all this."

"You're right," said Oliver, carefully stepping forward. "But there's someplace I think we should check out first."

"The park is about to open," she said. "We don't have time to take in any rides."

"I know," he said. "I'm more interested in sightseeing."

"What? What sights?"

"All of them. Come with me."

Chapter Six

Elias was lying back on his elbows, the stem of a flower between his teeth. He'd normally be sound asleep in his bed at this time. Still, he thought, maybe this morning thing wasn't so bad. The aroma from the new coffee shop on Main Street was intoxicating. Even though he'd never tasted coffee, Elias entertained the idea of sneaking over to see if he could somehow swipe a sample. He looked over to mention it to Kimball, but of course the brainy cat wasn't next to him.

"Now where did he...?" Elias started. He looked up. Kimball was wrapped around Walt's shoulders like a fur cape. With his telescopic lenses over his glasses he was scouring Adventureland for Oliver and Lilli, as well as any humans heading their way.

"Where are those two?" Kimball wondered aloud. "I'm starting to worry."

"Relax. They're talking to the Oracle. Maybe he's wordy. Heck, the Oracle's supposed to know even more than Thurl, and you know how he can go on."

"We really need to get back inside," Kimball continued, starting to sound jittery. "I can already see cast members milling around. It won't be long until this street is flooded with people. I wonder what the Oracle is telling them?"

"Hopefully where this stinkin' key is so we can grab it." Elias looked toward Adventureland. "I guess they have been gone a little whi..." Elias stopped talking. There was a rustling in a dense arrangement of plants. A pointed pink snout came sniffing out of the palm fronds.

"See, even you think it shouldn't be taking them so long," Kimball said.

"Hey, stuff it," Elias hissed. "I see something!" He rolled over onto his belly and bent his tail, pointing it in the direction he was looking. "Over there by those palms!"

Kimball followed Elias' tail and turned a focus knob on his glasses. Magnified it was clear as day. A black head with a pink snout poking out of the bushes, giving them both a clear view.

"*Genus Rattus*," Kimball sneered. He carefully slid down the statue like oozing syrup, not wanting to tip off the rodent. By the time he reached the pedestal the other two rats had popped into view. Mister Brown and Mister Gray.

"That's them," said Elias.

"Just like Oliver described," Kimball added.

"Good." Elias rolled his head around his neck and cracked his knuckles. "I was hoping we'd get a crack at 'em. This is should be easy. And fun!"

"No, Elias, what are you thinking? You can't go picking a fight now."

"Why not?"

"For one thing, it's broad daylight," said Kimball. "Apparently the hamster on the wheel that powers your brain hasn't gotten up yet, either. Didn't I just tell you the park is about to open. People. Everywhere. Not good."

"But, *rats*," Elias protested like a whiny child being denied a new toy, gesturing desperately. "They're right there. It won't take long. Look at them!"

They watched the three rodents conferring and pointing in numerous directions, thinking they were in the park undetected. The black rat was pointing at the castle. Elias was certain he heard one of them squeak something about Fantasyland.

"That's right, you little dirt mops," Elias whispered. "Right this way. Come to poppa."

"Easy Elias," Kimball mumbled under his whiskers.

Apparently Fantasyland was voted down. The other two rats, Mac and Murray, were pointing at Tomorrowland. Finally, the rats all nodded and scampered off in the direction of the rotating metal planets, white spires pointing toward the heavens, and spinning rockets in a constant orbital chase of Tomorrowland. They ran right through the space rock gateway and on toward the curving walkways of Innoventions.

"Wha...what?" Kimball stammered in shocked disbelief. "They...they're going into Tomorrowland." He watched in horror, unable to believe they would dare enter his favorite land; the place he revered as sacred ground. "They can't just go in there."

"Um, I beg to differ," Elias said, arching an eyebrow as they watched the three vermin disappear into the futuristic side of the park. "There they go, my friend. Probably hopping onto Space Mountain right now. Maybe dropping little rat pellets all over Star Tours while they're at it. Who knows? Too bad we can't do anything about it, huh?"

"They...they wouldn't," Kimball started, jaw hanging like it was on a hinge. "They couldn't. I don't...*rat pellets*? That's just unconscionable, for *any* species."

"Hey buddy, that's what rats do. I mean, if we're just going to stand here and do nothing."

"I can't even...."

"You're right," said Elias with a wicked grin, "I can't either." He tore off through the flowers, sprang over the curved guardrail, and made a running landing onto the asphalt, chasing after the rats. "I'm going after them!"

"Not without me," Kimball spat. He stopped short of hurdling the rail to slide the cover back over the tunnel. He pushed it down until the turf was once again flush with the real grass. "Sorry, guys," he said, looking toward the Tiki Room. "You're on your own."

Kimball caught up to Elias in front of the entrance to the Buzz Lightyear Astro Blasters. As usual, the brazen alley cat wasn't even attempting to hide. He was standing under the blue, bean-shaped sign, his silver chest puffed up, making his black stripes even more pronounced. His pale green eyes scanned this way and that. Elias was a born hunter. He may have looked like just a regular tabby on the outside, but inside he had the heart of a panther. He loved the chase. It was like a game.

When Elias knew there was a rat nearby, his predatory instincts kicked in. So Kimball, who under other circumstances would have been quite content to spend his days in a human home, specifically some cozy den with a pillow below a full bookcase, could only imagine what the prospect of catching these three mutant rodents was doing to his feral brain.

"Any sign?" Kimball asked after catching his breath.

"Not yet. They're definitely in here. I can smell them."

"None of the attractions are open yet. There's nowhere to go. They're probably still running."

"Oh, no," said Elias. "They have a mission. They're not scavenging for food. I'm sure their orders were to check every nook and cranny of this park. What they don't know is Elias has a mission too, and it's *them*"

"Uh, oh, you're speaking in the third person. And you're monologuing."

"Admit it," Elias said, ignoring his comment. "You want to catch them just as badly as I do."

"I just want them out. I shudder to think what you would like to do with them."

"Shoo them out, they only come back," Elias said flatly. He patted his stomach. "Once they're in my belly, that's the end of the argument. They looked pretty plump and juicy, too!"

"I think I'm going to be sick," said Kimball, clapping a paw over his mouth. Under his yellow fur he was sure his face was turning green.

"I'm kidding," Elias snapped, raising his finger. "Now be quiet. I heard something."

"What was it?" Kimball whispered, ducking down instinctively as if he'd somehow become invisible.

"I'm not sure yet." They both heard a loud crash, followed by a clanging sound. "Whatever caused that!"

"Get your filthy claws off of me!" a strange, high-pitched mechanical voice screamed. "*I* am not some scavenger's buffet!"

"Over there," said Elias, already starting to run, "by that big rocket thingy!"

"Rocket thingy?" Kimball said, rolling his eyes. "It's Redd Rocket's Pizza Port. Do you know what anything in this park is called? Seems they had time to search for food after all. Pizza Port is an excellent choice, I might add. Not that you would know apparently, but for rodents who would be perfectly happy with leftover crusts and...."

"Will you shut up and come on already?" Elias called back over his shoulder.

"Oh right," said Kimball, realizing Elias was long gone and breaking into a stride after him. "I'm just saying, Disneyland is your home. It wouldn't kill you to get over to this side of the park once in a while."

"You can give me the full tour, right after we catch these three *RATS!*"

Elias stopped in his tracks. The three rats came racing out from behind Pizza Port. They didn't seem to notice him or Kimball. They were in panic mode. Their wide eyes were focused straight ahead and they had dropped to all fours, their claws clicking rapidly across the asphalt. Then Elias saw why they were running. Actually, he wasn't entirely sure *what* he was seeing. A garbage can, seemingly like all the other rectangular metal trash receptacles stationed around the park. Except this one was rolling after the rats at high speed. It was silver with a blue T on the front, and white door panel that read PUSH.

"Come back here, you slimy sewer dwellers!" the high-pitched voice squealed again as the metal door flapped in and out. "Try climbing inside me again! I dare you!"

"Okay, Kimball," Elias muttered, "I admit it. This is your turf. Do all the trash cans talk?"

"It really is like you don't even live in this park," Kimball laughed, cuffing him on the shoulder. "That's PUSH. Don't worry, he's a friend. In fact, he accompanies me on my rounds sometimes. Hates rats almost as much as you do. Maybe more. At least you don't have them climbing inside your mouth looking for drumsticks and half-eaten slices of pizza. Or do you?"

"But how does it...is there someone operating him? Should we be hiding?"

"It's fine. Come on," said Kimball running after the trash can. "PUSH is different. He's special, like you. Besides, he's following the rats, so we should be following him."

Elias just shook his head. He'd seen a lot of crazy things living in the park, but clearly there were still some surprises left. This time it was him running off after Kimball. The lanky yellow cat was catching up to the trash can, which was trucking along at an impressive pace for a metal box.

"Kimball!" said PUSH, apparently becoming aware of the cat running up beside him. Admittedly, it was hard to tell what he was seeing since he had no visible eyes. "What are you doing out in the daylight?"

"The same thing you are, it appears," said Kimball. "Chasing rats. We really need to stop these three."

"I'll say," PUSH responded. "The fat brown one tried to climb into my stomach looking for breakfast like I was just another garbage can. As if I wouldn't have been cleaned out the night before even if I were!" He slowed to a stop right in front of the monorail station, and the end of the Tomorrowland border. Neither could see the three runaway rats now. Every breezeway ahead was empty. They must've ducked into a hiding place.

"Which way did they go?" Elias panted, catching up to them.

"Not sure," answered Kimball. "Did you see, PUSH?"

"No, I'm afraid not. I'd guess either the Matterhorn or the Nemo submarines. Unfortunately, this is as far as I can roll. The time is 8:42am. The park will be open in a few minutes. I cannot risk getting caught roaming the park freely, again. I need to keep my canister clean. My Florida counterpart was already decommissioned. What will you cats do?"

Kimball looked at Elias. "We'll keep going," he said. Elias nodded.

"Good luck then," said PUSH. He turned and rolled his way back into Tomorrowland where he would park out of sight until guests began to arrive. PUSH loved to surprise unsuspecting tourists, and particularly enjoyed interacting with younger park guests. Until, that was, they tried to drop a melting ice cream bar down his shoot. He paused and rolled back toward them. "I do wish I could come along and help."

"No, it's better you stay out of trouble," Kimball said, patting the side of the can. "Although, if they ever really do threaten to shut you down, there's an animatronic cat inside Pirates of the Caribbean. I've been thinking, maybe I could modify its brain circuitry to accommodate your personality chip. Then you could join us."

"Do you mean I could be a Cat of the Castle? You would do that for me?"

"Of course, buddy," said Kimball. "We could always use new members. You'd make a fantastic cat!"

"Uh, Kimball," Elias mumbled, "I hate to break up this moment. Seriously, I'm feeling the love here, but we should get moving."

"Your blunt friend is correct," said PUSH. "I must be going as well. Be careful." The trash can swiveled around and rolled away. It once again disappeared behind Pizza Port.

Kimball watched PUSH go, then turned back to Elias. The grey cat was staring at him with one eyebrow raised.

"What?" Kimball asked.

"The trash can would make a good cat?"

"Well, why not? He knows every corner of Tomorrowland, even if he can't get around them all. Plus, he knows all the technical specs. You don't even know which ride is Space Mountain."

"And it's really affecting my life," Elias snorted. "Well, what do you think? Should we check out the subs, or the mountain?"

"It's obvious. The Matterhorn. All those tunnels would be too tempting. Last thing they'd want to do is risk getting stuck in a submarine. Once the hatch got shut, they'd be trapped like, well, rats. Wow, can you imagine if that was where the expression originated from?"

"It would alter time and space," Elias said dryly. "Whatever you say. You're the resident genius. Besides, to them Matterhorn Mountain probably looks like a giant wedge of moldy cheese."

The two cats ran to the Matterhorn. It was an imposing snow-capped mountain with a narrow waterfall pouring down the side. It towered high in the sky between Tomorrowland and Fantasyland. They ran up the walkway to a Swiss chalet with multi-colored shields hung across the wall. It was the loading area of The Matterhorn Bobsleds. Human guests would pile into long, sled-shaped cars and journey up and around the mountain before they'd come flying back down to splash through a pool of water. The two of them pressed their backs against the wooden wall of the chalet.

"Could you really do that?" Elias asked, as if they were in the middle of a conversation Kimball wasn't aware of.

"Could I really do what?"

"Turn the trash can into a cat," Elias said, stretching sideways to peer up the side of the Matterhorn.

"Oh, that. Well, yes, I believe so. With PUSH it wouldn't be too difficult. As long as I could find a way to convert the animatronic skull housing to accommodate PUSH's personality chip. PUSH was part of a secret living character project Imagineering was toying with. With PUSH they were a little too successful. The artificial intelligence program they created became sentient."

"That's funny," Elias remarked, half paying attention. "The garbage can became sanitized?"

"No," Kimball palmed his own face with a paw in frustration. "Sentient. It's when an inanimate object, something that is not alive, like a garbage can, or a chair, or let's hope someday *your brain*, is able to think."

"So that's why he can roll around on his own, and talk to us, and all that without an operator or a remote control."

"Exactly. When Imagineering realized what a living character PUSH was, they decided it was safer to scale back the project. PUSH is completely peaceful, but there are obviously safety concerns about living animatronics with free rein over the park. Imagine if the Evil Queen came to life, or those giant cobras from the Temple of the Forbidden Eye."

"Yeah, that would be weird," Elias said distantly, not really listening. His eyes were trained on something else. "Stay here. I want to check something out."

Elias leapt forward, rolled over his shoulder, and sprang up behind a nearby trash can alongside the queue area. Once he was sure no one was watching, Elias leapt up on top of the can. He leaned over the front and was about to look inside when he glanced back at Kimball. He nodded his head suspiciously at the can. Then made a strange duck-bill with his paw, opening and closing it, as if it were talking.

"No," Kimball whispered, quickly understanding what Elias was asking, and trying at great pains not to laugh. "It's just a regular trash can."

Elias pushed it open with his other paw held out, claws in the air, in case one of the rats or anything else sprang out. There was nothing inside but a fresh, clear plastic garbage bag. He looked over at Kimball and made circles around his eyes, then pointed up at the mountain. Kimball flipped his binocular lenses back down and shielded them with his paws.

"See anything?" Elias whispered, as he slid back down to the ground.

In the distance behind them, the sounds of a brass band began to fill the air. With his binocular lenses, his eyes looked enormous. They exchanged a worried look. They both knew that music meant the front gates were only moments from opening. Guests would soon be allowed on Main Street, U.S.A., and shortly after they'd be queuing up for the Matterhorn.

"Alright, Bill," a human voice sounded just around the corner, "time to warm up the mountain."

"You got it," another voice answered, slightly more muffled and sounding as though it were coming from behind the wall.

"We've got humans," Elias whispered, hugging the other side of the trash can.

Kimball removed something that looked like a gray tuna can with a crank on the side from his tool belt. He fastened it over one of his lenses. With a pull of his paw, he stretched it out forming an adjustable telescope. Kimball crept to the edge of the chalet and carefully bent the tube to the right. Inside were tiny mirrored lenses that, when lined up properly, allowed him to peak around corners undetected.

Kimball turned the crank and the telescopic lens inched out farther and farther. Sure enough, he saw a man in short-sleeves and tan pants with a name tag, obviously a manager, waving his radio at the window up above. Kimball twisted another small crank and the lens twisted around and looked up until he could just see another Matterhorn cast member in a white shirt with tightly rolled sleeves and yellow flowers embroidered up the front. The younger human gave a thumbs up out the window. As he did, a train of two empty white bobsled cars with a green streak across the side rolled past the loading bay and headed up the track into the mountain.

"Oh, dear," said Kimball, rolling his lens back in, "this park is definitely opening. They're warming up the ride."

"The rats are here somewhere," Elias muttered, scanning the mountain. "I can sense it." Another train of bobsleds, this one with a purple streak across the side, was rumbling down the tracks toward the load area.

Standing just a few feet from the tracks, the cats could feel the vibration under their feet. "But there's only one way to be sure."

Elias bolted around the side of the building and without losing a step, dropped to four legs as he shot past the park manager, and quickly squeezed through the metal bars of the fence meant to separate waiting guests from the tracks. Without slowing, he pushed hard with his back legs and leapt right over the small empty moat and landed on the cushioned seat of the front car. Up above, the operator had only briefly noticed some dark grayish black blur dart past.

"Was that a cat?" he asked through the radio.

"Huh?" the manager replied, looking around. "Was what a cat?"

"Never mind," the kid said. "Probably a shadow or something." He turned to grab his plastic mug of coffee with Mickey and the gang on the side. Out of the corner of his eye, another blur, this one yellow and brown, rushed by down below.

"Elias," Kimball shouted, bounding into the last car. He barely cleared the side of the sled and clumsily crashed against the seat as their train disappeared into a cave. "Are you crazy? What are you doing? Scratch that, what are WE doing?!?"

"Ha! Good question," Elias laughed, looking back at his friend. "Eyes open. We're on rat patrol!" He pounded the seat with his paws and gave a joyful howl! The cats were rarely able to steal a ride on a park attraction. Elias figured even if he was working, he was going to enjoy every moment of this one.

They began to rise as their sleds were pulled deeper into the mountain. A cool wind blew in Elias' face. There was a horrible growl of something ferocious. Kimball dropped to the floor board. Elias laughed, figuring the sound probably cost Kimball one of his nine lives. Through an opaque window of ice something barked at them, and Elias saw a distorted face tracking their sled with blazing red eyes. His back instantly bristled and his claws slid out. That thing was definitely too big to be a rat. They turned a corner and sunlight streamed in through cracks in the mountain, illuminating a cavern where the mangled wreckage of other bobsleds littered the snow.

"Do you see anything?" Kimball called up, trying to straighten his glasses on his furry face.

"Um, no," Elias answered, quickly examining the ominous display as they sped on around the corner. "No rats, anyway."

Realizing they were in sunlight again, Kimball ducked for fear of being spotted. He hoped Elias had the sense to do the same, but of course the brazen gray kitty held his head up, sunning himself in the warm beams. Kimball raised his head again, just in time to come face-to-face with another unexpected creature. It was a monster right out of a frozen nightmare. This abominable beast was the size of a large human, draped in thick white fur with a horrible blue ape-like face and long sharp fangs like a lion. Its eyes glowed red and it roared as they passed, its hulking arms outstretched with thick blue fingers and claws that swiped at them.

Kimball shrieked and buried his head in the seat of the car, pulling his sweater over himself as if for some protection. His tried to reassure himself it was only an audio-animatronic, a machine, safely bolted to the attraction floor. But in the moment, staring at its flesh and fur and slobbering snout, it was hard to find comfort in logic. He imagined it tearing their bobsled, with them still inside, to mangled pieces of metal.

They continued on, zipping through the mountain. Slowly, Kimball pulled his sweater down and composed himself. They'd left the Yeti far behind. Still, his ears were perked up for any more roaring, or even a suspicious snarl or snort. All he heard over the *clickety-clack* of the wheels on the track was the obnoxious sound of Elias, watching and laughing with glee from the car ahead of him. The gray cat was cackling so hard, he couldn't catch his breath as tears streaked his furry cheeks.

Kimball was angry, and embarrassed, but at least they quickly rolled into another open area where there was plenty of sunshine, and no abominable snow beasts. The bobsled raced around corners and up and down hills in the track. They came to another junction in a well-lit cavern of the mountain. For the first time since he'd jumped aboard, Kimball remembered that the Matterhorn had been built with two sets of parallel tracks to increase the number of guests it could accommodate. Across an icy opening he caught sight of another two-sled train rolling by, only a few feet ahead of their own. He knew at once they had picked the right attraction, because in the front seat he spied three sets of pink ears and snouts, with grubby pink fingers gripping the safety bar for dear life.

"Elias," he shouted, pointing. He fumbled to flip his binocular lenses back down.

"I know, I know," said Elias, still laughing and facing back toward Kimball. "I'm sorry. I shouldn't laugh, but you should have seen your face! It was priceless. I hope they took one of those photos we can see at the end!"

"No, Elias! Look! It's the rats!"

"What?" Elias asked, spinning around to see what Kimball was pointing at. It was too late. The other train had sped off out of sight. He shrugged his shoulders with his paws in the air. "What are you talking about?"

Kimball slapped his forehead in frustration, almost knocking his glasses off. He carefully inched his way to the front of his car, just as they rolled up a small hill. He grabbed on to the safety bar just in time as his whole body caught air. For a moment he looked like a long yellow and brown flag hanging off the sled as it raced along the track. He dropped back to the seat with an *oomph!* "They were just there!" he shouted, cupping a paw to his mouth. "All three of them were in the sled with the red streak. If you'd have been looking forward, you would have seen them too!"

Elias turned around and gripped the front of his car. If Kimball was right, he wasn't going to miss them again. It didn't take long. They zipped around a few more corners, alternating between open sunlit passageways and dark caverns, when they rolled up to another set of tracks just beyond the stalactites and stalagmites. Just ahead he could see the back end of the red-and-white bobsleds. Kimball was right! Their wormy pink tails whipped around in the wind as they sped down the track.

The rats were clueless, busy enjoying the ride with no idea they were being pursued by two felines. Elias preferred it that way. He swung his hind leg up onto the front panel of the sled, climbed over the safety bar, and carefully crawled onto the hood, digging his claws into the fiberglass surface.

"What do you think you're doing?" Kimball called out. "Are you nuts? They're going to be peeling you off these cave walls with a shovel!"

It was no use. Elias could barely hear him. He was crouched on the front of the speeding ride vehicle. His black vest flapped in the wind. *Just get close enough*, he thought. The wind was whipping against his body but Elias braced himself for any unexpected dips or turns. His claws dug deep into the paint. Finally, the right moment presented itself. Both trains emerged in the sunlight on an outer ridge of the mountain. *Come on*, Elias thought, gritting his teeth. Just a few more inches. They rocketed past a waterfall. Up ahead was a fence, or at least sticks hung across poles to pass as a fence. Elias took note. If he missed the bobsled ahead of him, that fence might be the only thing to keep him from plummeting to the ground far below.

"Elias, this is crazy!" Kimball shouted. "You miss and you'll go right over the edge. And I wouldn't count on landing on your feet!"

"She'll be comin'...'round...the mountain when she...comes," Elias sang to himself, ignoring Kimball's warnings. Steadying himself as they sped along the bumpy track, his arms were outstretched like a surfer. His leg muscles were tight, bracing for the launch. "I'll be comin' 'round the mountain...to snatch some rats."

The tracks were about to lead right back into a dark tunnel. It was now or never. Elias wasn't going to risk losing them at the bottom. He shimmied to the very nose of the bobsled. Just as the rats' car was touching the entrance of the cavern, he jumped, pushing off with his legs and tail. Elias knew halfway through the air he was going to fall short. He hadn't been close enough to their train after all. Rather than land inside the bobsled, his body crashed into the back of it.

Elias desperately reached out and managed to lock three claws into the cushioned headrest of the last seat. His arm instantly ached as he hung there, bouncing off the back of the sled. His tail was dangling just above the tracks. Elias reached up and sank his other claws into the seat, praying the vinyl covering wouldn't tear from his weight. Above him the purple sleds, with Kimball peering down at him in horror, passed by as the tracks had diverged again. With a great grunt Elias managed to lock his arms around the seatback. He hiked his leg up over the back of the car and with a considerable scream he hoped the wind and clacking wheels would cover, he pulled himself inside.

His body might have hurt, but Elias refused to acknowledge it. He scrambled to his feet and quickly hurdled over the three seats of the back sled, even as they raced along at breakneck speed. He skipped across the hood without even using his claws and jumped into the next car. He didn't stop until he was in the middle row, just behind the oblivious rodents. They were hooting and hollering like teenaged humans. Suddenly, the sled slipped around a corner and there, even closer than before, was that same ferocious Yeti.

Its red eyes blazed and it bellowed another nightmarish roar. The startled rats shrieked with excitement. Only this time there was an added effect. Their three hearts stopped simultaneously as furry arms forcefully grabbed them and squeezed, pulling them painfully together. The unseen grip tightened as their sled shot out into the bright sunlight and they were momentarily blinded.

"Hello, boys," Elias said, leaning over them.

Murray the brown rat managed to turn his head and see what had a hold on them. It was not a snow beast, but it was just as terrifying. A gray cat with black stripes, squinting green eyes, and a devilish grin on his face as he licked his sharp incisors.

"C-C-Cat!" Murray screamed. The three of them squirmed, trying to break loose.

"I don't think so," said Elias. "You three are mine." He looked up to see they were rapidly approaching the end of the line. Up ahead was a pond of water the sled would splash through, and after that the unloading area would be right around the corner. So would human ride operators and attendants. It might cause a scene if a cat in a vest pulled up to the station clutching three rats.

"What are ya gonna do, cat?" the black rat, Fred, spat. He snapped his teeth trying to catch Elias' finger. "You can't pull all three of us outta this car. Even you ain't that coordinated!"

Elias thought for a moment. The rodent was right. Trying to get himself and three struggling, oversized rats out of a moving bobsled without getting seriously hurt seemed unlikely. Even if he could somehow make the leap, they'd surely break free once everybody hit solid ground. He looked around, trying to think quickly. The truth, he decided, was there actually was no time to think. So, Elias did the next best thing—he improvised.

"You know what I think?" Elias said, making a sniffing sound. "I think you rats need a bath." Without another word or warning, Elias pulled their three bodies tight against himself, drew a deep breath, and leaned over the side of the bobsled, falling over the edge.

The rats screamed. All four of them fell through the air for a brief, terrifying moment, before splashing into the pool of water below. As they sank down to the dark concrete floor of the murky pond, the rats kicked, clawed, and scratched to get free. Elias wasn't entirely sure why he'd done that, or what he was going to do now. Regardless, at least their current predicament was keeping the rats from running loose in the park or finding the key, so technically he was doing his job. And doing it well, he might have added, if he wasn't afraid to open his mouth at the risk of swallowing Matterhorn pond water.

Elias could feel his breath running out. Maybe that's what caused his grip on the squirming rats to loosen. Mac, the tall gray one, managed to slip between his arms and began to frantically paddle toward the surface. I don't think so, Elias thought. He kicked his legs off against the bottom, torpedoing upward. His head burst out over the surface with a splash and he drew a deep breath. Both of the other rats still trapped in his bear hug started coughing and desperately gasping for air. He could see the fugitive rat's pink nose and ears breaking the surface, as he made his way toward the shore.

"You maniac," Fred yelled, coughing up pond water. "You murderer!"

"Murderer? You're still alive, aren't you?" Elias mumbled at the rat, almost disappointed. "I promise you right now, if this vest shrinks from getting wet, you won't be much longer."

Fred seized the moment while the cat's defenses were down and chomped hard on his paw. Elias roared in pain, and as the rat had hoped, released his grip. Both rats paddled so hard it looked like they might actually take off in flight like ducks from a lake. Their gray friend was already out of the water and heading for the asphalt, leaving tiny puddles in his wake. The other two were catching up. They scurried up onto the grass and mud. They ran quickly across the sidewalk, under the safety rails, and almost to freedom when WHAM!

They collided into their gray friend as they suddenly found they could run no further. All three rat heads painfully *clunked* into each other. When the stars in their eyes finally cleared they realized they were trapped in a net. A tall lanky yellow cat in a brown cardigan was holding the handle and blinking down at them through huge round spectacles.

"Going somewhere?" he asked. "This net is for retrieving lost caps, sunglasses, and plush Mickeys and Donalds that weren't properly stowed in the ride vehicle. I don't know that it's ever been used to capture trespassing *rodentia* before. Do I turn you in at the Lost and Found, or just toss you into the trash compactor?"

"Tra-trash compactor?" Murray stammered. "They've got one of those?"

"Care to find out?" Kimball bent down and grinned.

"Kimball," Elias grunted, standing on the sidewalk, fur dripping wet and shaking his swollen paw. "Where did you get…?"

"You wouldn't believe how simple it is to pick the lock on a fifty-five year old supply closet," Kimball said. He added, "I might drop off a suggestion card at Guest Services."

"You rats are dead meat," started Elias, wringing water out of his tail.

"We don't have time, Elias. The park is literally opening as we stand here. We have to go."

"Not before we get some answers out of these three."

"You heard him," Fred said. "You better go hide, cat. Otherwise, you'll be chased out just like us!"

"Besides," said Mac, "we'd never tell you anything. There's nothing you can do to make us talk! We're no rats!" Even his two accomplices gave him an askew look.

"Okay, so we *are* rats, but not that kind!"

"Refusing to talk, huh?" said Elias, absently looking around. Across the breezeway he spotted the yellow tops of the Nemo submarines parked in their wide lagoon. "Kimball, what else did you see inside that supply closet? Anything sticky?"

A few minutes later the three rats found themselves stuck, literally, to the hatch of a bright yellow submarine. A line of subs just like it sat docked at the loading station, waiting for the day to begin. The cats had wrapped them in strong, silver duct tape.

"Boys," said Elias, standing over them, blocked from the sight of any ride operators, "it might be time to reconsider this no-talking policy. If you thought that shallow pond across the street was scary, wait 'til this baby submerges. They used to call it 20,000 Leagues Under the Sea for a reason."

"Actually, Elias," said Kimball, standing next to him, holding the role of duct tape, "these subs don't actually…*oof!*" Elias had elbowed him in the gut.

"You wouldn't dare leave us here," Fred challenged.

"Oh, wouldn't I? Come on Kimball. These guys aren't going to give us anything. Let's just head back to the castle. Won't matter what they know or don't know once they're at the bottom of the lagoon."

"Ah, yes," said Kimball, finally catching on. "That's right. Well, gentlemen, if any of you change your mind, you'll just have to tell it to the fish."

"That reminds me Kimball," Elias chuckled, "is that giant, submarine-eating squid still down there? I can't remember."

"You know, I'm not sure. I guess they'll find out."

The two cats turned to hop off the sub. They heard the whinny of the motors as somewhere, a ride operator had started the attraction. The entire vessel began to vibrate underneath their paws. The sub lurched forward and began to roll out into open water. Though muffled by the metal shell, they could hear a human voice speaking below, welcoming passengers aboard. It was only a recording of course, but when they heard the captain's voice announce they were preparing to dive, the rats began to panic.

"Wait!" Fred screamed.

"We'll talk," Mac added desperately. "Mintz! Doctor Sorrell Mintz! He made us this way. He hired us to find some magic key. Claims it will give him control over this place, and then we'll have all the food we can eat!"

"Mintz must be Oliver's friend, Doctor Owl," said Elias.

"Doctor Owl," the dimwitted Murray chuckled, "I love that. He really does look like...!"

"Murray!" Fred growled.

"Must be one in the same," said Kimball, leaning over the rats. "We already know about the key. Where is it?"

"We're not sure," Mac admitted. "Doc thinks it's some place high. That's why we were checking out the Matterhorn."

"That's right," Murray the brown rat chimed in. "We didn't see nothin', though. Nothin' shiny up there, except them crystals."

"You said the doctor made you this way," Kimball said. "How? What exactly did he do to you?"

"It was some weird blue powder," said Mac. "Like glitter, or dust. I don't know. He sprinkled it over our heads one day and next thing you know, we understood every word he said.

"Yup, and he says a lot," Murray added.

"Blue pixie dust," Elias said, meeting Kimball's eyes.

"Just what we were afraid of," Kimball nodded. "It certainly makes sense."

"Has Mintz used it on any other animals?" Elias demanded. "Other rats, or anything else—maybe dogs or something?"

"No, no," said Mac. "Just us. At least, as far as we know! The Doc is pretty mysterious."

"Yeah," said Murray, "but we live in his kitchen cabinets. We'd know if there was other animals around. And there wasn't. Except that dumb raccoon that knocked over the trash cans that one...."

"Shut it, Murray," Pete hissed at him. "It's just us."

"Mintz always says the stuff is precious," added Mac. "Said he only had a little bit, and couldn't get more until we find the key. Maybe it opens a storage cabinet around here or something."

"Listen, cats, bottom line here is we don't know where the key is," said the black rat. "Neither does Mintz. He brought us because we can sneak around better than he can. That's the truth. We don't know nothin' else!"

"I'm afraid I believe them," said Kimball, after a moment. "They're just his minions. Really, *really* dumb minions."

"Yeah, I do, too. They're too stupid to trust with too much information." The sub passed along a rock wall with some tree limbs growing out over it. Elias jumped up and grabbed one, pulling himself up. "Let's go, Kimball."

Kimball quickly followed suit, climbing up onto the branch just before the submarine began to turn away and float out of reach. He looked down at the helpless rats stuck to the sub. With his free paw he saluted. "Bon voyage, gents!"

"Hey, what are you cats doing!?" Fred screamed. "We had a deal! Cut us loose!"

"Yeah, get us off of here," said Mac as they floated farther away. "We told you everything we know! You can't just let us drown on this tuna can!"

Below they could hear the voice of the captain calling out, "Dive! Dive! Dive!"

"Come on, cats," Mac yelled out again. "This ain't funny!"

"It is from where I'm sitting," Elias called back.

"Calm down," Kimball added, cupping his paws to his mouth. "You won't drown. You won't even get your fur wet. The submarines never actually go below the surface. It's all just a show."

The desperate rats looked confused. Was the yellow cat telling the truth? He seemed a bit more trustworthy than the gray one.

"Unfortunately, he's right," said Elias with an audible sigh. "You won't drown. You won't even get wet. On the other paw, the maintenance workers with shovels and buckets waiting for you back at the dock will be very real!"

"Elias," Kimball tugged at his vest, "we need to get out of here before those same workers spot us as well."

"Aw, man, I wanted to watch," Elias growled. He waved to the rats struggling to free themselves from the tape as the submarine floated into the lagoon. "Boys, it's been a lovely cruise."

The two cats climbed through the branches and hopped off onto the stone wall surrounding the lagoon. From there it was an easy leap to dry land. They were right between Nemo's Submarine Voyage and the curve of the Autopia track. Elias began to run back toward the Matterhorn.

"Where are you going?" Kimball called out after him.

"Home, brainiac," he stopped. "We can cut back around the mountain and head straight to the castle."

"Not anymore," said Kimball shaking his head. "I'd bet you my glasses there are hundreds of guests marching up Main Street as we stand here arguing directions. And there will be thousands more behind them. We need to head north, around Fantasyland, and work our way back."

"Oh, that's not risky at all," Elias snarled sarcastically. "That's going to take twice as long, nitwit."

"It's our only choice. You go the other way, you'll be marching directly into a sea of humans. Going up and doubling back is our best option, mathematically speaking. The crowd will split at the hub. Roughly one-third will go left into Adventureland. Let's just hope Oliver and Lilli steer clear. Another third or so will head right into Tomorrowland, the same way we came. Not our problem."

"What is your point?" Elias asked tersely.

"The final group," Kimball went on. "They'll cut straight through the castle into Fantasyland." He began mumbling to himself, making invisible notations in the air. He flipped open his pocket watch. "Those guests are our concern. By my calculations, albeit hastily determined...given the time and how far up Main Street the first guests should be by now, assuming they're walking at a standard human pace...and of course, judging by the current marching medley, and of course the position of the sun...."

"Will you spit it out already?!?" Elias roared.

"We've got about five minutes before guests hit Fantasyland!"

"Sheesh, why is that so hard for you?" Elias shook his head. He took off running past Kimball on all fours and around the other side of the Matterhorn.

"Just remember, we're supposed to avoid cast members, too," said Kimball, quickly stowing his watch inside his sweater and dropping to chase after him.

They cleared the mountain and made for the pass between the Alice in Wonderland dark ride and the Mad Tea Party spinning cups. Kimball had never been on the Alice ride inside the building, but he'd seen plenty of pictures of the colorful characters inside. But those tea cups!

He'd made the mistake of sneaking a ride on those whirly, swirly tea cups once and it was not a pleasant experience. Especially just after trying his first—and last chimichanga.

There was a group of cast members in blue tunics with black stripes and red diamonds up the front assembled behind Alice. They began to filter out to their various work stations just as the two cats rounded the corner. They quickly changed course, ducking through the Tea Cups. They would have to cut past the Storybook Land Canal Boats, which meant traveling even farther out of their way, increasing the chances of being seen.

"This would be a great time to have some sort of invisibility cape," Kimball muttered between panting breaths.

"I don't think they have those in this theme park," Elias answered.

"Or better yet, one of the quick escapes. There's rumored to be one camouflaged among those big fuchsia leaves around Alice, but no one recorded the location. Besides, the spring would be so old, it probably wouldn't even work. But wouldn't it be fun to hop on, pull the release, and fly?"

At this point there were cast members all over, opening up drink stands, shops, and taking position at the various attractions. The two cats were hugging every planter, trash can, and rock they could find. At one point, Kimball tapped Elias on the shoulder as a cast member wearing a striped shirt and maroon string tie walked past pushing an ice cream cart, humming to himself and paying them no notice. The two hid behind a shrub until he was gone.

"I don't think the coast is going to get any clearer until the park closes," Elias said. "Just follow my lead. When I say run for it, run, and don't stop for anything. Some human might see us, but they won't have a prayer of catching us."

Elias crouched low, placing one paw on the asphalt. His tail shot straight up like an antenna, scanning the airwaves for impending danger. Kimball readied himself. Every cast member in their general vicinity was preoccupied or staring in another direction. This was the time. "Run!"

Elias dropped his tail like a hatchet and took off. Kimball ran after as best he could. His legs were longer, but Elias was so close to the ground he was hard to catch. The flying elephants of Dumbo and the regal horses of King Arthur's Carrousel were just colorful, shiny blurs out of the corner of their eyes. The cats focused on the castle. Nothing else in the world mattered. Through the center they could see the back of the Partners statue, and a massive crowd of park guests wearing short pants and sunglasses, smiling, pointing, snapping pictures, and marching deeper into the park.

"Code red!" Kimball shouted, finding the power to speed past Elias. He raced around the corner of the castle, alongside the salon for little princesses called Bibbidi Bobbidi Boutique. He reached the flower bed beside and began searching frantically for the specific branch that opened their hidden passage. Then he realized it wasn't necessary. The stepping stones were already standing over the surface of the moat and their door was open. Standing in the archway leaning on his staff, green eyes blazing like emerald fire, was Thurl.

"Well, hurry on," Thurl snapped, waving for them to get inside. "Or would you have me invite some family from Cleveland in as well?"

The two younger cats crossed the slippery stones and scrambled inside the castle. The stones were just slipping back beneath the water and the door softly sealing shut when a handful of guests came around the corner looking for Snow White or Pinocchio. A young girl with black hair in pigtails tied with pink beads tugged at her father's elbow, pointing and proclaiming she was certain she'd just seen a kitty's tail disappear into the side of the castle. Her father just looked down and chuckled, shaking his head.

"You have some wild imagination, sweetie," he said, leading her on to Fantasyland. "Come on, Cinderella is this way, and I'm pretty sure there's no kitty in the castle. Same as your closet."

"What on earth happened?" Thurl demanded, banging his staff on the floor. "I saw the two of you running into Tomorrowland from my window. If not for my nervous pacing, I might not have seen you coming back through Fantasyland just now with your tails between your legs. What is going on? Taking a mad tour of the park? You do understand if any of you winds up in some cage at Anaheim Animal Control, there's *nothing* I can do to save you!"

Elias and Kimball took turns explaining everything that happened, from following the rats into Tomorrowland, to meeting the talking trashcan (Elias decided not to mention Kimball's offer to bring PUSH into the Order) and riding the Matterhorn, and interrogating the rats on top of a submarine. By the time they finished, both cats were out of breath from the telling, and Thurl was nearly as exhausted from listening.

"Well, that certainly explains that," Thurl said. He hopped up onto a chair at the table and poured water from a ceramic pitcher into three pewter drinking dishes. He slid one in front of each of the cats, and lapped cold water from his own. Finally he sat back on the red cushion. "Given the circumstances, I suppose you had no choice but to leave the rats tied to that submarine."

"Taped, sir," Kimball corrected. "Duct tape, in fact."

"In any event," Thurl continued, annoyed, "this still does not explain where Lilli and Oliver ran off to, or why they haven't come back."

"They're not back yet?" Elias asked.

"Clearly not. Just as you were tearing off into Tomorrowland, I spied the two of them, creeping out of the Tiki Room headed toward Adventureland, instead of the tunnel like they should have done. I lost sight of them after that—curse my old eyes. Oh, this is my fault. I should have gone to the Oracle myself, or at least let you all wait until nightfall. Nothing has gone to plan so far. And now the park is open, and full of humans."

"Maybe they ran into more cast members," said Elias. "They're probably just taking the long way back, like we did."

"Or hiding until nightfall," added Kimball.

"I hope you're right," said Thurl. "It sounds like the rats are taken care of, at least for now. Which means Doctor Owl is on his own until the park closes. Still, I have this overwhelming sense that he did not go far."

Chapter Seven

While Elias and Kimball were chasing rats through Tomorrowland, Oliver and Lilli were on the other side of the park.

"Oliver, you know I trust you," said Lilli as they traversed deeper into Adventureland. "What is it you want to see?"

"Well, if we need to look over the park to find the key, there's something I want to find first. Careful."

He ducked down and gestured to her to do the same. They were passing between the Adventureland Bazaar gift shop on the right and Tropical Imports which sold fruit and snacks and cold drinks on their left. Just inside Tropical Imports a young woman was stocking bottled water in an ice bath near the open window. Oliver ducked and rolled, popping back up against the sandy wall. Lilli quickly slinked up behind him. Her fur was almost a match for the beige plaster behind them. She peered inside the store and watched until the girl moved away to find another box of waters.

"It's clear," she whispered, pointing forward with two stubby brown fingers. Oliver crawled past the shop as quickly as he could with Lilli right behind him.

"You're not making any sense," Lilli said as they sprinted past the Jungle Cruise entrance. For just a fleeting second, they both gazed off past the dock at the forest beyond, imagining it full of live jungle animals. Lilli pushed him forward. "We're already trying to find one mysterious object. Do we really need another scavenger hunt?"

"You just said you trust me. The Oracle said we need to look over the whole park. I think he might have meant that literally. So I want to go somewhere we can look *over* the whole park."

"Alright, I guess that's a plan. Kind of stupid, but it's a plan. Personally, I'd prefer we start looking from the safety of the highest castle tower. You know, where we live and hide from all the people about to come stomping through this park?"

"We can try that later," said Oliver, shaking his head. He was staring up at the veranda of the blue faced River Belle Terrace restaurant across the street. Oliver found himself momentarily captivated by the aroma of frying bacon and sausages wafting out of the kitchen. He shook his head and tried to ignore his growling stomach.

"I was thinking," he said, "as long as we're in this neighborhood, we should start with a tree."

"A tree? I've been in one tree already today. Really, it was enough…." She looked up in the middle of her sentence and saw they were standing before a wooden staircase with bamboo rails and rope nets for sides. Overhead an oval-shaped sign grew right out of the thick-trunked tree.

"Tarzan's Treehouse," she read aloud. "I get it." The tree was massive, unusually thick and tall, with platforms and bridges erected all the way to the top, like a literal jungle gym. She shrugged her shoulders. "Well, it's a high place, alright. I thought you needed to find something first."

"You thought right," Oliver said bounding up the stairs. "Fortunately, it's already here, somewhere. At least, I think so. Come on!"

"So, you're still not going to tell me what you're looking for then?" Lilli shook her head with a sigh. She followed him up the stairs around the tree trunk until they reached a rope bridge hanging over the Adventureland street, which guests would soon be passing under. An old rowboat sporting a huge gash as though it had slammed hard into some rocks hung precariously overhead by ancient looking ropes. Oliver waited at the end, pretending to be checking an invisible watch and tapping his foot.

"Very funny," she deadpanned, brushing past him as though offended, but really fighting an urge to smile. "Just come on, and mind thy head!"

Oliver felt momentarily bad. He turned to apologize and looked up. He saw the wooden beam hanging over them painted with a warning: "Mind thy head." He shook his head and chuckled. They passed a large open book welcoming them to Tarzan's jungle home. The cats climbed higher and higher, constantly discovering new perspectives of the park between the outstretched branches and leaves of the massive tree. The backside of New Orleans Square. The jagged fiery rocks of Big Thunder Mountain standing tall in Frontierland.

They reached the top of another staircase where the floor leveled off. There was a makeshift bedroom with walls of bamboo and ship's wood, roped off from the gangway. A door on the side was smashed in. Inside, furniture was overturned and scattered about. The curtains hung haphazard and torn about the room, wafting in the morning breeze. Another book sat open on display. On the page was a black-and-white sketch of a leopard and a few brief lines explaining this had been the home of a young family, Tarzan's parents, after they were shipwrecked at sea.

"Until the fateful night of Sabor's attack," Lilli read softly.

Suddenly, from right over their heads, came an awful, ghoulish cry, causing Oliver and Lilli to leap back in terror. Poised over them, perched in the bamboo celling rods, ready to strike, was the same leopard from the book in full color and size. Pale eyes, long, razor sharp fangs, and bright blood-red mouth open to bite. They both caught their breath and looked at each other with relief, then chuckled. It was a statue. The attraction was full of life-sized figures from the movie.

"I'm guessing that's Sabor," Oliver chuckled, holding a paw to the white patch on his chest, feeling his heart race.

"That could give kids nightmares. Or other cats."

"Easy cousin," Oliver said to the statue, only slightly embarrassed for nearly falling over backward in terror. "Look at those fangs. Glad he's stiff."

"He would be a killer alright," said Lilli. She was tracing the lines of the leopard's back and legs with her eyes. "But look at those muscles."

Oliver watched as she gazed almost longingly at the statue of the wild jungle cat. He suddenly felt very inadequate as a feline. "I guess, if you go that sort of thing."

"Relax hot shot," she grinned, sensing his discomfort. "I'm just saying, I'd love to have a leopard's speed and strength. Check out those claws. Imagine the damage a beast could do with even *one* of his paws."

They came to another book in a corner that overlooked Frontierland, this one with a sketch of a gorilla. Oliver couldn't help but duck, scanning the branches overhead. There were no gorilla statues hidden in the trees to startle them. The cats reached a staircase leading down under the thatched grass roof of another room. Inside they discovered a gorilla. A gentle, smiling female with brown fur and a kind face. In her arm she held a happy human baby.

"That's something you don't see every day," Oliver commented. "I never knew gorillas and people were so friendly."

"It's in the story," said Lilli matter-of-factly. "She adopted Tarzan as a baby after his parents were killed. You really should stop to read the books."

Inside another room Oliver and Lilli discovered a young woman with auburn hair tied in a bun wearing a yellow dress. She was holding a small pad and a quill, and across the room Tarzan himself stood, wearing little but his long hair and a loin cloth. Between them sat a large sketchpad on an easel that, like a magic mirror, reflected the young lady's drawing of the tree-surfing jungle lord. Oliver had his paws on the window ledge, poking his head inside, hopeful this was the right spot. His black tail was twitching anxiously.

There certainly were a number of artifacts from the shipwreck. There was an old sepia picture of a well-dressed couple, who he figured for Tarzan's parents. There was a tiny mirror and books on every shelf but not the instrument he sought. After another moment he sighed with frustration. Then Oliver remembered the next chamber over, on the other side of the wall. He quickly skipped across the walkway and Lilli scurried up behind him, excited to see whatever he discovered. Sadly, when she found him,

Oliver just stood there, shoulders slumped with a confused look on his furry face, staring at a giant ship's wheel before a picture window the family had reclaimed from the ship.

"I take it this wheel isn't what you were looking for."

"I don't get it," Oliver said, sensing Lilli's impatience growing. "The ship's wheel is here. The ship's window is right there as well. Wouldn't it just make sense to keep all the ship parts together?"

"Oliver, this is a tree. Ship parts don't make sense up here, period. Now come on, enough of this secret game. We have to go."

"No, we still have a little time to look around."

"No, we don't," she said. She gestured at the next set of stairs. "Look, these lead *down*. We've reached the end of the attraction. And I'm tired of chasing you around the tree, especially when you haven't even told me what we're looking for. Come on." With that Lilli began walking down the winding steps.

"A telescope," he said sullenly. "I was certain I remembered seeing a telescope in one of the scenes. Guess I was wrong."

"A telescope?" he heard Lilli repeat in the distance. "I imagine that could come in handy, back up there."

Oliver sighed and followed after her, resigned to having led them on a wild goose chase. His memory must have been wrong. He'd wasted their time, putting them at greater risk of being seen. They had better just get to the street and figure out the safest route back to the castle. Surely the tunnel was out of the question. The boys would have been smart enough to close the hatch. Well, Kimball would have. He imagined them both safely back inside the castle now with Thurl wondering where the heck he and Lilli were.

"Hey, Ollie, you coming? Or will you be living in the treehouse from now on?"

"I'm coming," he muttered, heading down the stairs. "Sorry I was just...."

Oliver stopped. Lilli was leaning against a bamboo rail down below, in front of yet another show scene. It looked like an outdoor laboratory or a study. There were books, glass bottles, a globe. There was even a complete human skeleton leaning against a wall. And there was one more thing.

"Good," Lilli said absently, examining one of her claws. She nodded her head toward the scene. "I thought you'd like to know there's one more room. And I may not be the scientific prodigy that Kimball is, but I'm pretty sure that's a telescope."

There it was. Mounted on a tripod. The old, worn brass telescope he'd remembered seeing when he was young. Time had left the once shiny metal finish dulled and dusty, in need of a good polishing. Appearances didn't matter. All Oliver cared about was whether it worked or not.

"Of course," he said, slapping his forehead with his black-and-white paw. "I'm such an idiot."

"No argument here," she smirked. "All of this belonged to Jane's father."

"OK," Oliver said, trying to scrounge what memories he had of the story. "The professor?"

"Looks like they set up this little laboratory for him when he and Jane decided to stay in Africa with Tarzan."

Oliver slid under the bamboo railing and stuck one eye up to the lens of the telescope. He swung it around on its tripod and it made an ear-splitting squeal, like it hadn't been moved in years. Oliver hoped the noise hadn't attracted any attention. Satisfied they were still in the clear, he pointed it out at Adventureland through the dense palms. Through the dusty glass he could only see light and blobs of unclear images. Oliver huffed on the lens and gave it a wipe with his vest. He did the other side as well. Oliver again held it to his eye, then screwed up his face, still unsatisfied.

"Oh, give it here," Lilli commanded. She snatched the spyglass and spit on the big lens. She gave it a good wiping with her sleeve, then did the same thing with the smaller eyepiece before handing it back. "Now try."

Oliver had no response. Sure enough, a little spit shine and the telescope worked like new. Well, new enough. He unscrewed it from the stand and carefully lifted it off the tripod, stowing it safely under his arm like a loaf of bread.

"Come on," he said, ducking back under the rail.

"Home, right?"

"No. Up."

"Up?" she asked, tilting her head back to stare up at the tree. "Back through the treehouse again? Oliver, we just came through it. This is the exit. We can get out right here and...."

"No." Oliver tucked the telescope snugly into his waist belt where his beloved plastic sword once hung. He extended his claws, jumped up at the side of the tree trunk, and began scaling its smooth bark. He grabbed the first branch he came to and looked back down at Lilli below. "This time we're taking the express lane, straight up."

A natural climber, Lilli simply shrugged and began to follow after him. At least she figured out what Oliver had in mind. A telescope, tall trees holding up Tarzan's Treehouse, and the Oracle's instructions to look over the whole park. She wished Oliver would've simply explained what they were doing, and what they were looking for in the first place. Sometimes he tried to seem so cool and mysterious. It wasn't him. He was smart, and curious, sure, but also a bit cautious, and excitable. Although, she thought, it was kind of cute. Lilli shook her head and continued to climb until she was just beneath him. Oliver already had leaves and twigs caught in his fur. That would be a mess to get out. She was grateful for her short, smooth beige fur.

"You know," Lilli grumbled as she clawed her way up the tree, "if you really wanted the highest vantage point of the park, the Matterhorn would be my pick. It's taller than any of these trees."

"I thought of that," he said, climbing from branch to branch, his black-and-white fur occasionally disappearing in a cluster of green leaves. "However, the Matterhorn also has human climbers going up and down the side all day. We'd have to wait until the park closes, at which point it would be dark."

Oliver looked down at her again and then his eyes accidentally looked past her and he became dizzyingly aware of how far up they were. His eyes widened and he had to take a deep breath to keep from losing his balance. He shook his head, turned his face back upward, and continued to climb. "Besides," he went on, "these trees are plenty high, I'd say."

The two cats clawed and jumped their way through the highest branches and thick green leaves until they were soon perched at the top. They could see all of Adventureland, New Orleans Square, and most of the park spread out beyond. They could even see over attraction buildings to spy the hustle and bustle of the park's backstage areas. Small vehicles rushed back and forth as did costumed cast members pushing carts and carrying boxes and register tills. All safely hidden from the eyes of the park guests, and too busy rushing to get to their particular part of the park to bother looking up, let alone notice a vest or a lavender tunic. Even if someone had noticed them, there was a real chance they might just forget a cat with a telescope *wasn't* part of the attraction. After all, this was Disneyland!

Oliver put the eyepiece to his left eye and squinted the other. As he did so, his lip curled in one corner, revealing a slim white canine. Lilli couldn't stop from letting a giggle escape. He lowered the instrument and looked at her with confusion.

"What's so funny?"

"I'm sorry," she laughed. "It's just, well, when you did that you looked like a kitty pirate!"

"Gee thanks," he said, feeling self-conscious. He turned away and looked back into the telescope, this time trying hard to control his lip.

"No, Oliver I'm sorry," she said, not wanting to hurt his feelings. "That's not a bad thing. It's kind of cute, actually."

He lowered the telescope. "Really?"

"Sure. I like pirates."

"Hmm," he said, cracking a slight smile again. He looked back through the telescope lens, his snarl intensifying. "Avast ye scurvy bilge rats! Fetch me that horizon!"

"Alright swabby, don't overdo it."

"Oh, right," Oliver coughed, straightening up. Oliver scanned the park, gazing over the rooftops of Main Street, U.S.A. and on toward Tomorrowland. Admittedly, he wasn't sure what to look for. He'd kind of hoped once he had the telescope, something would just jump out at him. After all, the Oracle said the Imagineers hid the key someplace easy to find but hard to access. Still, that could mean a million different things. In fact, it didn't specify a high place at all. And why did she say she liked pirates? That could mean a million different things, too. Oliver shook his head.

"*Concentrate*," he muttered quietly.

"Who, me?" Lilli asked.

"What?" Oliver said, before realizing he'd spoken. "Oh, uh, nothing. I was just, you know, thinking out loud."

"Gotcha. See anything?"

"Just the usual stuff." He peered at Fantasyland, though much of it was blocked by Sleeping Beauty Castle and the Matterhorn. He scanned the Matterhorn but spied no trace of anything gold. Slowly panning to the left, his view suddenly became very orange. He turned the end of the brass tube until the picture came back into focus. He was staring directly at Big Thunder Mountain in Frontierland. The craggy mountain range surrounding a runaway mine train roller coaster might be a good spot. "Big Thunder would make a great hiding place."

"Definitely hard to reach," Lilli agreed. "Any of those rocks and crevices would work."

Oliver scanned the entire mountain, looking for any trace of the key. An unusual glimmer. A misplaced reflection of the sun. Nothing stood out. At least nothing that might indicate a hidden key. Perhaps the fellow spinning around in a bathtub was sitting on it, Oliver sighed, watching an animatronic bather on the side of the mountain. Oliver slowly swept over Mickey's Toontown. It was pretty far away and this old spyglass wasn't that powerful. Wouldn't have been much good at sea, he thought. No wonder Tarzan's ship wrecked.

"Ollie, the park is open. I can hear the Adventureland music down below. There will be guests all over the place any minute. We have to go."

"You're right," Oliver answered with a sigh, feeling frustrated. He lowered the telescope in defeat. All this adventure in Adventureland and still no closer to finding the elusive Disneyland key. It was time to give up, for now. Hopefully, wherever the key was, it would remain safely hidden until nightfall.

Just then, Oliver saw a brief flash. Not a light. It was like a momentary glimpse of a shooting star. He returned the spyglass to his eye. The flare had come from Splash Mountain. Sure enough, as a small white cloud passed in front of the morning sun, the light hit it just right. There was something shimmering inside the hollow old tree that sat over the waterfall on Chick-A-Pin Hill. Easy to see. Immensely difficult to reach.

"I don't believe it," Oliver said excitedly. "I think I've found it!" He couldn't believe his luck. His hunch had paid off. "Lilli, I think I found the key!"

"What? No way! Where? Let me see."

Oliver handed her the telescope and pointed it toward Critter Country. "Right above the opening where the logs come out, inside the tree. Wait for it. Wait for a flash."

After a moment, Lilli caught sight of it, too. A small reflection gleaming off something metal at the top of the attraction. "Wow! Do you really think that's it?"

"What else could it be? Everything up there is brown and orange. It's an old tree. I don't think there's supposed to be anything shiny inside that trunk. We've got to get up there before Mintz spots it."

Lilli put the telescope down for a moment and looked directly at Oliver, concerned. "You do realize this just made things *immensely* more complicated, right?"

"You mean Baxter," Oliver said flatly, understanding exactly what she meant.

"No Castle Cat has set paw on the mountain for years." Lilli put the telescope back to her eye. "There's a reason it's off-limits."

"I know, but this is bigger than Baxter. He'll either let us up there, or..." Oliver's words trailed off. He didn't want to sound like some tough guy. He didn't feel tough at all. That was Elias' job. In fact, Oliver felt nervous at the prospect of entering Splash Mountain. This would be one mission where Oliver would be happy to let fearless Elias take the lead.

Yes?" she smiled, giving him a curious eye. "Or what?"

"Or I'll let Elias deal with him while I run up the side of the hill," he answered with a forced smile.

Lilli laughed. They stared at each other for a moment, not speaking. Both understood the mission had indeed gotten more serious. Lilli started to hand him the telescope but heard something. She put it back to her eye and turned it toward the hub.

"Well, there's nothing we can do about Baxter or that key right now," she said. "Especially if we get caught. Look!" She pushed the telescope at him. Oliver saw the heads of hundreds of park guests walking right up the middle of Main Street. "Come on!"

Lilli dropped down to the next branch and began the climb down. Oliver couldn't argue. Nor did he have time to return the spyglass. He carefully rested it securely between some branches. He'd have to remember to retrieve it later. And if he forgot, another Disneyland urban legend would be born. He followed Lilli down the tree from branch to branch, skipping a few at a time. Finally they reached the ground near the exit.

"We better go the long way," said Lilli, pointing farther into Adventureland.

Oliver agreed. They couldn't head back to the hub now. Better to stay ahead of the crowds and work their way around. Soon they were rounding the corner into Frontierland, their claws slipping across the freshly hosed streets. They ran past the Golden Horseshoe theater and were startled by a clutch of cast members standing in the doorway, looking over a tablet. The cats exchanged a quick glance indicating they couldn't stop now.

They darted past the shooting gallery, where luckily nobody was shooting this early. They followed the path that ran past the striped tent of the Royal Theatre and there, looking more welcoming than ever, was their castle.

The stones belched their way through the water. The secret door began to swing open. The two cats raced across the slippery stones before they were fully in place. Oliver's back paw hit a slick spot and he flipped tail-over-whiskers. He was so turned around, he looked up to see the moat. Something grabbed his tail and yanked. It was Lilli; her legs stretched between the last stone and doorway ledge. Kimball ran up behind and helped steady her. Elias pulled on Kimball's tail, and with a combined effort they hoisted Oliver into the castle. The cats tumbled to the floor in a heap. As the wall quietly swung shut, Thurl stood over them, eyes ablaze, shaking his head.

"I can't believe the lot of you," he said, exasperated, shaking his staff. "Disregarding my warnings. Roaming the park in broad daylight. Narrowly racing through that passageway in the nick of time. Be glad this isn't Disneyland Paris. I'd have left you to the dragon under the castle!"

"Well," Kimball muttered, "technically it's not a *real* dragon."

"If you say so," grunted Thurl.

Thurl instructed them to return to their rooms and rest. He knew they had a long night ahead and would need energy. The five cats reassembled at their table that evening. Dinner plates were set out before them, laden with shredded chicken and salmon mixed with steamed rice. Alongside each plate sat a wide-rimmed drinking goblet of water. The food appeared each evening on a cart by an unseen courier. It had been this way since Walt's time. It was part of the deal he promised Mr. Lincoln. A safe home and full belly in exchange for protecting the park from vermin. Tonight, the vermin would be bigger than usual.

"Eat, young ones," said Thurl quietly, standing at the end of the table. "You need strength. You cannot be effective if you're hungry."

"What about you?" asked Lilli. She gestured to his own plate standing in front of his empty chair at the table's head. "You need to eat as well."

"I confess to my hypocrisy, my dear," Thurl said with a soft smile. "I am too concerned to eat. From what the Oracle told you, this is more serious than I feared. This Mintz, Oliver's owlish friend, seeks to settle a very old grudge. He will return tonight, with or without the rats. He's carried that anger, all those hurt feelings, for so long that he won't give up. I pity him. But if he finds the key, it could be devastating."

"Yeah," Elias muttered though a mouthful of fish, "we'll be homeless again"

"I can't go back to the streets," Kimball worried aloud, pushing his plate away. "I'm an intellectual, not an alley cat!"

"We're not going to let anything happen," said Oliver. He looked at Lilli who nodded. "Lilli and I think we found the key. At least, where it's hidden."

"You're kidding," Elias sneered, rice falling off his face.

"Where, dear boy?" Thurl asked hopefully. "Where did you see it? This is wonderful news! Why didn't you tell us this right away?"

"It's not entirely wonderful," said Oliver.

"It's at the top of Splash Mountain," Lilli added. The room went eerily quiet for a moment. Even the lanterns seemed to stop flickering.

"Uh oh," said Kimball.

"I see," Thurl finally said, tugging at his beard.

"It doesn't matter," said Oliver. "It's not going to be easy, but I will get it. Somehow."

"The kid's right," said Elias, punching a fist into an open paw. "Forget about Baxter. I've been dreaming of running into that guy. Somebody needs to shake some sense into that backwater hairball."

"Baxter's not alone in that mountain, you know," said Kimball.

"Kimball is right," said Thurl. "Baxter and his compatriots know every nook and cranny of that mountain. They've explored every tunnel and passage. They have the element of surprise. And they have no reservations about punishing intruders, even cats."

"*Particularly* other cats," Kimball added. As a young stray, he had wandered into Critter Country seeking scraps for his belly from the nearby Hungry Bear restaurant. He climbed onto the base of Splash Mountain for a better look, and was lucky to escape with his tail still intact. He never even got a good look at Baxter. Just a flash of fiery orange hair and green eyes and yellow fangs. "Baxter is a monster."

"No," said Thurl softly. "That would be easier to understand. He is, in fact, a cat."

"I don't get it," said Lilli. All their lives, at least since coming to the park, Thurl had warned them to stay away from Splash Mountain. Chick-A-Pin Hill, as the mountain was actually called, was off limits. It had its own protector, of sorts, who didn't take kindly to visitors. "What's his problem with us?"

"His problem is he used to *be* one of us," Kimball answered, still looking at Thurl. The other cats followed his gaze.

"What Kimball says is true," said Thurl with a sigh. It was finally time they heard the truth about Baxter, especially since it appeared they were about to meet him. An air of sadness began to permeate the room as the old cat spoke. It clearly upset him to think about, let alone speak of, Baxter.

"Baxter was a member of the Order once, just like all of you. He sat at this table, just as you do. Baxter was always different. He was bold and fearless, much like Elias. He was smart, like Kimball. Of course he possessed a strong appetite for human food and drink. That last one didn't help matters. In our youth he was agile and quick, like Lilli. And once, at least for a brief moment, I thought he might be a natural leader. Just like you, Oliver."

Oliver looked down at the table. The words made him feel uncomfortable. And he imagined they grated at Elias' nerves like cheese. Elias had already been part of the order for a few years when Oliver arrived. Sometimes even Oliver thought Elias should be the leader. He was courageous. He would stop at nothing to protect his home. Still, he was also impetuous and would leap before he looked, if no other paw reached out to hold him by the tail. Oliver worried that one day Elias might have enough of taking orders. He feared the day Elias might be spoken of, like Baxter, as a cat who was *once* in the Order.

"I was correct," Thurl went on. "Baxter has become a leader. A leader of rabble—of ne'er do wells and criminal creatures. And he is indeed bold. Bold enough to bound right into the kitchens of the park restaurants and take food. Just as he was bold enough to steal some of our precious blue pixie dust to create his own misguided Order.

"Baxter learned survival in the streets of another city before he wandered onto a boxcar and woke up in California. That's how he eventually came to Disneyland. He joined the Order but never completely adopted the philosophy, to serve the park, not reap personal rewards. I think he felt owed somehow. A dangerous belief."

"So he left the Order?" asked Lilli.

"More like he was tossed," said Elias.

"It is true," said Thurl. "Baxter began to sneak his friends from the streets into the park at night when he was meant to be on patrol. Once altered, he and his band began raiding the snack counters. They caused damage in gift shops. They would turn on attractions at night for their own private parties. And not just here in Disneyland. Baxter and his crew would even sneak across the borderland to pillage the other park."

"California Adventure?" Lilli gasped. "That's not even our jurisdiction."

"Precisely," said Kimball. "He probably figured Thurl and the Order couldn't keep an eye on them over there."

"Plus the restaurants offer more adult-oriented beverages," added Oliver, listening intently. "Who knows what that stuff will do to a cat's brain."

"When I confronted him on these offences, he called me a fool for serving humans," Thurl said. "Baxter said Disneyland is a giant playground and we should take advantage of it."

"You mean treat it like his own personal scratching post," said Elias.

"For Baxter," Kimball interjected, "more like litter box."

"We reached an impasse," said Thurl. "Baxter's attitude could not stand. Nor could his actions. The Order voted to revoke his membership. We demanded he leave the park. Of course, we were fools to think he would comply. He ran to Splash Mountain. I led the Order inside Chick-A-Pin in Hill to smoke him out, but we were ambushed. We should have expected that he'd have his own gang waiting inside. A terrible brawl ensued, with some of my cats bearing the worst of it. Baxter's boys had higher ground, and the element of surprise. They took some damage, of course, including Baxter himself."

"His eye?" Kimball whispered, pawing at his own face.

"Yes," Thurl nodded. "Again, my own naivety. Good cats were hurt because of it."

"No, Thurl," said Oliver. "That is not on you. He had a home in the park, in the Order. Baxter chose to disobey. He chose to attack. "

"Oliver's right," said Elias, surprising everyone. Perhaps, his face revealed even himself. "We may not always get along, but we're still a family. Castle Cats are bound together. We believe in our cause, and in our home. If he couldn't deal with that, he never should have signed up!"

"Regardless," Thurl said, clutching his walking stick, "after that night I vowed never to let any Castle Cats be harmed fighting one another again. Not even Baxter. That is why I've allowed him to hole up inside Splash Mountain, along with his band of drunken reprobates. He has, to date, accepted the uncomfortable truce. I shudder to think the state of the hidden coves and corners of that mountain."

"We'll give you a full report when we get back," said Elias.

"He's right," Oliver added, "we'll get the key, with or without Baxter's permission."

"I really hope it's *without*," Elias snarled.

"Boys, please," said Thurl, "arrogance is a soldier's enemy. Baxter is not to be underestimated. He may not be the cat he once was, but he's strong, and clever. He knows that mountain which is something neither of you can say. I would not allow you to attempt this mission if the key were not so important."

"How many others are in there with him?" Lilli asked.

"Don't ask me," said Kimball, "I didn't have time for a head count."

"At least three others, perhaps more," said Thurl. "In the years since our last encounter, who knows if his family has grown? Baxter is fickle. It's easy to fall in and out of his favor."

"If only there was a way to get up that hill without going inside," Oliver said.

"If I thought they could be trusted," Thurl pondered, "I would enlist a few birds to fly to the peak of Chick-A-Pin Hill and snatch the key for us."

"Flying is not a bad idea," said Kimball. "Perhaps with the right parts I could work up some sort of flying machine. Or maybe a zip line we could launch from the top of the Matterhorn. Then one of us could swing over, grab it, and get back."

"There's one problem with that plan," said Lilli. "Zip lines only work in one direction."

"Drat, she's right," said Kimball. "Foiled by the laws of physics once again! I don't suppose anyone knows how to walk a tightrope?"

"There's not going to be any zipping," said Oliver. "Or flying. Kimball, these are great ideas and in another situation they'd probably help, but there's no time to design anything effective. Let alone find the parts to build it."

"I'm afraid he's right, son," said Thurl, patting the arm of the crestfallen feline engineer.

"We do it the old-fashioned way," said Oliver.

"That's right," added Elias. "We walk right into that mountain and if Baxter has an issue, I'll deal with him. Kimball and me!"

"*What?*" Kimball spat. "Can we go back to my zip line idea, please?"

The four younger cats ate dinner without saying another word about the mission ahead. Even Thurl finally sat with them and picked at his own plate. Best to put up a positive front, he reasoned. It would be better to appear confident in their abilities and not worried they might not be ready to face a nastier, more conniving cat and his gang. For a moment he considered calling off the plan. They could take the gamble that Mintz would never find the key. Or better yet, that Mintz and his rats would come face-to-face with Baxter. After all, while he let cast members do their jobs by day, Baxter had no hesitation taking on human trespassers after hours. There was a well-known story in the park of a couple of troublemaking teenagers who tried to climb Splash Mountain after dark. They were caught by security running through Frontierland with torn clothes and scratches all over their faces and arms, crying about some wild orange monster. Thurl knew exactly what rough beast they'd encountered. He had chosen not to share that story with his young friends tonight.

Soon it was time for the Cats of the Castle to leave the castle. The fireworks had fizzled away. The park was long closed. Oliver stood first and looked around the table at each of his friends.

"If anyone needs to get anything from their room, go now," he said, trying to sound confident, like a leader should. He wished he felt that way.

"We will be heading out the side door in the next five minutes." Elias and Kimball disappeared up the spiral stairs to their floor. Lilli stayed behind.

"I'm as ready as I'll ever be," she said with a smile when they had gone. She extended her claws. "These have never failed me in a jam."

"Hopefully it won't come to that. Maybe if we're lucky, Baxter and his boys will be sleeping off one of their field trips across the promenade."

"Yeah, sure," Lilli smiled, trying to be encouraging. "We should have Elias lay a trail of churros from Splash Mountain to Toon Town to draw them away!"

"Good idea," Oliver laughed. "Why didn't I think of that?"

"Duh, because you're a boy," she said with a wink.

The other two cats came bounding back down the stairs. Kimball was tightening his belt which looked much bulkier than it had before. Elias stepped right up to Oliver until they were almost nose to nose. Oliver felt uncomfortable. What was Elias doing?

"You really think you're ready to lead us, kid?" Elias growled. "'Cause I don't. You're not ready for this job."

Oliver stared back, never breaking his gaze. Inside he was panicking, feeling anger and fear churning in his gut. Why was Elias doing this, especially now? Was this a challenge?

"Not without this," said Elias, glaring at Oliver. Then, as if he couldn't control it anymore, his gray mouth broke into a grin. From behind his vest he revealed a new sword. It had a wide gray blade that curved like a crescent moon. The handle was shiny gold plastic with a matching finger guard. He laid the souvenir weapon on the table. "Go ahead. Pick it up."

Oliver didn't know what to say. He picked up the sword. It was heavier and sturdier than his old one. At the end of the hilt was a round red jewel. Oliver held it out and gently sliced at the air. This was a nice sword. This was the sword of a leader.

"I saw it in an Adventureland gift shop," said Elias. "It's new. From some movie. I figured it would make a nice replacement for the one you lost in the mansion."

"I don't know what to say." The other cats looked on with smiles on their faces. Oliver tucked the sword into his belt. "I can't believe you thought of me."

"Alright, take it easy," Elias chided, paws out. "Don't cry or anything. Just figured some extra protection couldn't hurt tonight. I can't be everywhere. Now come on, let's go." He cuffed Oliver on the arm and turned for the secret door.

"I, uh," Oliver stammered. "He's right. Come on everybody. It's time to go."

Thurl tripped the sconce back and the door opened. The four of them leapt out one by one across the stones to the path on the other side of the mote.

The wall of the castle closed softly behind them. The sky was black with only the bright white moon shining above. They could hear music playing softly off in the distance near Main Street and the gates. Around the castle, all was quiet. There wasn't a human in sight, not even a cast member.

"What do you think, fearless leader?" Elias asked. "Do we cut through Frontierland to New Orleans Square? It's a straight shot to Splash Mountain."

"I don't think so," said Oliver. "Baxter will see us coming the minute we come around Rivers of America. What do you think, Kimball?"

"Oh, well, I agree. There's no guaranteed way to get there undetected, assuming Baxter and his cohorts are awake and alert. That said, the safest way might be the longest way."

"And that is?" Elias snorted.

"Cut through Fantasyland and around Big Thunder Mountain."

"Then what?" asked Elias. "We steal a canoe and paddle our way around Tom Sawyer Island?"

"Follow the railroad," said Lilli, seeing where Kimball was going.

"Precisely. We walk the tracks. They run right over Critter Country, and into a tunnel through Splash Mountain. Plus, we'll have tree cover most of the way."

"Great idea, Kimball," said Oliver. "It will be like sneaking in through the backdoor."

"Assuming Baxter doesn't have anyone watching the tunnel." said Lilli.

"Well, yes," said Kimball. "There's always that."

"Anyone disagree?" Oliver asked, looking at each cat. They shook their heads. "So be it. We cut through Fantasyland and make our way to the tracks."

Oliver held out his paw. Lilli locked eyes with him and put her brown paw on top of it. She turned to look at Kimball. He put his yellow paw over hers. They all turned to Elias. He grinned and nodded his thick gray head. He placed his paw on top of the pile. They all exchanged smiles and without another word, took off into the night toward Fantasyland.

Chapter Eight

Every attraction in Fantasyland was dark, but the white street lights shone brightly. The carousel, Dumbo, Alice's Mad Tea Party; attractions that were usually alive with thousands of lights and sounds sat quiet and still. The park seemed peaceful. The quartet of cats hurried past the tracks of Casey Jr's Circus Train and made their way around the east side of Big Thunder Mountain. That's when something else disturbed the peace. The echoing sound of heavy footsteps pounding the asphalt, heading in their direction.

"Hide!" Oliver shouted. The cats scattered, diving behind trees and trash cans. Kimball sprinted right up the walkway into the shadows of the Thunder Mountain queue. From behind a closed up turkey leg stand, Oliver could just see him adjusting the lenses of his glasses. No doubt he had some form of night vision lenses for a better look at whoever was coming.

It wasn't long before they saw who it was. Louie and Pete, the same guards he'd seen the night before on Main Street U.S.A, and at the Haunted Mansion. They had rushed out of Mickey's Toontown in a hurry. Pete was in the lead, with his longer legs. Louie brought up the rear, panting like mad.

"Pee...Pee...Pete," Louie called out as he jogged along, "wha...what...are we...running for?"

"He's not gettin' in tonight," Pete called back.

"Hu...who?"

"Whoever cut the hole in the fence behind New Orleans Square," said Pete. "I bet it's the same crackpot from last night. Why else would he cut all the alarms and camera feeds along the northern perimeter of the park? He wants in!"

"Crackpot from last night?" Oliver wondered aloud. Had to be Mintz. Somehow he'd cut the alarms. But how?

"Hu...how could...he?" Louie huffed. Finally, he sputtered to a halt. "Pete... stop running for a second! How could someone cut the alarms from outside? I thought it was impossible."

"Good question," Oliver quietly agreed.

"*That* I haven't figured out yet," said Pete, circling back around to Louie. He too stopped and bent over, hands on his knees, catching his breath. "We gotta get in better shape, Lou."

"I know," said Louie, his uniform shirt growing darker with sweat. "If only… we didn't get an…em-employee…discount…at the Confectionery! Those fudge squares…are so good! Maybe I should…stick to the…candied apples."

"Louie," Pete looked up in disbelief, "they're *candied*! Get it? Caramel! Chocolate! Heck, I saw one covered in chunks of peanut butter cups!"

"Yeah, but they're apples," Louie reasoned, finally straightening up. "That makes 'em healthy."

"You're hopeless," said Pete. "Come on, we gotta get over there. If it is the same weirdo with the scarf from last night, I want to nab him before the other guys get over here."

"Man, I love that apple with the peanut butter cups," Louie mused aloud, a blissful gleam in his eye. "I could go for one right now. Or two. And those fudge squares. Ooh, a fudge square on an apple! Soften it up a little and spread it over the caramel and the candy pieces, maybe with some warm caramel corn…"

"Will you knock it off?!?" snapped Pete, tugging at Louie's elbow to get him moving again. Just then Pete's radio squawked to life.

"Pete!" the voice called. It was Forte, the night supervisor. "Pete! What's your current location?"

"We're on the north side of Thunder Mountain, Tony," Pete answered, still shaking his head at his partner's appetites. "Officer Prima and I just heard about the alarm issue on the radio. We're headin' over to check the fence breach from last night. Just in case it's not a coincidence."

"Good thinking," Forte responded. "I don't believe it was an accident myself. I just checked out the server room with Eisner from maintenance. Those wires were deliberately cut."

"Cut?" said Pete.

"Actually that's being kind," said Forte. "They were mangled. I mean, it literally looked like they'd been chewed through."

"That's definitely no glitch," said Pete.

"Yeah, glitches don't eat wires," added Louie. "But who could get in there to do that?"

"I don't know, Lou," said Pete, "but it's no coincidence. Some guy breaks in last night and we chase him off. Then tonight the alarms are cut. And cameras, too. Somebody's up to something."

"It gets weirder," Forte added. "Apparently some guy walked right into the park this morning, claiming to be a doctor from the city or something. We cross-referenced the security camera feeds. I'm pretty sure it was the same guy from the mansion last night. His name is Sorrell Mintz. Turns out he's been on the 'no entry' list for years."

"Whoa, this Mintz guy really wants to come to Disneyland," said Louie. "So you figure he's the one that cut the wire?"

"Can't say for sure," Forte said. We can't pull up tonight's feed. Still, seems pretty likely. I want teams checking every inch of fence out there. I've already called in some extra shifts tonight, at least until we get the cameras and alarms up and running again. My brother Vinnie's a sergeant with the Anaheim PD. I asked if they could put some extra patrols on Harbor Boulevard, as a favor. We need all the eyes we can get. Stay sharp, boys."

From his hiding place, Oliver looked up at the sky. What was the man on the radio talking about? The moon was bright, but it wasn't full yet.

"We're on it," said Pete. He clipped his radio to his lapel and the two trotted off around Rivers of America toward New Orleans Square. As soon as they were out of sight, Oliver crept back out into the open. He waved his paw in the air, signaling the others it was clear.

"D'you guys hear that?" Elias asked, appearing from behind a trash can—which he'd given a quick shove before ducking behind to make sure it wouldn't talk and give away his hiding place. "All the alarms on this side of the park were cut."

"Has to be Doctor Owl," said Oliver.

"But how?" Kimball asked. "It would be nearly impossible for him to enter that server room. If he'd managed to get that far, he'd still need an access card. I can't see how Mintz could even get inside the park. After this morning's encounter, his picture will be taped up next to every security monitor."

"Boys," said Lilli, shaking her head. "You heard him. The wires looked like they'd been chewed. Mintz didn't bite through electrical wires. Clearly it was his stupid rats."

"No way," said Elias. "We taped them up good. Those rats are in a cage somewhere, if they're lucky. Or at the bottom of the submarine lagoon, if *we're* lucky!"

"It doesn't matter," Oliver said. "The park is vulnerable. Doctor Owl could be inside right now. And that hole in the fence is not far from Splash Mountain." Oliver quickly lowered his voice to a whisper, on the odd chance anyone was within ear-shot. "Whether he knows the key is there or not!"

The cats dropped to all fours and began to run toward the north end of Frontierland. They hadn't gotten far into Big Thunder Ranch when behind them they heard a thunderous metal crash. All four cats skidded to a stop and spun around, rearing back up onto their hind feet with claws extended, ready for a fight. They saw nothing. All was quiet. The attractions remained perfectly still. There was no trace of movement. Not a soul to be seen anywhere.

"Okay, that was weird," Lilli whispered.

"Those rats," Elias snarled. "If they did escape, they're going to regret it."

"Everybody relax," Oliver tried to reassure the group. "We're all just a little jumpy right now. It was probably a guard poking around back there or something. We can't worry about it. Our job is to keep moving forward."

None of the cats felt reassured that the mysterious noise had been nothing, not even Oliver. Still, agreeing they had to keep going, the cats continued to run. Had they been on the other side of Big Thunder Mountain, or if Kimball had some crazy lenses that could peer through solid objects, they would have seen a trash can lying on its side in front of Rancho del Zocalo Restaurant.

It looked as if something had crashed into it in a hurry, or maybe even intentionally knocked it over, hard. They might have paid particular attention to the large indentation in the side of the can. A dent bigger than any one of them. They might have also caught a fleeting glimpse of the ferns in the landscaping behind it trampled and torn away as someone, or something, made its escape.

The Cats of the Castle turned off the paved path, ducked under a handrail and headed for the trees. Soon they found the train tracks. They were grateful it was late at night and no trains would be coming this way for many more hours. Of course, that didn't stop Kimball from quickly leaning over and pressing a yellow ear to the iron rail.

"Better safe than roadkill," he said as they all stared at him in disbelief.

"You mean *railroad* kill," Elias laughed.

"Kimball, I thought you loved trains," said Oliver.

"I do. I love watching trains. Even love being *on* trains. Just not in front of them as they're barreling forward at high speed."

They followed the tracks at a quick pace. Down below at the bottom of the hill, the light of the moon reflected off the water. The dense pine trees had a silvery glow about them. The cats followed the curve of the track around Rivers of America. They soon passed a shed marked "Livery."

"We're getting close," Oliver said.

They carried on a few more yards in silence. The trees got thicker and blocked out more of the moonlight, making the travel much darker. They were cats, so maneuvering through darkness was like second nature, but it didn't help their nerves. The four of them seemed to move in closer to one another as they walked along.

"Everybody freeze!" Elias suddenly whisper-screamed.

"What is it?" Oliver asked, feeling panic rising in his chest.

"There's something down there. Right on the ridge. I don't know if they can see us."

Oliver turned and squinted to see what Elias was talking about. He was pointing down the hill where the trees grew thinner and farther apart. Sure enough, there were strange creatures standing in formation along the hillside. Some indeed were looking toward the tracks and the cats now frozen with fear.

"Elias," Oliver said with a sigh, "those are deer. More importantly, they're not *real* deer. They're deer statues."

"Wha?" Elias grunted. "They're not real?"

"They are real statues," said Kimball, palming his face, "but they're not breathing. And they're definitely not a threat to us."

"Well, they almost gave me a very real heart-attack," Elias grumbled, embarrassed. "I may be short a life now."

"Listen, it's okay," said Oliver, trying to be reassuring. "Thurl told us to be extra-vigilant and watch our tails. That's what you did."

"Come on, scaredy-cats," Lilli called out, already walking down the tracks again. "Or do you need to visit a little kittens' box now?"

"Come on," Elias spat, cuffing Kimball in the chest.

"Oof!" Kimball exclaimed. "What was that for?"

"You were there."

Soon they could make out a clearing up ahead in the moonlight, surrounded by wood railings. There were tables and chairs set all around it. It was one of the dining decks of the Hungry Bear restaurant. The shadow of the large restaurant itself came into view just beyond it. Like a big frontier cabin in the woods, Hungry Bear Restaurant sat nestled against the trees across from Splash Mountain. Just below its peaked roof was a long wooden sign with the restaurant's name and an image of a golden bear in a bright blue bib licking its lips.

"Almost there," Elias muttered, sniffing the air. "Everybody keep your back hair up."

"Gross," Lilli whispered.

"Um, just a reminder," Kimball called out, "there will be a bridge along shortly."

"Yeah," said Elias, "and what's your point?"

"Well, first of all we'll be high above concrete. I recommend not falling. Also, we'll be completely exposed."

"Kimball's right," Oliver nodded. "And not too many escape routes. Only straight ahead or back."

"Or down," added Lilli.

"Right," Oliver said. "Let's try to avoid that one. If we do run into any humans, particularly security, then it's every cat for himself. And herself. Just get away safe, whatever it takes. Head straight to the castle as quickly as you can."

"That goes for you, too," said Lilli.

"What?" She was staring right at him. Her face was a mixture of concern and criticism, as if she knew he had no plans of giving up tonight. "Oh, I, uh...yeah, of course."

She put her paws on his face and squeezed his cheeks. "I mean it, Oliver. No cat gets caught tonight. If we get in trouble, get out. You don't run, I won't run. No cat left behind."

"I'm with the lady," said Elias. "We're in this together. Band of felines."

"Cats of the Castle," added Kimball.

"Fine," said Oliver, suppressing his smile. "Then here's how it's going to go when we get to the other end of that bridge. I'm following these tracks straight in."

"Into the belly of the beast," Kimball mumbled.

"Elias, you and Kimball are going up the side of the mountain. It's dark so you'll have plenty of cover."

"Now why would I stay outside?" Elias argued. "You might need some muscle."

"You are our strongest climber," Oliver said. "If anything happens to me, someone's got to get to the top and grab that key. You're our best bet."

"You got me there."

"And I have a sneaking suspicion Kimball has something in his belt to assist with the climb," Oliver smiled, placing a paw on Kimball's shoulder.

"Would you expect any less?"

"Is there any chance I could persuade you to climb up the mountain with them?" Oliver asked, turning to Lilli. She was already shaking her head.

"No way, Oliver. I don't go the safe route. I'm going in. Who would look out for you?" She flipped up her hood.

All four cats scurried across the bridge as quickly as they could, heads and shoulders slouched as if that would magically keep them invisible. Within seconds they were surrounded by the shadows of a tunnel. They were officially inside Splash Mountain.

"Keep your eyes peeled, lady and gentlemen," Elias mumbled. "It just got real."

They were immediately shocked to hear howling and wailing and music. Loud music. Elias, Oliver, and Lilli locked eyes in surprise and fell to their bellies like lizards.

"I wouldn't worry about that," said Kimball who was up on his knees, peering down through an opening in the train tunnel wall. His furry face was bathed in a flashing orange-and-pink colored glow.

"What is it?" Oliver whispered.

"Come see," Kimball grinned, lights dancing off his glasses.

They crawled over and joined him. There was a long series of openings in the tunnel that provided riders on the train a clear view into the attraction as they passed through. Below, fully illuminated and rocking back and forth in the water, was an old Mississippi paddle wheeler. On the deck of the boat, chickens were swaying and singing and shaking tambourines in a mutual celebration. On the river banks, alligators, birds, and turtles were all joining in the party, singing along to the happy medley.

"The park is closed," Oliver whispered. "This shouldn't be happening."

"They don't seem to know that," said Elias.

"Maybe Baxter and his boys just keep it on all night," Lilli wondered.

"Maybe," said Kimball. "Or maybe they turned it on to distract unexpected company while they prepare to strike." The other cats all stared at him. "What? I'm just speculating."

"So what should we do now?" Elias asked.

"Stick to the plan. You and Kimball get outside and start climbing. I don't need to tell you to be extra careful. Just get to the top. Nothing else matters."

"Hopefully you two will be up there waiting," Elias said, "with that crazy key in your paws."

Elias and Kimball crept back to the mouth of the tunnel. Kimball peeked out and made sure the coast was clear. No sign of security, no sign of Baxter's gang. He nodded to Elias. The gray cat pointed at him and then directed his paw at the north side of the mountain. He gestured to the south and then himself, implying he'd be taking that side; the side most exposed to the park. It was Elias' way of looking out for him. His bright yellow fur might be more easily spotted climbing Chick-A-Pin Hill. Elias had darker fur and could hug the shadows, virtually disappearing. Kimball nodded back.

They put their paws out and bumped knuckles. Then Elias grabbed onto to the side of the tunnel and sunk his claws in. He hoisted himself up and around. In a split-second he was out of sight, scaling the rough terrain of Splash Mountain. It only took a minute for Elias to realize climbing this mountain wouldn't be as easy as he'd let on, but there was no turning around. He searched in the dark for crevices and little ledges to pull himself up. It was especially arduous as the "dirt" of the hill wasn't earth at all, but fiberglass and concrete, covered in paint and patches of grassy turf. He'd need his claws sharpened when this was all over.

Kimball, always the less impulsive of the cats, flipped down his specially crafted night-vision lenses. They were crude, to say the least, given the materials he was able to scrounge around the park. Thick round plastic rims encircling green lenses with duct tape wrapped around plastic housings that covered the array of wires and circuits. Resourceful as Kimball was, the materials that night vision required were hard to come by in a theme park. Fortunately, there had been a security and law enforcement expo at the nearby Anaheim Convention Center the winter before.

As if by some miracle, at least to the crafty cat, a pair of police-grade night vision goggles had been found on the floor of a Small World boat. They were promptly taken to the lost and found, and promptly removed by Elias. For Kimball, it was like Christmas morning. He carefully took them apart and studied every wire and screw. It took him two days to reverse engineer the insides and create this lightweight version he could clip over his own spectacles.

He scanned the tunnel and then looked out at the Hungry Bear. Everything appeared bathed in emerald. He leaned out and turned his head to look up the mountainside. The cliffs, the grassy knolls, the knotted branches, all bright shades of eerie green when viewed through the night-vision. He found the right gaps and grooves in the wall and crawled up onto the side of the hill. Kimball reached around his back and unclipped a cord of rope. High above he spied a tree stump jutting out of the hill. At the end of the rope was a hook with three pointed prongs. He let out as much rope as he could, trying to judge the distance to the stump up above. Sinking the claws of his free paw into the side of the mountain, he began to whip the rope around, like a cowboy about to lasso a calf.

Faster and faster the hook began to spin, making a *whoosh whoosh* sound as it passed near his head. As soon as it reached proper velocity, Kimball released the rope and the heavy grappling hook launched into the air. Of course he had some concern as he hadn't been able to properly calculate the distance or angle at which to let go, but sometimes, he reasoned, you just have to wing it. The hook flew right past the branch he'd aimed for, but as hoped it dropped back down around the other side. When the rope caught, Kimball yanked back on the line and his hook dug a sharp prong into the stump. The line went taught like he'd snagged a big fish. Kimball clipped the loose end to his belt, and dug his back claws into the fiberglass mountain. He began pulling himself, hand over hand, walking up the side of Splash Mountain.

Back inside the railway tunnel, Oliver and Lilli were strategizing how best to enter the attraction without being noticed. Lilli nodded toward the holes in the side of the tunnel looking down on the show scene. She suggested they make a dive for the water.

"That's a long drop," Oliver said. "And I don't think the canal is that deep. Plus, I'm pretty sure this scene is the end of the attraction. We need to go up."

"Then what do you suggest? Go back outside and walk in through the turnstiles? That shouldn't draw any attention at all."

Oliver thought for a moment. "Yes, that's exactly what we're going to do."

"Very funny. Wait, are you serious?"

"Why not? If somehow they were expecting trespassers, what are the odds they'd expect them to walk in the front door?"

"I hate to say it," Lilli nodded after considering his plan, "but I have no argument. Every other idea seems just as crazy anyway."

They exited the tunnel the same end they entered. The park was quiet. No guards around, and no cleaning crews in sight yet. Just dim lanterns and street lights. Oliver's ears perked up at the distant sound of clanking dishes being washed at the Hungry Bear. Oliver hugged the corner of the tunnel opening and shimmied his body around. On the other side he found a level area covered in grass wide enough to stand on. It appeared there was a good flat stretch they could follow around the hill. Somewhere not far above they could hear rushing water gurgling by. Oliver recognized the knocking of the log bumpers as they bounced off the sides of the canal.

"We'd better stay low," he said as Lilli appeared around the edge. They both dropped to all fours and took off down the path. It led all the way to the front side of Splash Mountain. The path narrowed, and the terrain became more difficult to maneuver. Oliver put his front paws on a rock ledge and looked down toward the road below. He saw a concrete path lined with rails. Up ahead was an oversized birdhouse. Oliver knew it housed a sculpture of Br'er Rabbit, the hero of the attraction, and blue letters that read "Splash Mountain." There was also a smaller sign pointed like an arrow marked "Entrance."

"That's it," he whispered. "We need to get down there."

"Then I guess we're climbing." She swung her tail over the rocky edge and felt around with her paw until she found a nice smooth rock to step on. Even for cats the climb was difficult. Climbing curtains was one thing, but mountains were further back in their DNA. Within a few seconds she looked down and saw the walkway just below. An easy drop for a cat. Lilli let go and fell gracefully to the concrete, landing softly on her feet.

"Wow, she's good," Oliver whispered. He swung his legs over the side of the ledge and clumsily flailed his back paws in the air trying to find a step. As Oliver planted his foot on what looked like a sturdy black rock, it turned out to be a mere shadow. His foot passed through darkness and he lost his balance, sliding down the side of the hill, frantically trying to sink his claws into the red hill. Oliver hit the sidewalk flat on his back. Dazed, he struggled to get up quickly and brushed off his fur. The pads of his paws stung and he had scraped his nose in the fall, but he played off the embarrassment.

"Are you okay?" Lilli asked, stifling a chuckle. She didn't want to hurt his feelings, but it had looked pretty comical as he awkwardly tumbled down the hill.

"Yeah, of course," he said, a little wounded. "It wasn't that high. Come on." He turned away as if he was going to walk, but then gestured for her to go ahead. Not wanting to make him feel worse, she hurried past. Only then did Oliver lick the top of his paw and rub it across his stinging nose a few times.

"Oliver, look," Lilli whispered after a few moments. She was standing at some wooden steps leading up into an old barn. It was the attraction entrance. Both cats felt knots in their stomachs. They were about to enter a favorite attraction among the humans, featuring a water ride and fun-loving, singing characters. At least that's how the maps described it. Neither had even ridden it. This had always been "no cats land."

Oliver wrapped his fingers around the handle of his new sword. He hoped for the best-case scenario. They'd get in, get to the top quickly, find the key, and get out unnoticed. But Oliver couldn't help feeling somewhere in the mountain, unseen eyes were well aware of their presence. Getting out of Splash Mountain without a confrontation seemed unlikely. He thought he'd actually prefer to face the three talking rats from the mansion again. A haunting wind whistled through the open barn windows.

He and Lilli locked eyes. "For Disneyland," he gulped.

"For Disneyland."

The two of them followed the winding path through the barn, past old farm tools, yokes for hitching oxen to a plow, broken crates, and bags of feed. Soon they were in an underground corridor leading through the mountain. It was quiet. Lanterns flickered on the walls every few feet, but otherwise there were no signs of life. Just two cats and their shadows sliding along the wall beside them. There was no music playing, so perhaps the final show scene had just been left running by mistake. At least that's what Oliver told himself.

Finally, they reached the loading area. There was a plank platform, and a fence of wooden sticks. A river of water flowed below with a belt that kept the logs moving. Each vessel would pull up to the edge and stopped long enough to let passengers board and exit. Each log sat six humans in a single-file line. One came whooshing up in front of Lilli and Oliver. There was a jack rabbit carved on the nose of the log, like a hood ornament. The gate in the stick fence swung open automatically.

"Well," said Lilli said, taking a deep breath, "I guess we're going for a ride."

They hopped down into the front of the log. Both were instantly treated to the unpleasant sensation of cold water soaking into their tails from the wet seat. The log pushed off with a jerk, causing them to fall back. They cruised around a bend, passing barrels and kerosene lanterns and up ahead the track began to rise. Old wooden signs in white lettering warned "Keep your hands and arms inside" and "Remain seated."

"Are those really necessary?" Lilli commented, reading each as they passed. "Who would actually stand up?"

"Humans," Oliver shrugged.

Up they rose, the little rabbit's nose turned toward the sky, carrying them up the mountain. They leveled out again in a concrete river that curved to the right. Lilli nudged Oliver and nodded at the backside of the Haunted Mansion in the distance.

"How scary is it in there?" she asked.

"Huh? Oh, the mansion?" he said, caught off guard. "It's definitely spooky, but it's not so bad. It's a lot worse when there are three rats trying to gnaw your tail off."

"I'd like to see it sometime. Without the rats, of course. Maybe when all this is over we could sneak off our patrols one night and take a ride."

"I, erm, that is," Oliver stammered. Lilli wanted to spend time with him on a ride, alone, without the threat of an evil rogue cat or vengeful human looming over them? He suddenly felt emboldened. His chest felt so full he wished Baxter would appear right in front of them. He wasn't afraid of anything. Well, more or less. "Sure. I'd love to. I mean, that would be fun."

The log sailed on toward a paddle wheel churning through the water. Once again the track lifted them out of the water. The rolling belt carried them inside an old mill where an animatronic owl sat dutifully on a beam. It's head turned slowly as its glowing eyes followed their log. It gave Oliver an uneasy feeling. It was like the bird was watching them. They leveled off into the river again, slipping quickly under a wooden bridge. They were surrounded by high red dirt walls with grassy tufts hanging over them. Happy banjo music echoed off the sides of the ravine. Soon the walls broke and on their left they saw a green door surrounded by thick thorny brambles and sign that read "Br'er Rabbit."

They sailed around the hill at a pretty quick clip. Another sign pointed the way to the lair of Br'er Fox. Fox was the cartoon villain of Splash Mountain. They were hoping to steer clear of *any* bad guys on this trip. As the attraction drew them in deeper, they continued around the curve of the hill, passing barrels of melons and pumpkins. The river snaked through an open cavern where an old wooden mailbox bore the name Br'er Bear, the gargantuan oaf of a brown bear that did Br'er Fox's dirty work.

A few feet ahead Oliver spied a gate across the canal, blocking their passage. He opened his mouth to say something, but before he could the gate swung open and their log slipped down a small waterfall, splashing through the canal toward a cave. Oliver caught sight of three figures just inside the opening, but before he could focus, he was splashed by a wave of water that rolled over the front of the log. Lilli shrieked and giggled, but Oliver desperately wiped water from his eyes. Was this it? Was Baxter's gang hiding just inside the cavern ready to pounce. Oliver's claws extended on instinct. He had no intention of going down without a fight.

"Lilli," he started to warn her, his eyesight still blurry from the water.

"Oh look," Lilli laughed, nodding ahead.

All the adrenaline that had been pulsating through Oliver's system washed away as he rubbed his eyes. The figures he had briefly glimpsed in the cave weren't enemy cats. It was a gaggle of happy geese in straw hats, blue jeans, and red neckerchiefs, fishing and singing songs. A friendly gentleman bullfrog lazed on the back of a mellow alligator. All merrily sang a country greeting to the logs that floated by, even if there were no park guests in them at this hour. It was a happy atmosphere that seemed to celebrate life along their river. Oliver actually felt his concerns lift, at least a bit. No wonder the lines were so long for this attraction. He looked over at Lilli who also had a big smile plastered across her face. Her blue eyes were wide, taking in every scene.

They floated past a large bear in a blue shirt and red hat, hanging from a tree with his legs and paws in a snare. Across from him, a nasty fox in a yellow shirt shouted orders in a shrill, unnerving voice. That was Br'er Fox, and the large fellow dangling from the branches was his henchman, Br'er Bear. Fox kept ordering Bear to stop messing around and get down, though by the looks of things, he wasn't exactly hanging there by choice.

"Glad it's him and not us," Lilli said. Oliver had been thinking the same thing. Something about Br'er Fox didn't sit well. Oliver wasn't sure if it was the orange fur, the pointy incisors, or his all-around nasty demeanor. Fortunately, they had yet to see hide nor hair nor whisker of another cat.

They did pass all manner of other furry forest critters, including the brown bunny with an itch to travel, Br'er Rabbit. He was singing his intention to be moving along to an old friendly turtle. Oliver found himself tapping his paw to the music.

Until that is, they happened upon a darker section of the swamp. Up ahead was a wall of earth, and the big brown backside of Br'er Bear hanging over them, having tried to squeeze through a tiny crevice looking for Br'er Rabbit. Lilli pointed up and they both chuckled about old Bear's predicament. Then they found themselves in one of their own. Their log tipped forward and plunged into darkness. Wind whipped through their whiskers and the roar of rushing water echoed past. They both shrieked. Oliver might have been louder than Lilli. Both cats gripped the safety bar. They went rocketing forward, splashing water everywhere.

"Oliver, look!"

They were cruising under a swarm of eerie, glowing beehives with bees buzzing everywhere. After a few seconds sailing through darkness their boat slowed inside the dark cavern surrounded by glowing purple mushrooms with red, green, and yellow spots. It was like a crazy dream. Somewhere up ahead they heard a maniacal laugh.

"What is this place?" Oliver whispered.

"I was hoping you knew."

It appeared they were deep inside the mountain, maybe even underground. They were surrounded by geysers spitting water into the air, some erupting in powerful jets. Among them, emitting that lunatic laughter was Br'er Rabbit riding on one of the streams.

"At least he's here," Oliver said, in an attempt to sound reassuring, "so it can't be too dangerous, right?"

"I'm not so sure that he's a shining example of good choices," Lilli responded.

A long-billed stork in a red top hat stood on the banks with his wings outstretched. They sailed past a goose on the left with a singing brown chicken and behind them, peeking out over a rock, was the head of scruffy-looking raccoon wearing a floppy cowboy hat. His dark glassy eyes, one larger than the other, seemed trained on their log. His lip seemed to quiver as he watched them float by, revealing a sharp crooked fang. Oliver couldn't even see its body hidden in the darkness behind the rocks. The detailing on the hideous face was certainly impressive, Oliver thought. Even scary for a family attraction.

"Oliver something about all this doesn't feel right.

"I agree," he said, still craning to see over his shoulder. "I think we should jump out and try to make our way on foot. I feel like sitting ducks in this log."

"We should find Elias and Kimball too. I'm not so sure splitting up was the right thing to do."

"The good news is they're on the outside. Makes it easier for them to make a run for it if they get into a jam."

"I guess that will have to pass for good news," said Lilli. Suddenly her eyes went wide, but not with wonder. She was pointing up ahead. "Oliver, look!"

In the next scene Br'er Rabbit was all tied up and covered in honey. Br'er Fox loomed over him with a wicked grin. Oliver hoped this particular scene was just a coincidence and not a vision of their own future here in Splash Mountain.

"Looks like his luck ran out," said Oliver, trying to lighten the mood.

"No," she said, physically turning his head. "Look! Right in front of us!"

They were cruising toward an empty log sitting in their path. With a loud thump they rammed into it. Their heads rocked forward and back. The abandoned log didn't budge. Something was holding it there. Oliver looked behind them. It wasn't good.

"Hang on!" he said.

Another empty log came barreling into theirs from behind. It knocked them back against their seat before again crashing them into the log ahead. The cats heard a slow, deliberate sound, like a *clunk-clang, clunk-clang, clunk-clang*. It grew louder until someone appeared from behind a rock. They could only make out the stout silhouette. He was immersed in shadow, but he was bulky, with a pot belly, and walked with a limp. The figure leaned heavily on a thick, heavy staff. It was metal and weighed a ton, judging by the sound. There was something affixed to the top; a figure of some kind, with wings.

The stranger began to chuckle as he came closer, occasionally making an odd clicking sound with his tongue. With one last loud *clunk-clang*, he emerged into the dim light a few feet away. A large cat with matted orange fur, except for a spot on the left side of his face where no fur grew, but three scars disappeared under a black eyepatch. A patch, it bears mentioning, emblazoned with a pirate skull and crossbones.

His other eye was wide and yellow, with an emerald pupil floating in the middle. Locks of his orange hair were braided and bejeweled with metallic pins of random Disney characters—souvenirs no doubt lost in the waters of Splash Mountain. The top of his head sported a wide-brimmed hat with one torn ear stuck through the side. A single strap of his green overalls lay across his broad body to the shoulder.

Oliver recognized the tarnished brass bat at the top of his staff. The unwieldy walking stick was in fact a green queue post from the Haunted Mansion. In his other hand he clutched a brown jug with three X's scrawled across it. He lifted it to his lips and took a loud swig. When he pulled the bottle away from his face, droplets ran down his chin fur and his face scrunched up in a grimace. Baxter fixed his one good eye on the two of them and began to laugh.

It was too late to be turning around.

Chapter Nine

"Well, well," Baxter finally spoke, clicking his tongue between his incisors. He spoke in a playful, sing-song voice with a thick bayou drawl. "Look at these little lost kittens, caught without their mittens."

"We didn't come for trouble, Baxter," said Oliver.

"Oh, looky now," said Baxter, his face lighting up. The orange cat sauntered over to stand right above their log. He bent down, turning his head to keep his good eye on them. "I do find it discomforting when a complete stranger throws my name around so freely, as if we're kin."

"My name is Oliver," he said, wrapping a paw around the hilt of his sword. "This is Lilli. We are Cats of the Castle."

"You don't say," Baxter exclaimed in mock surprise. "I presupposed by the blade at your side that y'all wandered over from the castle. That, or ya got real confused and mistook this waterway for Pirates of the Caribbean."

"We came on purpose," said Oliver. "If you'll let us get what we came for, we'll leave again. There's no need for any trouble."

"Well now, cats o' the castle," Baxter said, "I don't know what particular brand of gumbo ol' Thurl's been feeding you, but I've never started no trouble in my life." Baxter's smile faded and his yellow eye squinted. "I just don't back down when trouble finds me. Now, it was *you* that came into my home, and *you* that found me. So tell me, is you *trouble*?"

"We're all in trouble, Baxter," Lilli spoke loudly, "Even you! The park is in danger."

"Danger?" he smiled. He raised his paws and looked around the cavern. "No danger in here, *cher*. Least, not for me."

"There's a human sneaking around the park that wants to shut it down," she said. "Shut it down for good. Even Splash Mountain."

"Ha! They can't shut down my mountain," Baxter laughed. "Look around you, kitten! They used to try every night. Me and my boys just turn it back on. They finally gave up trying. We have a celebration every night! That's why I chose Splash Mountain as my proper home. It's always a party in here. The perfect place for ol' Baxter to plant his flag. You cats have your castle—I have mine."

"No, Baxter," Oliver explained, "we don't just mean power it down for the night. There's a key—it was made for Mr. Disney by fairies. It has the power to shut off the magic that runs through this park. If that stops, the whole place goes dark, forever."

"And your party will be over," added Lilly.

"Mm hmm," Baxter straightened up, raising an eyebrow. "S'that right? And I suppose ol' Thurl who hasn't seen me in years, not since he clawed up my face, that is, sent y'all here to warn me? Out of the goodness of his snow-white heart."

"You don't understand...," Oliver started.

"What I understand is y'all are trespassing in my home," Baxter roared over him. "An indefensible violation of the unspoken *detente* we set years ago. Such an infringement must be dealt with most judiciously, with extreme prejudice! Boys, scoop 'em on up outta there."

"Boys?" Lilli said. For a moment, they'd forgotten Baxter didn't live alone. Before she could turn, a heavy net of wet rope dropped over them, instantly weighing them down. Neither could see their assailants but they heard thuds as other cats jumped into their log. Lilli could see dirty toe claws on the front of the log, as the heavy net pushed her head down.

There was grabbing and pushing and pulling. Everything was a blur. Oliver and Lilli felt a great tug then toppled over sideways as they were hoisted out onto the ground. Both Castle Cats hissed and tried to slash with their claws, but it was no use. The net tightened and pulled their paws tight against their sides. They felt themselves being dragged through the attraction, bumping over rocks and bumps in the ground.

"Lilli," said Oliver. They had somehow ended up back-to-back in the net. He couldn't get a good look at anything. Thick rope covered one of his eyes. They were sliding along the hard ground fast. "Are you okay?"

"Not really Oliver. I'm trapped in a net that smells like dead fish. But I'm not hurt, if that's what you mean. Can you reach the ropes with your claws?"

"No," he grunted, trying again. "Not enough to matter. My paws are stuck tight."

"Alright boys," they heard Baxter snarl, "this ought to do. Let 'em loose."

The net was pulled up forcefully, before it opened up and spilled them onto the hard, wet ground. Oliver landed on his back and bumped his head. He stayed there a moment, sprawled out, looking up. Two vultures stared down at him, dressed as undertakers.

"Olli, are you alright?"

He looked over and saw Lilli crouched a few inches away. She was looking at him with concern. He also noticed her claws were bared on all four paws.

"Yeah," he answered with a wince as he lifted his head, "I think so. Can't say for how much longer, though."

They could feel the metallic *clunk-clang* reverberating through the ground beneath them as Baxter came near. His thick braids decorated with shiny pins like knotted orange lanyards dangled over their heads. Up close they saw the thin scar that ran from his chin, through his bottom lip, and then continued on, ending at his pale nose. They could see the bare pink skin around his eyepatch and the deep maroon scars that slithered out below it. The horrors of the great battle fought years before, which had, until this moment been only words Thurl had spoken, were etched forever in Baxter's weary face. In another situation, Oliver thought, he'd feel sorry for the wounded cat. Until he spoke, that was.

"So you kittens couldn't resist sneaking a night ride on Splash Mountain," Baxter said with a click of his tongue. "Well, I can't say I don't understand. You two ain't the first to pass this way. Nor will ya be the last, I reckon. But I assure you, y'all won't be coming back for another turn."

For the first time, Oliver and Lilli caught a good look at Baxter's accomplices. Three motley hill cats stood behind him. One was tall with dirty gray fur which he'd weaved into dreadlocks on his head. He wore cut-off jeans tied with a rope. When he smiled he had one particularly long, sharp incisor. The next had short brown fur and bright orange eyes. He was stocky like Elias, and wore a faded Disneyland t-shirt that was too tight for his body. On his chest he'd affixed a plastic cast member name tag that read "Ernie. Cleveland, OH." The third of the cats was wiry with a patchwork of colored fur—black, orange, white, and brown. Even his eyes were mismatched, one blue and one green. The green one appeared to wander independently in various directions. He occasionally laughed out loud at some secret joke. And he was chewing a thick wad of cat nip. Oliver could smell it.

"Oh, I'm sorry," Baxter chuckled behind them. "Where are my manners? Allow me to introduce my associates. These would be my dear brethren of the hill, and as you've come to know them, keepers of the nets. That tall, gray drink of water is Fang. Ernie is, well, the one wearing the name tag which conveniently reads 'Ernie.' And finally, that crazy quilt of many colors is our dear brother 'Nip.'"

Baxter leaned in close to Lilli's ear and put his paw to his mouth. The thick odor of rotten banana and paint thinner on his breath made her eyes water. "As you may have surmised, Nip's a few strings short of a full ball o' yarn, but bless him, he means well!"

"Baxter you have to listen," said Oliver. "The whole park is in danger. Your party will be over! Doctor Owl will shut down everything!"

"Wait," Baxter said lifting a paw, "did you say Doctor Owl?" He exploded with laughter and shook a stubby orange finger at them. "You can't be serious? Y'all expect to scare me with tales of *Doctor Owl*?"

"It's not his name," Oliver tried to explain, feeling scared and now irritated. "It's just something I made up...he looks like an...he's dangerous! That's what matters!"

"And he hates cats," Lilli added. "We heard him say he's allergic to us. This human will do whatever it takes to get rid of us all. He'll bring in an entire army of rats. Or worse."

"Worse?" Baxter clicked.

"Yes, worse," said Oliver stalling. "We think he may have other animals working with him. He stole some blue pixie dust. For all we know he has a horde of stray dogs ready to run down Main Street."

"Dogs," Baxter repeated softly, taking a half-step back. His jowls shook. Baxter lifted his trembling paw and gulped down a mouthful of stinky brew from his jug. He wiped the back of his paw across his mouth, staring off absently. "I hate dogs."

"Think about it Baxter," said Lilli. "We won't be fighting each other. We'll all be fighting to keep our homes. Fighting to stay alive."

"Wouldn't be the first time," Baxter replied, snapping back, eyes darting toward her.

"Yes," said Oliver, "but we can avoid that. It doesn't have to be like last time."

Baxter slowly felt at the patch over his eye. He ran his paw down his scars. Fighting other cats had been bad enough. The idea of a human with rats, maybe dogs, the mortal enemies of felines everywhere was too terrible even for him to imagine. Or believe, he thought to himself, eyeing up the black-and-white cat. Doctor Owl? This could be a trick. That's what it was, he thought, taking another sip. A trick by old Thurl to draw him out of the mountain. He sent these two young'uns to do his dirty work.

"Enough!" Baxter screamed, hurling the clay jug against the wall, which exploded with pieces of pottery and sticky brown liquid. "Talking rats? An owl doctor with a magic key?!? Enough lies and deceptifications! You little kitties are spies, sent by my enemy Thurl!"

Baxter pounced faster than they would've expected for his size and grabbed Oliver by the scruff of his neck. "Get the girl!" he ordered. "Let her watch how I deal with spies in my house of love."

"Baxter, we're not...*gah!*" Oliver tried to explain, but the grip on the fold of his neck pulled tighter. It didn't necessarily hurt, but it didn't feel great, either.

"Shut it you!" Baxter spat. He dug a brass bat wing into Oliver's side. "This is my world! The mountain is my kingdom! You should not have come!"

Baxter began to drag him up the path. Oliver could hear the rushing water and turning conveyor belt nearby. He struggled to break free from the older cat's grip. In desperation he let out an angry, feral *yowl* and swiped his claws, just hoping to land one good shot. He felt one claw rip across Baxter's thigh. The orange ogre hissed and kicked at Oliver, but his rancor quickly turned to a chuckle.

"That all you got?" Baxter taunted. "You see my pretty face? You see these scars, boy? I've taken on stronger, scarier critters than you and been the last cat standing. You tried to sneak honey outta the wrong honeycomb. Now you get stung!"

With a loud grunt, Baxter threw Oliver over the side of the ledge. Lilli screamed. Oliver felt himself falling and closed his eyes tight, sure it was the big plunge. Instead, he landed with a splat against the wet conveyor belt. Immediately he began to slide backward. Oliver grabbed for one of the notches in the belt that propelled the logs. He looked up and saw moonlight. He was a only few inches from the top of the incline. From there the only way out was down.

"Enjoy the briar patch, kitten," Baxter called. "I imagine it's a different experience without a log around you! You'll have to let me know. Oh, wait, you probably won't be able to."

His three thugs laughed like jackals, clutching Lilli's arms tight. She watched with terror as her friend, her fellow Cat of the Castle, rolled closer to the edge, helpless. Maybe he had a plan, she thought. Maybe he could jump to the side at the last minute, or grab onto a random rock or tree branch.

"Watch closely, darlin'," Baxter said, limping over to her, rubbing the scratch on his leg that was bleeding down his orange fur. "This is a preview of what awaits."

Oliver braced himself, his back arched and his tail straight. His head darted all around, but there was nothing to do, nowhere to go. Even if he did jump for the sides, chances were he'd slip on the wet belt and tumble over the edge, or worse, fall into some unseen gears. The sound of rushing water echoed all around the dark cavernous flume, mixed with the maniacal laughter of Baxter and his goons behind him. This was it.

Oliver readied himself. The night air blew across his whiskers as he rolled to the top. For a moment the belt slowed and he looked down over the edge to watch as water rushed all the way down the steep mountain flume, then vanished into darkness under the briar patch—a mass of twisted, thorny vines. Maybe we cats really do have nine lives, he told himself. For a split second Oliver looked out over the park. He saw the pink castle glowing in the distance. His beloved home where his mentor who had cared for him awaited their safe return.

Oliver also thought of Lilli, caught in the grasp of those feline thugs. Were they planning the same fate for her, or something even worse? The thought made him angry. Lilli was tough. She took care of herself, but this time she was outnumbered. More importantly, she was his friend.

"I'm the leader of the Cats of the Castle," he growled. "I can't give up." Oliver dug his claws back in, determined to survive this ordeal, somehow, and help Lilli. He turned, looking back into the mountain, imagining somehow he could hang on, despite the current, and gravity.

Oliver suddenly felt his back paws rolling over the side. He lunged forward, but he was too late. The world fell out beneath him. He was sliding. He desperately clawed at the belt, trying to hook in, but it was no use. Down he slid. Oliver looked over his shoulder and saw an eerie white mist clouding over the briar patch in the cool night air. For a moment it felt like his body was floating in mid-air before he began to fall. A ride log would just glide down the flume, and level out at the bottom, causing a big splash and lots of cheers. There was to be no leveling out for him. His body would tumble all the way down, bouncing off the track and rocks alongside it, before hitting the bottom and being sucked into the current. Oliver closed his eyes. He was doomed, and without that key, so was Disneyland.

Oliver let himself fall, slipping and bumping along the inclined track, feeling gravity pull him down. Then all at once, there was a rough jerk. He stopped. Am I dead, he wondered? He could still hear the roar of falling water. He opened one eye. The briar patch was but a few feet from the white tip of his tail. Something was holding him, suspended in mid-air. Something unseen was holding him—even pulling him up again. Disneyland truly was flowing with magic. Was this also pixie magic or something else—something even more mysterious?

"And you're supposed to be the leader of this circus," growled a familiar voice above.

Oliver swung his head around to see an upside down Elias, arms outstretched, with a tenuous grip on his vest. Beyond Elias, standing on a ridge halfway up the hill, gripping the other end of a rope that held them both there dangling precariously, was Kimball. His yellow face screwed up tight, revealing his fangs as he struggled to support their combined weight. The rope was slung over a thick root of the old gnarled tree that sprouted out of the mountain. He was grunting, wincing painfully as the line, which he'd tied around his own body for added support, slowly tightened, like a constricting snake.

"Please...hurry!" Kimball called.

Elias quickly surveyed the sides of the flume. He saw a bit of rock sticking out just enough to make a narrow ledge.

"Kimball," he yelled over his shoulder, "we need one good swing to the right!"

Kimball rolled his eyes but nodded. He gritted his teeth and tugged to the left as hard as he could. When he felt it swinging, he pulled back to the right.

"You're...both...going...on...a...DIET!" he growled as he yanked it with all his might, releasing a primal roar like some ancient saber-toothed cousin.

Oliver and Elias felt themselves swinging sideways, then falling as the rope went loose. Just as he opened his mouth to scream, Oliver landed on solid ground with a thud. Elias landed right on top of him, knocking the wind out of his lungs.

"I don't know...how you were there," Oliver said, catching his breath, "but, am I glad...you were. Thanks!"

"Thank Kimball," said Elias. "He saw somebody creeping into the mountain through that same opening. Couldn't tell if it was you, Baxter, or what. Figured we better check it out. I'd love to take the credit, but the reason I was hanging there the moment you came spilling out, well, that was mere coincidence."

"Either way," Oliver smiled, shaking his head. "Besides, I don't believe in coincidence anymore. Not in this park."

"What, something put me there on purpose? Who, Uncle Walt? Tinker Bell? Come on, I don't believe in that hocus pocus stuff."

"No?" Oliver asked. "Then what are you doing up here? We're cats wearing vests, Elias. We can talk. We were sent on a quest by a Tiki god to find an enchanted key before some talking rats get it first. And you don't believe in magic?"

Elias was quiet a minute. "Okay, you got me. Come on. We gotta get Kimball and find that key."

"No, wait," Oliver exclaimed. "Lilli! We have to help Lilli! They've still got her in there!"

Elias looked up at the opening. "Look, Lilli's smart, and strong. She can get herself out of a pinch. She'd want you to save the park."

"She's outnumbered," Oliver said, getting to his feet. "I'm have to help her."

"No, you and Kimball get to the top and grab the key. You're the heir of Mr. Lincoln, remember. I'll go help Lilli." He turned and reached for a rock to start climbing the hill.

"No," Oliver demanded, putting a paw on his shoulder. Elias spun around and the two cats locked eyes. "You gave me this sword. You said I'm the leader. Well, we are a team. We rise or fall together. We are all going to help her, together."

Back inside the mountain, Lilli was indeed in a tight spot. Baxter's boys were dangling her over the rushing water. She was struggling to break free, the whole time fighting back tears as her mind replayed the vision of Oliver going over the edge.

"Aw, come on, boss," Fang pleaded playfully with Baxter, "can't we keep this one? She's real *purrty!*"

"Yeah, boss," said pot-bellied Ernie. "She's real slinky. I bet she could get right through the back window of that churro stand. Nimble, too! She could probably snatch us some fresh turkey legs in broad daylight."

"Heck, I bet she could get us into Club 33," added Fang. "We could eat fancy, like white Persian cats on red velvet pillows." All the hill cats laughed.

"I wouldn't steal anything for you," Lilli hissed. "I'd feed fleas before I ever fed parasites like you!" Her eyes narrowed and she stared directly at Baxter, whose smile faded into a look of discomfort.

Fang slid a gray paw over her mouth. Lilli seized the opportunity and bit down, sinking her fangs deep into his nubby fingers. She knew his paws were filthy, but it was worth it to hear his cry. The other two cats squeezed her arms tighter, threatening to throw her into the canal.

"Enough," Baxter ordered. "You see, idiots? This kitty's no good to us. She's one of Thurl's. She's a Cat of the Castle. She'd never join our merry band of misfits." He hobbled over and took hold of her muzzle with his strong orange paw. "These cats are the enemy. And enemies receive no quarter."

"My team will succeed," Lilli growled at him. "They'll find the key and they'll stop Doctor Owl. Then they'll come for you. All of you. I guarantee it."

"I'm sorry, sweet wildcat," he clicked his tongue. He pushed her face away. "I'm afraid not. The penalty for trespassing is death. That's the law of our mountain. Who am I to challenge the law, particularly my own? Boys, let this one join her boyfriend."

"Let the cat go," came a deep, gravelly voice, like a blender full of rocks. It came from the shadows behind them. Baxter squinted to see who it was.

"Excuse me," the orange cat called to the shadows. "Who goes there?"

"I need her," the rough voice replied.

Lilli felt the paws gripping her loosen. She watched Baxter's eyes widen and his paw slid down his staff as though he were preparing to use it as something other than a cane.

"Pray, tell," Baxter demanded. "Who are you?"

"Doesn't matter," the voice responded with zero emotion.

"This is my mountain, friend," said Baxter, stiffening. "She's my prisoner to do with as I please. You show up unannounced, and unseen, and say you want her? I'm disinclined to acquiesce. 'Fraid you'll have to claim her down below, wherever she washes up."

"I'm taking her now," the voice growled. "Let go of her, and walk away."

"Boys, seems we have another intruder in our midst," said Baxter. "And apparently his momma never taught him 'bout minding his manners. Deal with him. I'll watch the girl."

The three cats pushed Lilli toward Baxter who quickly snatched her by the arm and spun her around roughly. She was finally able to see the large, thick silhouette making demands from the darkness. The dim light reflected off its glassy red eyes. The thing, for there was no telling at first what it was, stepped forward into the orange-and-pink light. It was a raccoon, more or less, though unlike any she'd seen before. This creature was enormous, by raccoon standards, with dirty, matted gray fur and uneven black stripes, hunched over by strong, heavy shoulders, which made his head hang low. His left eye, yellowed and bloodshot, bulged out further than it's squinty counterpart, which blended into its black mask of fur. A single long fang peeked out from a tear in his lip that never healed properly.

The raccoon wore ripped corduroy pants about to burst at the stitches around its massive thighs, but revealed impossibly thin gray calves and clawed black feet. In his paw, Lilli noticed he was gripping a crumpled cowboy hat. This was clearly not just an ordinary scavenger out tipping over garbage cans. Scars cut across his face and body from many late-night scrapes. His big eye zeroed in on her.

"Where's the key?" he asked directly, as if the other cats weren't even present. He sounded like he'd been gargling broken light bulbs. This monster knew about the key, Lilli thought? He must be another minion of Doctor Owl.

"You know I've heard just about enough about this infernal key," Baxter moaned. "Fang! Ernie! Nip! What are you ignoramuses waiting for? Get him!"

The cats looked at each other, unsure about this character. Ernie just shrugged. "It's only one raccoon," he reasoned. "Come on, boys."

All three lunged forward, claws out, ready for a fight. The intruder leapt back, drawing the hill cats into the shadows. There was ear-splitting hissing and yowling. The sounds of scuffling and hollow punches and claws swiping. Within seconds, Fang's thin gray frame came soaring backwards through the air, tumbling to the ground at Baxter's feet. His eyes were shut tight and his lips mumbled gibberish they couldn't understand. His visible fang had been knocked crooked in his mouth.

"Fang!" Baxter exclaimed. Lilli felt his grip loosen a little. His paw trembled. He was shaken.

Shortly after they heard a terrible cry of pain, followed by a splash. Ernie, the stout brown and currently unconscious hill cat rolled by, slumped in the front seat of a ride log. He was headed helplessly for the mouth of Chick-A-Pin Hill and the waiting drop.

"Aren't you going to help him?" Lilli asked in shock as Baxter stood by, watching his incapacitated friend being whisked toward the flume.

"He was a good soldier," was all Baxter said, removing his hat and holding it at his chest.

"Hard to believe you were ever a Cat of the Castle," Lilli said.

"What would you have me do? Dive in after him? He's in a log. He'll be fine. I think."

"It's what any one of us would do for another. That's our code. Don't you believe in honor?"

"Honor," Baxter spat. "That what you call it? I tried honor once. All it ever got me was a nightly plate of tuna. My way is better. Besides, I've still got Nip. He may not be the brightest bulb on the Christmas tree, but he's a fighter. Nip's too dumb to know fear. You watch, kitten. This masked bandit doesn't stand a chance! Ol' Nip will send him to the great garbage dump in the sky. Then, of course, we'll get back to carryin' out your sentence."

There was a horrible *merrower!*

A blur of furry patchwork colors sailed over their heads and landed with a smack against the wall. Poor Nip slid down the rock and disappeared into the shadows behind the attraction scene. The raccoon stepped forward, unhurt and unfazed. He held out a black paw and opened his clawed fingers, letting a clawful of brown-and-white fur drift gently to the ground.

"Now, give me the girl," he grumbled at Baxter. The orange cat was speechless.

"My dear kitten," Baxter finally spoke after taking a moment to size up the situation, "I have decided the honorable thing to do is grant you a full pardon." He pushed her forward toward the raccoon. "I'm afraid you're at the mercy of this, er, gentleman's justice now."

Lilli spun around and watched in disbelief as Baxter, who'd always been described as a fierce, terrible fighter, tipped his hat, gave the raccoon one last, terrified glance, and hobbled off quickly. He headed for the last ride scene featuring Br'er Rabbit tied-up and begging for his own life while a shadow of the fox laughed over him. Baxter pushed his orange paw against a stone in the wall which opened up a cutaway door. Baxter paused for just a moment, glancing back toward them. Lilli was certain she saw an embarrassed, ashamed look cross his orange face. Then he disappeared into a secret passage, letting the hidden door slam shut behind him.

Lilli turned slowly and faced the raccoon. He glared at her, his mouth hanging slightly open. He breathed loudly and his clawed fingers continually opened and closed. He made no moves. In fact, he seemed strangely relaxed. This was just business for him. He was indeed the scariest thing she'd ever laid eyes on.

"The key," he finally spoke. "I heard the black-and-white cat say it's here. Show me." He spoke slowly and without emotion. Just a deep, guttural growl of a voice.

"Listen, I don't know where it is," Lilli said.

"Your friend went over the waterfall. You don't have to."

"Honestly, I don't know." Lilli gestured toward the cavern wall. "We, uh, came in here hoping Baxter might know. You know, Baxter, the very slow orange cat that just went that way?"

"You're lying," he grumbled, his eyes never blinking. "Tell me where it is now, or I'll make you tell me."

"That's no way to talk to a lady," said Lilli with a nervous smile. She needed to stall. If nothing else, maybe Elias and Kimball would have enough time to get the key and get off the mountain. "Why don't we start over? What's your name?"

"Don't have one," he said flatly, in his low growl. "Never needed one. Doctor calls me Scavenge. Now tell me where the key is, or I toss you over the side of this mountain...and not the side with water."

"So, Scavenge, you, uh, *do* work for the Doctor, then?" she asked, confirming her suspicion. "You must know his rat friends."

"Rats," Scavenge sneered. "Rats are useless scum. They are sloppy. And weak. Doctor should have sent me the very first night."

"Well, see, there you go. We have a few things in common. We both hate rats. We don't have to be enemies. In fact, I think...."

"Enough talk!" Scavenge shouted, lunging over her, his lip quivering. Even his pointy black ears twitched with anger. "I will tear this mountain to the ground with you trapped inside."

"Oo...okay," she said, nervously. She spied shredded electrical wiring stuck between his jagged teeth. That explained the mystery of the sabotaged alarms, she thought. His breath smelled like hot garbage left in the sun, and as he snarled over her, a long strand of drool dangled from his lip, swinging precariously over her face. Lilli almost wished he would throw her off the mountain, rather than endure another minute in his company. She turned her head away, fixing her eyes on his feet and his crooked black toe claws standing on top of the same wet, mildewed net the cats had used to bind her and Oliver. She remembered how the hill cats pulled them along the ground, and as it got wet, the net seemed to get heavier.

"You know what?" Lilli said, throwing her hands up. "You're right. You got me Mister Scavenge. It is here. We don't know where, exactly, but it's somewhere near the bottom. Around the loading area, in fact, where the guests board their logs."

"Load area," he repeated. Scavenge took a step back, slowly, eyeing her with suspicion. He scratched at his chin as a flea did a backflip off his gray chin. "Don't believe you. What were you and the black-and-white cat doing all the way up here?"

"Fine," she sighed, giving him a coquettish smile and batting her blue eyes. "You got me again. You're too smart, Scavie! It's actually hidden at the top of the mountain, inside the old tree." She pointed up at the dark cavern top above.

"Up there?" he mumbled. Scavenge followed her paw and gazed up, taking a step forward so both his feet were on the net.

"Yep!" she said. "That's the spot." As soon as he looked up, Lilli bent down, grabbed hold of the net, and pulled it up as hard as she could, until the heavy ropes went taught, looping around his ankles. She yanked it toward her and Scavenge fell flat on his back. Before the raccoon knew which way was up, Lilli leapt nimbly over his body, pulling the net over his head. He began to roll around and swing his arms wildly. This only caused it to get tighter around him, and his arms got stuck in the squares of the net. Within seconds he was caught in the soggy net, like a fly in a spider's web. He growled and savagely bit at the ropes. It was thick and damp, but Lilli could see his sharp yellowed teeth would work their way through eventually. This was a temporary solution.

Suddenly there was a loud *thump*. Lilli jumped, thinking it was Baxter, returned to help the raccoon finish her off. A second later, one of the ride logs came floating along, bumping off the sides of the canal. Another log had come loose.

"Oh, look," she said in a sweet voice, "your ride is here. At least you have a better chance than you were going to give me." She kicked her foot into his side and shoved him over the edge into the log. He hit the floor of the boat with a thud. Lilli could hear the rabid raccoon gnashing his teeth and making guttural, feral sounds as he tried to fight his way loose.

"Lousy cat!" he roared as he flopped around the bottom of the boat like a caught trout. "I'll get you! There's more than one way to skin a caaaaaaaaaaaaaaaaaa...!"

She watched the log disappear over the edge. Lilli ran to the cave opening and leaned over to see Scavenge slip beyond the briar patch. He'd splash down below and level off, then be carried back into the attraction and the riverboat celebration. He'd most likely be fine, she figured, but hopefully it would take him a while to gnaw his way to freedom. Especially with a few more gallons of water soaking into the ropes. Just long enough, Lilli hoped, for some cat to get to the top of the hill, find the key, and get it back to the castle. She felt sad again, thinking about Oliver. Was there any chance he was okay? And where were Elias and Kimball?

"Guess it's up to me," she said softly, straightening her shoulders and steeling her resolve. "A woman's work is never done."

Lilli licked her claws and dug them into the side of the mountain wall. She climbed around the edge of the cave opening and felt cool night air on her fur. She pulled herself out onto a big boulder in the face of the hill. She found just enough flat space to stand on. Another empty log appeared at the top of the flume over her shoulder, thunking loudly against the sides due to the lack of weight before it plunged into darkness below. She stepped down onto the ledge to figure out the quickest route to the top.

"Lilli!" a familiar voice called out. She turned around and couldn't believe what she saw, or rather, who. Perched atop three big rocks on the other side of the cave entrance, bathed in bright silver moonlight, was Oliver.

Chapter Ten

"Oliver?" Lilli gasped. She couldn't believe what she was seeing! Was it a hallucination? Some ghostly apparition. "You're alive! I mean, *are you?* You're not a ghost? Are you?"

Oliver laughed and made a running leap, clearing the falling water, and landed on the ledge. Unfortunately, the pads of his back paws were wet and he slid clumsily, barely stopping right in front of her. Only slightly embarrassed, he opened his mouth to assure her he was very much alive but before he could, Lilli wrapped her arms around his neck and squeezed the speech (and breath) out of him.

"I'm so happy you're okay!"

"I was going to say the same thing," Oliver chuckled.

"Ahem, if you two are finished catching up," Elias cleared his throat. He had appeared on the other side. He nodded his head toward the gnarled tree growing out of the mountain over their heads. "The key?"

They let go of one another, blushing under their fur. Oliver looked past Lilli's shoulder into the attraction.

"Where's Baxter?" he asked. "How did you get out?"

"Was he the lump tied up in the bottom of that log?" Elias added.

"No, Baxter showed his true colors. He's a coward without his boys, like most bullies. Baxter slithered into his hole. The lump was something worse."

"Worse?" They both asked.

"Scavenge," she said. "Doctor Owl's mutant attack raccoon. He's been dusted, like us. Seems to have made him even nastier than your average rabies-infected raccoon. He took down all three of Baxter's boys."

"I guess I owe him for that," Oliver said. "Are you okay to continue on?"

"Are you kidding?" she scoffed, pushing him away. "Scavenge knows where we're headed. And he's not the type to give up and crawl home."

Suddenly Kimball's head appeared, or rather dropped right between their faces, hanging upside down. He had his big green night-vision lenses on, giving him the appearance of a strange bug. He was dangling by his rope like a spider.

"You scared us," Lilli laughed, pushing him away. Kimball swung out over the water fall and he looked up to look down just as another log slipped over the edge, just inches from his nose.

"Cool!" he marveled as he slowly swung back toward his friends. "So, hey, are you guys coming, or what?"

He turned himself upright and held the rope with one paw while he fumbled with something on his belt. With a whizzing sound like a fishing line being cast over water, Kimball rocketed upward into the air, flipped over backwards, and landed on his feet on a grassy tuft above them. He unclipped the rope from his belt and tossed it down to Oliver. One by one the other three climbed up to the little plateau just below the old tree.

"Alright, Oliver," said Elias, looking up at the top of the tree, "it's your show now."

Kimball, you've got the climbing gear," said Oliver, looking up at the old tree. "Do you want to climb up and get this crazy key? Then we can all go home and let security deal with raccoons and mad doctors tonight"

"No, no," said Kimball. He held out his grappling hook to Oliver. "This is your mission. You thought to use that telescope and climb up the treehouse. We might have searched for weeks and not come up here. You should do the honors."

"He's right," said Elias. "You brought us this far. It's your score. Should be an easy climb from here."

"But hurry," Kimball added. "I'd estimate another log will be coming over in about 12 seconds and you'll be dangling in its path in about 10!"

"No problem." Oliver smiled and rubbed his paws together. He couldn't help feeling a surge of pride. Here they were, working together as a team. Maybe he *could* be a leader. Oliver took the rope and scanned the treetop. The trunk was split at the top like a Y; the perfect little nook to catch the hook on.

"Stand clear," Oliver said, letting out some slack on the hook line.

Kimball inched away as much as he could given there was only so much space to stand, even for cats. Elias and Lilli climbed down to a grassy ledge just beneath where they could watch. Oliver began to swing the hook around in a circle. It made a buzzing sound as it picked up speed, rotating faster and faster. Oliver gave one last look at the spot he wanted the hook to connect with, then let it fly. He was greatly relieved when, even though it hooked onto the taller split of the trunk, it slid down and dug right in at the middle where he'd wanted it to go all along. Oliver gave it a yank and sure enough, it was caught tight.

"Oh, Oliver, I almost forgot," said Kimball. He removed a small cylinder from his belt. He handed it to Oliver who looked at the strange plastic tube with confusion. "It's dark up there. You'll need it."

"What is it? A flashlight?"

"Better. Something I thought up after I got lost exploring the Jungle Cruise at night. I call it an Illuminator."

"How does it work?"

"When you're ready, just pull on both ends," Kimball answered. "You'll see. Hey, that's funny. You will see, once you use it. You'll be able to see in...."

"*Alright*," Elias butted in. "He gets it Kimball. Go on, Oliver. We're still on Baxter's turf. Let's get this done."

Oliver nodded. He put the Illuminator in his belt and smiled at Kimball. Retracting his back claws, he pushed off from the ground and swung out over the waterfall. Oliver quickly shimmied his way up the rope, paw over paw, drops of water splashing his dangling black tail. After a moment he looked back down at his friends. Lilli was holding her paws together tightly. Kimball had his claws crossed. Oliver even caught Elias mouthing, "You can do this, kid."

Oliver didn't have much farther to go. He pulled himself up until he reached the thick roots of the old tree. He hooked his arm around one and pulled himself up. This was it. Oliver let go of the rope and climbed inside the dark stump. There was little ground to stand on; just a ledge of roots. It was like balancing on the rim of a manhole. The hill shook as another empty log dropped below. Nervously, Oliver stretched out his arms and dug his claws into the sides of the tree. This was definitely where he'd seen the sun gleaming off the key. Right now he couldn't see much of anything.

Oliver reached for Kimball's Illuminator tucked in his belt. Kimball said pull the ends. Oliver dug his back claws into a root to keep his balance, grabbed each end of the tube and pulled. He felt the ends extend and there was a click like something locking in place. Something inside it made a strange *swishing* sound. But it was still quite dark inside the tree.

"Okay, Kimball, what else am I supposed to do?" he mumbled. As if in answer, a ghostly blue glow appeared in the center of the tube. Then it suddenly flashed at each end where Oliver could see two little mirror-like discs had opened up. In a moment, the whole tree lit up with eerie blue light. Whatever was making the light in the center was amplified by the mirrors at the ends. The strange tool Kimball invented truly was an illuminator.

Oliver slowly panned the light across the walls and after a moment a flash reflected back in his eyes. The key? There was a thick mess of straw and grass and pieces of shredded park maps packed tightly together. At some point a bird had built a nest in here. Oliver shined the illuminator to the top of the nest and stretched his neck to see in. There was no sign of the avian architect. No eggs, no baby birds, and most importantly, no angry momma bird. It looked long abandoned. The way those logs shook the tree, this probably wasn't an ideal nursery for new hatchlings.

Oliver reached his free paw out and grabbed the rope again. He put the Illuminator between his teeth and swung across to the other side of the tree. He found the root ledge even more narrow on that side. Oliver flashed the Illuminator across the nest one more time, certain the key had to be there somewhere. Maybe the nest wasn't even made by a bird at all. Perhaps it was a diversion left by whatever Imagineer hid the key here in the first place. As the blue light danced over the nest this time, there was indeed a flash of something shiny and metal. There, on that side of the nest, a corner of gold metal poked out of the compacted grass and straw.

Oliver got so excited he almost dropped the Illuminator. He clamped it between his teeth again and leaned out over the abyss, wrapping the rope around his right paw. With his left, he quickly dug through the nest material which was quite dry and brittle. Excitedly, he grabbed for the metal object and pulled it out, expecting to see the golden D-shaped handle, the jewels set within the body, and the jagged teeth of the key.

"Huh?" Oliver puzzled, with the Illuminator in his mouth. His heart sank. He immediately felt worse than if Elias had punched him right in the stomach. He wanted to scream out in anger and frustration.

It was not the key. It was a brass star-shaped badge. On the front was printed "Frontierland Sheriff" around a picture of Mickey's face wearing a cowboy hat. Oliver flipped it over. The pin was clipped shut, but the point was still sharp. There was a year printed inside it: 1979.

"No!" Oliver grunted. "No! No! No! I can't believe this! Just a piece of old junk some stupid bird picked up? No! That key's gotta be here!"

Oliver tore the nest to pieces but found nothing else. He flashed the light all around the inside of the tree, certain he wasn't wrong, that it hadn't just been a chance reflection caught off an old souvenir trinket. The key was in here. It had to be! He couldn't allow himself to believe otherwise. This whole journey, putting his friends in danger—it couldn't be for a stupid souvenir pin!

For a moment Oliver thought to hurl the badge out into the night. It made him angry just to look at it. Instead, he tucked it inside his vest to show Thurl and the others later. Maybe they wouldn't be as angry with him if they could see it was an understandable mistake. At least, *somewhat* understandable, anyway. Some leader, he thought to himself. Oliver clamped down on the Illuminator with his teeth and pushed off the side of the tree, swinging out into the night. He carefully made his way back down to the ledge where the others were waiting. They looked up at him with wide eyes.

"Well?" was all Lilli said.

"Do you have it?" Elias chimed in.

Oliver couldn't bear to even say it. He hung his head with a sigh.

"What's wrong?" Lilli asked. "Oliver, what is it? Where's the key?"

He didn't answer. He couldn't even bring himself to speak. He just held out his empty paws.

"You've got to be kidding me," said Elias. "It wasn't up there?! Are you sure you looked everywhere? What did we come all this way for?"

"I'm sorry, guys," Oliver said softly. "It wasn't the key. Just some old junk."

"I knew I should've gone," Elias growled, snatching the rope from Oliver's paw. "Give me Kimball's stupid Illuminations thing. I'll go find it."

"Elias," Oliver started, meekly. "I looked everywhere." He reached into his vest to show them what had caused the initial reflection. "I'll show you...." A rock in the mountain suddenly swung open, slamming against the side and startling them all. Oliver froze, his paw inside his vest.

"I'll take that key," growled a Southern drawl. Baxter appeared in the opening, eye narrowed. He leaned against the side of the secret door and took a long swig from a green glass bottle.

"Baxter," Oliver gasped, quickly tucking the badge back into his vest.

"This is Baxter?" Elias grunted, pushing past the others and taking a step toward him. "This shabby old rug is what everybody's so afraid of?"

"Tsk tsk," Baxter clicked. "Such disrespect toward your elder, boy! I'd be backing up, were I you."

"Baxter, it's no use," said Oliver. "It's over. Just let us get back down to the street."

"Oh, you'll be heading down alright," Baxter interrupted, holding out his free paw. "And you'll stay down this time. Unless you hand over that key, youngster."

"You know," Elias spat toward Baxter, standing his ground, "maybe it's because I was already in a bad mood, but I just met you, and I'm already sick of you. We're leaving, and we won't be giving you anything."

"You don't think so," Baxter grinned. "You don't seem to realize I've got the advantage."

"Advantage?" Elias laughed. He did his best to mock Baxter's accent. "I do declare, I reckon you have trouble with arithmetic, so ah'll explain it to ya. There's four of us, and only one of you!"

"You know, you'd be quite amusing," Baxter sneered after a moment, "if not for being so dumb. First of all, I am not alone. Your friend the raccoon was only successful at temporarily dispatching my men. While a bit worse for wear, they are alive. Second, and perhaps most important, as far as y'all are concerned, one of them is standing just below you at this very moment. You see, under your eight little paws is an old, unused maintenance panel installed during the early construction of this mountain. My boys and I have since discovered and, as they say, refurbished said panel to be part of our home defense initiative. It now serves as a trap door. Oh, and since it was, as I mentioned, unused, there is nothing below it. No ladder. No, if you'll excuse the term, cat walk. Not even a clear drop to the water. Only dead space all the way to a concrete floor. Getting the picture yet?"

Baxter looked directly at Lilli. "How many lives you reckon you've got left after today, kitten?"

"Aw, give me a break," huffed Elias. "He's bluffing."

"I'm not so sure," said Kimball, carefully sliding his foot through the grassy bluff. "While it was built long after the original quick escapes and trapdoors of our predecessors, Splash Mountain underwent many early structural changes, even during construction. This mountain could be full of unmapped maintenance panels and emergency exits."

"That's right," said Baxter, pointing his staff at them, then sliding a pointy brass bat wing across his thick orange neck. "Do you really want to take that chance? Or are you a very rare *flying* kitty cat?"

"Kitty cat?" Elias coughed. "Did he just call me a kitty...?"

"Forget it, Elias," Oliver said, stepping in front of him. He had a plan. He may have made a mistake by leading them into danger, but maybe this was how he could get them out of it. Even if he had to risk his own tail to do so. "I'm tired of this. You want the key, Baxter?"

Elias, Lilli, and Kimball all met eyes, but tried to mask their confusion.

"Now, perhaps you're hard of hearing, all those cold nights alone in an Anaheim alleyway," Baxter jibed. "Maybe you bumped your poor head when we bounced you down the flume. My demands were quite clear. You said that key has power. If so, I should be the one to possess it. Not some crazy human, and *not* Thurl or his delusional kitten squad."

"You know what? You might be right," said Oliver, turning around to face the others. He raised his voice as an empty log clunked up to the top of the flume. Oliver locked eyes with Kimball, then ever-so-slightly nodded toward Lilli and Elias, then at the dangling rope. "I mean it, guys, maybe we should give Baxter the key. He's strong, he runs this mountain. Sometimes you have to take a *leap* of faith."

Kimball squinted, then as it sunk in, the corner of his mouth turned up in a grin. He carefully stepped in front of the hanging rope and began to reel up the end, slowly wrapping it around his paw. Lilli on the other paw shot Oliver a concerned look, wanting to scream, "What are you doing?"

"And you, Baxter," said Oliver turning again to face him. He stepped up to the edge just a few inches away from where Baxter leaned out of his hidden doorway. He patted his side as he walked. "If you want this magic key in my vest, you're going to have to do something we cats hate."

This time it was Baxter with the confused look on his face. He squinted at Oliver and his lip turned up in a sneer, revealing his crooked fangs. "And what, pray tell, would that be?"

"You're going to have to get wet!" Oliver leaned back and took a running leap right off the side of the cliff, disappearing in the mist rising off the water rushing down the mountain.

"Oliver!" Lilli cried out. This was the second time in one night she'd watched her friend go over that flume. Elias stood next to her, his jaw hanging open, too dumbfounded to speak.

While he hadn't planned it out, Oliver's timing was perfect. He landed hard but square on the back of an empty log as it slipped down the falls. He somersaulted forward into the back seat. Oliver's heart was pounding from excitement. He threw his paws over his head and burst into a fit of childlike laughter as he raced down the mountain.

It was a momentary distraction, but it was enough. Up above, Baxter snarled, not believing what he'd just watched. He came to his senses and glared at the other three. Baxter clanged his staff against the side of the mountain twice. It was the signal to his henchcats. Now was Kimball's turn to act quickly, without any planning—something he despised.

"No time for goodbyes," Kimball said. He charged into his two dumbfounded friends like a bulldozer. "Elias, grab Lilli."

Elias instinctively did as he was told, hooking his arm around her waist, just as Kimball pulled all three of them over the side of the cliff. Right as they left solid ground, Kimball looked back and saw the spot where they'd just been standing fall away as the trap door swung down, grass and rock still attached, leaving a large square hole.

"Look at that," Kimball called out, seemingly unconcerned they were falling rapidly. "He wasn't bluffing."

"Kimball!" yelled Elias.

"Do something!" Lilli added.

"Oh, sorry," Kimball said, hitting a red button on the reel attached to his belt. The zipping sound stopped and the rope went taut. All three came to a quick stop with a jarring snap. They were near the bottom of the hill. Hopefully far enough from Baxter to climb to safety without another booby trap springing open. Kimball hit the release and they dropped to their paws.

"I declare I am in a state of befuddlement," Baxter growled above, unable to see the cats or determine their fates. "What is the matter with this ridiculous new breed of Castle Cat? Where is their sense of self-preservation?"

"That old crackpot Thurl's made 'em all plain nuts," remarked Fang, appearing in the door beside Baxter, wiggling his tender loose tooth. "That's what it is!"

"No," said Baxter, clicking his tongue. He stood silent, looking out at the castle in the distance. He took a long swig from his bottle and wiped his mouth on his furry arm. Baxter let out a sigh. "No, Fang, my boy, that ain't crazy. That's called valor. Noble courage, even in the pretty orange face of danger."

Down below, Oliver's log levelled out and cool night air tickled his wet neck. When his log hit the bottom a wave of water crested over his head and splashed down over his back. Not so bad, he thought with a laugh. Just around the bend he'd be floating inside the attraction for the finale they'd witnessed from the railroad tunnel. Unfortunately, he didn't have time to see it up close this particular ride. The log cruised alongside a rock wall. Oliver was fairly sure on the other side was a plateau of grass, and then a short drop to the street. Oliver stood up on the seat, not even caring if any humans were around, and as the boat turned back toward the mountain, jumped out onto the wall. Just as he struck an almost perfect landing on his back paws…

"*Oliver!*"

He nearly fell backwards into the channel. Oliver caught himself and turned to see Lilli, just across the water. Elias and Kimball were climbing down behind her. They both grinned at the sight of him. In a few seconds, another empty log came floating around the bend. The three of them quickly sprang across like in some kind of video game to reach Oliver on the other side. They all hugged, happy to be alive, and much closer to the ground. Elias clapped him on the shoulder, impressed by his guts and that daring escape.

"What can I say?" Elias nodded. "I'm impressed. Don't ever do that again!"

"We should get out of here," Oliver said. "We're not out of the woods yet."

"I believe it would be more appropriate to say off the mountain," Kimball started. They all turned their heads and stared at him with a groan. "That is to say, uh, I agree. There's no telling how many short cuts Baxter has throughout this attraction."

"You're right," Oliver said, "let's get moving." With that he turned and stepped out off the wall to run across the grass he had been certain waited on the other side.

"Oliver, wait!" Lilli called out, but far too late. His black-and-white paw swung in the air a second before sinking into very cold, wet "grass." In the excitement of the adrenaline-fueled escape, Oliver must have gotten confused. There wasn't any grass or ground at all, but a shallow pool separating the ride and the street. Oliver fell in with a splash.

"Was that part of his plan?" Kimball wondered aloud.

"I don't think so," said Elias, doubled over laughing.

Oliver floated below them, his chin above the surface, with a dazed look on his face.

"I got confused," he said, spitting water like a fountain. "We need to patrol Critter Country more often."

"Yeah, well, for what it's worth you've got the right idea," said Elias. "Even if you didn't mean it. The only way out is through. Much as I hate to say it, we're all gonna get wet."

The cats jumped in and waded to the other side. They crawled out and, making sure there was solid ground below this time, leapt over the rocks to the street. When they reached the asphalt they each dropped to all fours and shook out their fur, spraying water everywhere.

"I'm sorry, guys," Oliver swallowed hard. "I led you on this ridiculous journey for nothing. A mistake! It was just a glare in the sunlight. I should've known the odds were probably a million to one." As soon as he said that he looked at Kimball, expecting to hear a correction, followed by the exact mathematical odds. Kimball only smiled and nodded.

"There's nothing to apologize for," said Lilli. "I saw it, too. There was no way to know it wasn't the key. Even if we weren't sure, we had to find out."

"She's right, kid," said Elias. "I, uh...I'm sorry. I kind of lost it up there. I just wanted you to find the key as much as anybody. Truth is, we're going to have to check out every strange flash, weird glare, or odd shiny thing we see. That key could be anywhere. At least we can scratch Splash Mountain off the list. So actually, in this case, it's a good thing you're an impulsive housecat with a lot to learn."

The wet black-and-white cat managed a smile. His friends had his back. That felt good. Plus, there was comfort in knowing Baxter didn't have the key. And Doctor Owl was all over security's radar. They would all have seen his picture from the morning. Even if he did sneak into the park, every guard would have their eyes peeled looking for him. That bought the cats some time, Oliver figured. They could breathe a little easier for one night.

"We'd better get back to the castle," said Lilli. "I'm sure Thurl is pacing the halls."

"Yeah, come on," said Elias, specifically to Oliver. "Tomorrow we start all over again. Tonight, we've earned a rest."

Chapter Eleven

The Cats of the Castle agreed they could risk traveling right through the park, rather than going the long way around the railroad tracks. They'd just be careful to keep to the shadows as much as possible. They were all exhausted. Oliver noticed the Haunted Mansion and thought it appeared a little less scary now, after their harrowing adventure on Splash Mountain. At least in the mansion, you stayed dry.

Far across the Rivers of America, the majestic *Mark Twain* paddle wheeler sat docked for the night. The white paint seemed to glow in the moonlight as it reflected in the dark water around it. Oliver's tired brain drifted off to a vision of taking a leisurely cruise on the deck. In his vision, Lilli was with him, leaning wistfully against the rail. Their paws might accidentally brush against one another. They'd smile nervously, and then she'd point out the strange beam of light moving toward them.

Oliver's attention snapped back to reality. From around the dock where the *Twain* sat peacefully, a beam of light appeared. He didn't need Kimball's binocular lenses to recognize the unmistakable silhouette of a human carrying a flashlight.

"Everybody get down," Oliver whispered. They all ducked into some shrubs near the water.

"Security?" Lilli whispered.

"Maybe. Can't make out anything specific."

Kimball adjusted the lenses of his night-vision glasses only to discover one lens had cracked, most likely when they dropped down Chick-A-Pin Hill. "Sorry, guys," he said, covering the bad lens with his paw to focus through the good one. "I'm half night-blind. Not to mention the petrified tree is in the way. I think he has a hat on, *maybe*."

Kimball was right. From their vantage point the petrified tree that stood as a monument on the edge of the Rivers of America near Frontierland was blocking their view. The ancient remnant had been an anniversary gift from Mr. Disney to his wife, but was so big and heavy, she in turn donated it to the park. Now the massive stump, which Oliver often thought was shaped like a rocket ship, sat in a circular garden with a plaque commemorating the donation.

"I don't know why they keep that slab of deadwood," Elias muttered.

"Because it belonged to Mrs. Disney," said Kimball sternly. "And it's almost eight feet tall and weighs a ton. Perhaps we triggered a silent alarm. Or Baxter did."

"Nah, there'd be an army of guards heading toward Splash Mountain," said Elias. "Besides, they said the alarms were cut. Probably just switching up the routine, putting guards on solo detail to look for Doctor Owl. Covers more ground that way."

"I know exactly which raccoon chewed those cables," said Lilli.

"So the Doc's got security on a wild goose chase," said Elias. "Keeping them off their normal routine. Maybe this human is smarter than we thought, even if he does hang out with rats."

"Maybe," said Oliver. He looked around at their location. Seemed the best option was behind them. "Whoever it is, we need a better spot to hide until they pass."

"I say New Orleans Square," Elias offered, nodding his head over his shoulder. "It's perfect."

"What if he's heading that way?" Kimball asked.

"That's where the *hiding* part comes in," said Elias, scrambling to his feet. "Come on! Last one in buys the beignets."

"Elias, wait!" said Oliver. "I'm not sure that is the safest plan" It was too late. The brazen cat had dropped to all fours and taken off like a shot into the heart of old New Orleans.

"We got him," said Lilli, chasing after Elias with Kimball bounding by.

Oliver shook his head. He'd been through New Orleans Square a hundred times at night. It could get confusing, as it wasn't really a square at all but dark, weaving streets lined with tall, narrow old buildings, each affixed with intricately designed iron balconies, like the real French Quarter. Walt wanted it to be very authentic. They'd even hosted the mayor of New Orleans at the grand opening. Even a cat could get turned around. This plan didn't feel right. Shaking his head, Oliver chased after his friends. He paused at the opening. Up ahead he saw Kimball's bright yellow fur.

"I don't like this," Oliver mumbled. "Kimball!"

Kimball turned to see him and grinned. He took a step toward Oliver when suddenly, *fffffwit!* The brilliant cat was yanked into the air, upside down by his ankle. Oliver was too far away to intervene and too shocked to even understand what he was seeing. Kimball's glasses fell out of the darkness and hit the street where some of the lenses shattered. Oliver ran after him, and found his friend hanging by a wrought iron balcony. He was bumping into a red sign that read "Le Bat En Rouge."

"Kimball, are you okay?" Oliver asked.

"Um, I think so. It's just a snare. Someone set a booby trap."

"Oliver!" Lilli's voice called out from the other side of the street.

Oliver ran to the middle of the square and held out Kimball's Illuminator. In a few seconds the entire street was bathed in blue light.

"Lilli," Oliver called out. "Where are you?"

"Above you," she said, matter-of-factly. "Look up, Ollie."

There she was, dangling upside down, just like Kimball, a few feet over his head. Her tail kept whipping against an oval sign depicting a beach scene with a pile of gold coins, a shovel, and a skull. Off in the distance a pirate ship floated in the surf. Below the picture were carved the words "Pieces of Eight."

"Pirates," Lilli muttered with irritation. "Just my luck. After all I've been through today, I've been captured by pirates."

"Lilli, I'll get you down. Just stay right there."

"Not exactly going anywhere. Wait, Oliver, don't! This whole place could be trapped. Someone expected us to run in here."

"I'm beginning to think that wasn't a security guard," they heard Kimball say.

"We were herded in," said Oliver. "Like cattle. Whoever it was knew if they cut us off at Rivers of America, we'd most likely run straight into New Orleans Square. The perfect land to hide traps. Let me find something to climb so I can cut you down."

"I'm not a damsel in distress, Oliver. I can get myself down." Lilli bent her body up and began trying to claw at the rope around her ankle. While she made contact every other swipe or so, the cable was strong. It proved even more difficult hanging at such an awkward angle. "Okay, I could use something a little sharper."

"Sharper," Oliver said, looking around. "Got it! Hang tight!" Without looking he could feel her stare. "Sorry, bad choice of words. I'll be right back!"

Oliver ran over to Kimball's broken glasses in the street. A large piece of lens had come loose. One edge was chipped good, and razor sharp. Sharp enough to split a whisker, Oliver thought. He hoped that meant it could cut through the snare, too. Being careful to hold it by the thicker, less likely to slice a paw end, Oliver used the broken lens to cut a long strip from his vest. He tied the glass firmly against the broad end of his sword.

"Here," he said holding the sword up to Lilli. "Plastic or not, I knew one day carrying a sword would come in handy."

Lilli took it and bent herself up again, managing to grab the rope with her free paw to pull herself closer. She began carefully sawing the sharp lens across the snare line. It was working. Little by little the tightly wrapped fibers began to split and break away. She just had to go slow, to make sure the glass didn't come loose from the sword.

"This might take a minute," Lilli grunted. "Where's Elias?"

"I don't know yet." Then he saw movement at the dark end of the street. Elias came running out of the shadows, headed straight toward them. He looked like he'd seen a pack of Dobermans.

"We need to get out of here!" he shouted, pulling Oliver's elbow. "Come on, man! We need to find Lilli and Kimball and go!"

"Elias," Oliver said, digging his feet in until they both almost barreled forward to the ground. When Elias turned to face him, Oliver pointed up. "I already found them!"

"What?!?" Elias looked up in disbelief.

"And Kimball's right over there," he said, gesturing across the street.

"This isn't good, Oliver. I think I just met Lilli's new friend, the raccoon!"

"Scavenge is here?" Lilli called down.

Just as she spoke there was a deafening crash. At the end of the street, the large brute appeared. It was indeed Scavenge, looking more monstrous than ever bathed in eerie blue light. His wet fur clung to his bearish body. His scarred lip locked in an angry snarl. His squinty eye scowled at them while the other was popping out of his skull like a twisted cartoon not intended for small children. Drool dangled from his jaw. With his thick gray arms he was hoisting a heavy metal trash can over his head.

"Stand still, cats!" Scavenge demanded. "I'll smash both of you at once!" He heaved the can with a roar. Oliver and Elias dove away in separate directions as the metal receptacle smashed loudly against the street. One side of it was completely crushed. The cats exchanged knowing glances; the dent could have been their heads.

"This is bad," Oliver said, jumping to his feet. He glanced up at Lilli who was nearly finished cutting through the remaining strands of cable holding her captive. They heard a soft snap, and she dropped, flipped gracefully in mid-air, and landed on her back paws on cobblestone.

"Are you guys alright?" Lilli asked, ignoring Scavenge and helping them up.

"Yeah, we're okay," Oliver answered. He eyed the angry raccoon gearing up for another attack. "We have to do something to slow him down."

"Way ahead of you," said Elias who was walking right up to Scavenge, jumping up and down as he moved. "Hey! Yeah, you! The masked mutant!"

Scavenge stopped laughing. His scarred eyebrow arched.

"Yeah, I'm talking to you," Elias kept going. "You overgrown, ring-tailed rat! What's your problem?"

"Cats," Scavenge snarled back. "But not for much longer."

"You'll have to get through both of us at once," said Oliver running up beside Elias. Lilli was right behind him. Scavenge laughed again.

"Cats want to fight me?" Scavenge pointed a black claw and sneered, revealing a mouthful of jagged, misshapen teeth. "Scavenge is stronger than twenty cats."

"It doesn't matter," Oliver said, taking a step toward him. "We fight for the park. We stand for Disneyland. That's strength enough. What do you stand for?"

"That's right," Elias added. "Who are you working for again? Oh, that's right, some crazy human who looks like a bird. He's using you to get his revenge. Being a human's puppet sounds pretty pathetic, if you ask me."

"He has a point," Lilli prodded, stepping in front of the boys. "Big tough raccoon doing a human's dirty work. Do you really think the good doctor is going to reward you when this is over? You think if you get him the key, he'll give you all the turkey legs you can gnaw on? Guess again!"

"Don't see much human love for raccoons," Elias said. "Have you noticed the hats they sell in Frontierland? You'll be keeping the old man's head warm like Davy Crockett. Some reward for being his servant."

"Never," Scavenge spat. "Scavenge works for Scavenge! Scavenge is no puppet...or hat!"

The raccoon's eyes were glassy and bloodshot. He lunged at them with an awful, ear-splitting scream. Elias, Oliver, and Lilli braced themselves, claws out and teeth bared. The odds they could overpower him seemed unlikely. This was going to get ugly.

"Scavenge," a loud voice commanded from behind them. "Stop!"

Scavenge immediately dug his claws into the cobblestone, halting his attack. He glared down at the cats, his chest heaving. Oliver already knew who had called him off. They all turned around, and sure enough, standing at the entrance to New Orleans Square was a tall, thin human with unmistakable wings of hair, oversized round spectacles reflecting the blue light, and a red scarf pulled over his nose and mouth and tied behind his head like a bank robber in a cowboy movie. He wore his long gray coat, belted at the middle, and black rubber gloves, in which he clutched a heavy flashlight. It was Doctor Owl who had corralled them into New Orleans Square where his traps and Scavenge were already set for their arrival.

"Okay, I'm confused," Elias said over his shoulder. "Who was it Scavenge said he *doesn't* work for again? Because he sure stopped in a hurry."

"Keep talking, cat," Scavenge mumbled in a guttural growl behind his clenched teeth, just inches behind them. "Cats' time is coming."

"Lights," Doctor Owl commanded, as if there were someone listening they couldn't see. A second later, the lanterns affixed to the walls on either side of them flickered to life. Oliver switched off the Illuminator.

"Ah, much better." He pointed directly at Oliver. "You filthy felines have been nothing but trouble. I expected my plan to take a day, maybe two at most. But then *you* showed up! You've been under my feet at every turn!"

"And I'm still here now," Oliver said. "We're Cats of the Castle. It's our job to stop *any* vermin that creep around this park. Even the two-legged kind."

"Oh, snap," Elias added, putting a paw to his mouth and raising a brow. "I think he means you!"

"You're never getting that key, Mintz!" Oliver said firmly.

Though they couldn't see the man's expression behind the scarf and glasses, the cats could sense the surprise that washed over him. His brows arched behind his circular frames.

"So, you know my name," said Mintz, slowly walking toward them. The closer he got, the more they could hear the muffled sniffs behind his scarf. "That's good. You should know my name. Soon all of Disneyland, and the world beyond it, will know my name. You will give me the key now."

"Ollie, are you listening to this whack-a-doo?" Elias said with a forced laugh. "He thinks you have the key."

"I guess he knows I found it," Oliver said after a moment.

"Yeah, I guess he...," Elias started. He looked over at him with a cocked head. "Oliver, what are you doing? We already played this card once."

"No point in hiding that *I have the key*, Elias," Oliver went on, loudly, staring Elias down with eyes wide, hinting for him to shut up. He tapped on his vest so they could hear his claw clicking on metal. "It's right here in my vest."

Mintz raised his eyebrows wide in excitement. "You do! You have it!" He seemed ecstatic. It looked like he might start dancing an Irish jig in the middle of New Orleans Square. "You've done the hard work for me, you wonderful, disease-ridden dust mop! Now hand it over, and perhaps I won't throw you into the Rivers of America with a rock tied to your tail!"

"First, tell me what happens to the park," Oliver demanded, taking a step forward. "If I give you the key, you're going to shut down the park, aren't you? They banned you for breaking into Walt's apartment so you're going to shut down Disneyland."

"Shut it down!" Mintz laughed. "Of course not, you horrible little hairball. Oh, I admit I spent most of my youth dreaming of driving a bulldozer straight down Main Street, or swinging a wrecking ball through that castle. Wouldn't anyone in my position, having been shut out so unjustly? Punished for simple childish curiosity. All my friends were inside each summer, and on weekends, flying on Dumbo, spinning in tea cups, and riding caterpillars into Wonderland." Mintz stopped. He took a deep sigh as the front of his red scarf sucked in and then puffed out. His face turned up to the sky as if lost in a dream. "Oh, Wonderland—you have no idea how often I dreamed of riding through Wonderland!"

"This dude is a weeeeeirdo," Elias muttered from the side of his mouth.

"No, I won't be closing the park," Mintz snapped back. "In fact, I plan on keeping it running for a very long time. Mind you, I will be the only guest inside, for a while. The rest of the world can watch from outside the gates. They can stand on Harbor Boulevard, trying to steal a glimpse at all the wonder and excitement happening just inches away, but completely out of reach, just like I did!"

"So that really is what all this is about?" Lilli asked. "You're willing to go through all this trouble, even risk going to jail, because you never got to ride Dumbo?"

"That's a heavy chip on your shoulder there, pal," Elias said.

"Oh, no, there's more," Mintz grinned. "You haven't let me finish. The mollification of my childhood injustice is only sweet icing on the cupcake, you litter-box loitering miscreants."

Elias looked at Oliver with a shrug and whispered, "Miscreants?"

"I wish I could say a personal vendetta was all that I cared about. I'm afraid at the end of the day my motivation comes down to the basest human desire. You animals wouldn't understand. Humans need it. This park practically prints it."

"FastPasses?" Elias wondered.

"Money!" Mintz screamed. "Bushels of it!"

"How will the key get you money?" Lilli asked.

"It's simple," Mintz went on. "I will demand the deed to Disneyland be signed over to my name, along with a ridiculous sum of cash up front. I'm thinking one-hundred-million dollars sounds like a good place to start. Once the money and deed are mine, and I've had enough fun, the park will undergo a grand re-opening for all the sniveling, churro-munching public.

"Of course there will be some changes. This will be Mintz Land. I plan to immediately refurbish that beloved statue standing before the castle to resemble my own striking visage. And there will be personnel changes. No more cast members, or cats. My rats will collect admission, operate the attractions, and sell the sugary sodas and sweets. Every nickel from every child's balloon, every hat with silly black ears, it will all come flowing to the foot of my throne in the newly rechristened Mintzy's Castle! Oh, and believe me when I tell you, prices are going up, up, up!"

"This guy's beyond Fantasyland," said Elias.

"I can't let this happen," Oliver said quietly.

"Humans really are monsters when it comes to money." Lilli said.

"*AHSHPLOOSH!*" Mintz let loose one of his awful sneezes. If they didn't know better, they'd think it lifted him off his feet. "Ugh, you horrible beasts and your disgusting dander! Everything is about getting rich, you obstinate ocelot!

"What did he call me?" she said, charging forward with claws up and fangs displayed. Elias and Oliver each grabbed an elbow to hold her back. "I'm a Siamese, pal!"

"Watch how quickly the people pay," Mintz said, ignoring her. "After all, this is the happiest place on the planet. Shouldn't I be happy, too? He who holds the key controls all the magic of Disneyland! You want a piece of the magic? You pay *me*!"

"What do you suggest we do?" Elias looked at Oliver.

"You hand me that key," Mintz demanded, "or I order Scavenge to retrieve it for me. That is your only option. Otherwise, there'll be nothing left of you but a shredded green vest."

From behind them came warm, musty breath accompanied by a menacing chuckle. This close, Scavenge smelled like skunk spray and pond water. Yet over his feral noises, they heard something else. A strange hum mixed with a metallic rattle. It was coming from the park. The noise grew louder with each second, and it seemed to be getting closer. Mintz clearly heard it now, too. He spun on his heel just as the sound materialized inside New Orleans Square, now accompanied by wild hooting and hollering. That's when Oliver felt time seem to switch into slow motion. There was a blur of metal and orange and Mintz was launched into the air.

"Boys, look out!" Lilli screamed from over their shoulders.

Something, or more appropriately someone, blindsided him, tackling him to the street. His immediate thought was Scavenge had attacked. Any second he'd feel those sharp claws and jagged teeth. But no attack came. Instead he felt himself being rolled, albeit forcefully, out of the way. Oliver couldn't tell which way was up. Had Elias pushed him down? Was it Lilli? There wasn't time to find out. Oliver looked up and saw Baxter rolling down the center of New Orleans Square at high speed in a big gray washtub on wheels. The master of the hill cats had bowled Mintz over and was headed straight for Scavenge with no sign of slowing down.

The raccoon's eyes went wide, one more so than the other, and he tried to attack the tub, but his claws only slid on the slick street. Baxter leaned out over the metal edge, gripping his heavy iron staff like a baseball bat, and he swung for the bleachers, taking Scavenge out at the knees with a bone-blasting clang. The hulking raccoon howled in agony as he fell face first into the street. Baxter sped past, laughing like a mad clown, his orange paw raised in a fist.

"Hooo-wee, that was fun!" said a vaguely familiar voice standing over Oliver. He rolled over to see it was Ernie, the stout dark-haired hill cat in the tight Mickey tee. His face and arms bore deep red scratches and one of his eyes was now badly swollen, courtesy of his earlier encounter with Scavenge. But his whiskers were turned up in a grin from ear to ear.

Past him, Oliver saw tall, lanky Fang pushing Elias out of the way. He, too, was badly scratched and clawed with a number of tender pink patches. Oliver wondered what were the hill cats were doing there? Had they intervened only so they could kill him again themselves?

That's when the wild-eyed Nip, who had been pushing Baxter in the tub, leapt at Scavenge, landing on the brute's back while holding a large brown pot that read "Hunny," pilfered from another attraction. Growling and slobbering,

Scavenge attempted to get back up despite the excruciating pain in his knees, plus the weight on his shoulders. Nip slammed the pot down over his head. With a wide grin revealing flecks of cat nip in his teeth, the wild calico began banging on the pot with a mallet. The raccoon went flat again.

There was a crash around the corner like someone had thrown a box of cymbals out the window. One of the wagon wheels that was affixed to the tub came bouncing back toward them. In a moment, they heard the familiar clunk of a heavy metal staff on the bricks. Baxter reappeared, giggling like a loon, leaning heavily on his staff. He took a sip from a small glass jug hanging from a string around his neck.

"Well, I must admit it's been a while since I've been out of my mountain," Baxter spoke, surveying the current scene with his good eye. "But I recall this street being much cleaner."

Oliver got to his feet and cautiously stepped away from Ernie. Elias slipped in beside him. The two Castle Cats stood shoulder to shoulder, wondering if they were truly safe or not. Baxter's boys watched them, amused.

"Lilli," Oliver said, still eyeing the hill cats. "I think this would be as good a time to as any to go...."

"Get Kimball down?" she finished his sentence. "I'm on it."

She slipped off to the other end of the alley. Standing on her tip-paws she raised the sword to Kimball's outstretched fingers, warning him to be careful. The long, lean Kimball was easily able to slice away at his own snare. Lilli returned to stand between Oliver and Elias.

"Baxter," Oliver said. "We're not on your mountain anymore. We have no plans to bother you again."

"Nor I you," said Baxter, clicking his tongue. "I have made an executive decision. We have no more quarrel with you, Cats of the Castle. Least not today, anyway." He gestured his thumb back at Scavenge lying still on the street. "Can't say the same for that carpet-baggin', bag of carpet over yonder. He defiled the sanctity of my home. He brought harm to my men. Vengeance is mine, sayeth the orange cat."

"So you didn't come to finish us?" Oliver asked, not entirely sure he understood the old cat's strange speech patterns. Baxter shot out a laugh.

"We're all good?" Elias asked, gesturing his paw from their group to his. "No more bad blood between the hill and the castle?"

Baxter examined them for a moment, his green eye narrowing. Finally he sighed and smiled, adjusting the strap of his overalls. "Who among us knows the future?" he responded slyly. "Let me simply say I was impressed by the courage I witnessed today on my mountain. It was quite...noble."

He stopped and gave a nod toward Lilli. "Reminded me of earlier days when I sat at the table myself. Let Thurl know our detente has been restored, even if an uneasy truce it might be."

"Detente?" Elias whispered.

"It means no more fighting," Lilli said.

"We can live with that," said Oliver. "At least for now."

"Enough of this!" Mintz screamed.

All the cats looked to see him back on his feet, but now holding Oliver's sword in one hand and Kimball in the other, partly by the brown sweater, partly by the scruff of his neck. Kimball hissed and tried repeatedly to claw at the man's arm, but with no luck. "This whole theme park is infested with filthy felines! That ends tonight!"

Mintz threw the plastic sword at them. He reached in his coat pocket and removed a small plastic baggy containing little more than a pinch of something powdery that shimmered in the blue light. "One more surprise from any of you, I sprinkle the last of this blue dust over a pack of hungry Rottweilers and let them evict you!"

"Oliver, do you see that?" Lilli asked. "He still has some pixie dust."

"Oh, yes," said Mintz. "I've been holding on to this magical blue powder for a long time."

"You mean since the day you broke into Walt's apartment and stole it," said Oliver, sliding his sword back in its scabbard.

"Broke in?" Mintz dismissed, as if offended. "I was merely looking for a bathroom. The punishment was rather steep for merely being lost, don't you agree? They embarrassed me. Treated me like a common criminal!"

"And here you stand with the stolen property," said Lilli.

"Stolen?" Mintz spat. "I just happened to find this strange blue dust. How was I to know the power it possessed? I was merely a curious child. So I poured a pinch or two into my hand. I was just about to put it back when those security orangutans burst in. They gave me such a scare I instinctively dropped my hands to my sides without thinking. I forgot I was even clutching some in my fist, or that it spilled out into my pocket. Hardly the crime of the century."

"Maybe so, but it was still theft when you didn't return it," said Oliver.

"And now went and poured it over your masked mutant there," added Elias. "Not to mention the rabies-carrying three! I'm no expert in human law, but that sounds criminal to me."

"I've officially grown tired of you, tubby tabby," said Mintz, taking a step toward Elias. His furrowed brow quickly rose as he got closer. *"ACHOO!"*

When he sneezed, Mintz raised his arms higher, and Kimball along with them. It gave the yellow cat an idea. Kimball whipped his tail across Mintz's face. The irritated doctor began shaking his head from side to side. Kimball seized the chance to stick the end of his tail down into the scarf, making direct contact with Mintz's nose. That was all it took. He broke into a violent sneezing fit. They came fast and furious, one after a-snotty-nother, causing the man to shake and convulse with each outburst, swinging the yellow cat with him.

"KASHPLOOH! KERCHOOSH!" Mintz doubled over, his scarf flapping out with each sneeze. Finally his gloved hand lost its grip on Kimball's fur. Kimball quickly slipped right out of his cardigan and hit the street. He ran to his friends on all fours. They all put their arms around him, glad to have him back on their side of the street.

"It's over, Mintz," Oliver said. "Scavenge is out of commission. Your little henchrats are long gone. Now it's just you against four walking, talking, very irritated cats."

"One of whom feels very naked right now," Kimball hissed.

"Hate to quibble with you, son," said Baxter, stepping up behind the Castle Cats with his boys and locking his good eye on Mintz. "There's eight angry cats. You say this scrawny human sent that bloodthirsty bearcat you call a raccoon into my home? Well, Doctor whatever your name is, you just doubled your enemies."

"What is happening?" Mintz screamed. "Where are all of these...*sniff*... cats coming from? This wasn't in my plan!"

"You lost," said Oliver. "That's what happened. It's over. Your plan unraveled."

"Time to walk away, Mintz," said Elias. "Won't be good for your allergies if eight cats pounce on you."

"Oh, I don't think so," Mintz said with a runny sniff. "This game's not over yet, you menacing mau! There's still one more piece of my plan intact. It's a recent addition. In fact, I can't take credit. My otherwise useless underlings thought of it themselves."

Mintz turned and clicked his flashlight on and off three times. In a moment, Mac, Murray, and Fred appeared, dragging a burlap sack behind them. They chuckled as they heaved and ho'ed to pull the heavy bag along.

"I don't believe it," Elias said, mouth hanging wide.

"Believe it, you gullible gato," said Mintz. "Did you really believe these rats couldn't weasel their way out of any predicament? They're rats. It's what they do. To that end, much more admirable than lazy cats."

"Thanks, boss," said Fred, the black rat. The rats dropped the sack at Mintz's feet and scurried behind him. It was moving around. Something alive was squirming inside it.

"Get me out of here," they heard a familiar albeit muffled voice demand.

"Thurl?" Lilli gasped.

Mintz gave the bag a shove with his foot. It fell over sideways with an *oof!*

A shaggy white head and paw slowly appeared from the opening. Lilli ran for him. The three rats sprang at her with their teeth bared, ready to fight.

"Not so fast, toots," Mac hissed.

"Surprised to see us?" Fred asked, locking eyes with Elias. He was holding a roll of silver duct tape. "Wait 'til you see where we're going to tape up the old cat."

"I'm sorry, my young ones," Thurl said, struggling to his feet. His normally fluffy white face looked matted in defeat. "I broke the same rule I always insist of you. I let my guard down."

"It appears this game is still in my favor," Mintz said. He held out his hand. "Now for the last time, my key if you please."

Oliver hadn't expected this. They couldn't let anything happen to Thurl. He was their leader. More than that, he was the only father any of them had ever known. They needed a plan. The eight of them could easily rush them, but it was too dangerous. Thurl could get hurt. Oliver quickly realized that the times you need a good plan most were the moments there wasn't time to think of one.

"Fine, I'll give it to you," he finally blurted out, thinking on his paws. "It doesn't matter. The key's no good to you anyway."

"What are you talking about?" Mintz asked with a sigh. "Stupid cat, we've been over this already. In this park, that key is all powerful. Remember, the possessor controls the magic, etcetera, etcetera?"

"You don't understand, Mintz," said Oliver. "All this time we've been trying to stop you and your rats from finding it, when the truth is, we could've been relaxing in the castle, sipping pineapple floats. Even if you found the Disneyland key, you couldn't do anything with it."

"This is desperate babbling." Mintz looked back at his rats and chuckled. He bent over toward Thurl on the ground. "You let this one lead them?"

"It's a key, Doctor Birdbrain!" Oliver continued. "And even if we give you the key, you have no idea where to find its matching keyhole. Keys are useless without a lock."

"Oh mein kat," Mintz said, shaking his head. "Perhaps you should hold your little pink tongue before you speak so quickly. Point goes to me, for I know exactly where said secret lock is hidden!"

"You do?" Oliver asked, surprised. He had been bluffing. All that lock stuff just came to him on the spot—though it actually did make sense.

Mintz stepped over Thurl and walked down the street past all the cats who were watching him closely. The doctor stopped at a pale green door set back from the street. Beside it hung an ornate, oval plaque with the number 33. It was the subtle entrance to a private restaurant called Club 33. As far as Oliver knew, no cats had ever seen the inside. He'd heard there was an old-fashioned elevator that once carried Walt's personal guests to a private dining room. There was also some strange legend about a talking vulture.

"Behold!" Mintz called out with a flourish of his hands. His gloved fingers danced below the sign. "It almost breaks my heart to inform you, but

I wouldn't know the secret of this sign if not for your beloved master. In fact, he was almost too happy to reveal the location."

"That's right," sneered Mac, punching one spindly hand into the other. "I was actually disappointed at how easily he cracked."

"According to grandfather cat," Mintz continued, "all one need do is push firmly upon the face of the sign and it will open to reveal the secret lock that fits that key."

The cats couldn't believe it. Thurl told Mintz where the lock was hidden? That didn't seem like him at all, no matter how Mintz threatened him. Thurl had never even mentioned a lock. Although, Oliver thought, until a day ago he'd never even mentioned the Disneyland key. Thurl looked up at Oliver with sad eyes, his face revealing his shame at giving away such a crucial secret. But then, as if certain the moment was shared only by the two of them, the corners of the old cat's mouth turned up ever so slightly into a grin, the yellowed tips of his heavy white mustache bending with them, before quickly drooping again. He gave his young squire a knowing wink, and then his face fell sullen. It dawned on Oliver that perhaps the park didn't belong to Mintz just yet.

"It's been right here all along!" Mintz continued with his monologue. "Hidden behind this mysterious 33 for so many years. In fact, your old friend told me that's the real reason Disney built this secret clubhouse. It was just a ruse to relocate the lock." He placed his palm flat against the 33.

"The hole that fits that key," he said, flatly, as if entranced by the potential of power, "the conduit to all the magic of this park, and the power over it is right *here*!" Mintz pushed his palm against the sign.

"Cats," Oliver said out of the side of his mouth, "get to Thurl, *now!*"

"What are you going to...?" Lilli started to ask.

"You want this key?" Oliver yelled at Mintz, patting his vest. Mintz pulled his hand off the 33 and stared at the cat with one arched eyebrow. Oliver glared back. "Catch me!"

With that, Oliver took off like a shot, leaping over Thurl and all the rats, who fell over themselves trying to grab for his ankle or tail. He tore off down the cobblestone street on all fours, darting out of New Orleans Square.

"You want us to go after him, boss?" Fred asked.

"No, you idiots, guard the old one," Mintz ordered, eyeing the other cats advancing toward Thurl. "I'll handle this myself, as I should have done all along!" He turned and ran out into the park. The sounds of his black shoes tapping clumsily along the street faded as he chased after Oliver. The three rats turned to face the Cats of the Castle, who had been joined by four mangier, much more menacing newcomers they hadn't seen before.

"Get back, all of ya!" The gray rat stepped forward, claws ready to swipe. His compatriots exchanged nervous looks. They were outnumbered, out-clawed, and outsized. They both shrugged as if making an unspoken agreement then turned tail and scurried away into the park, splitting off in different directions.

"Bad form," added Kimball. "Perhaps we should've taped your turncoat friends to the *bottom* of that submarine."

"I respect your ability to turn a phrase," Baxter said, nudging Kimball with his elbow.

"Your odds just got worse," Elias chuckled. He feigned a yawn. "I almost feel bad for you."

Mac reared back making a defensive hiss. He clawed at the street and whipped his pink tail in the air. To the cats he just looked like the usual garden variety sewer rats they encountered in the night.

"Now would be a good time for you to follow your friends," Lilli advised with a sly grin. She pushed her sleeves up.

"Please *mon cher*," Baxter cooed, gently placing a paw on her elbow. "While I have seen what an impressive fighter you are, it would be my honor if you'd let us take care of this one, and his *bons amis*!"

"Well, you didn't come all this way down the mountain for nothing," Lilli answered with a shrug. "You know what the song says? Be our guests!"

Ernie, Fang, and Nip stepped around the lone rat cowering between them and Thurl. Knowing he was doomed, the rat finally turned and bolted off. With a wild battle cry, Baxter's boys took off in pursuit. Too old, and secretly rather sore from his washtub crash, the orange cat shuffled over and kicked away the old burlap sack. Thurl's ankles were still bound with silver tape. Baxter reached down, and with a single claw sliced through the bindings. He extended his paw and helped his former friend to his feet.

"You're gonna want to soak your ankles in warm water before pulling that tape off your fur," Baxter said. "Trust me, I know what it can do."

The old white Persian straightened up and looked at the stocky orange cat who once sat at his elbow as a Cat of the Castle. They hadn't laid eyes on one another since that terrible fight years before. Neither smiled nor frowned. Not a word was said. That same night, Baxter tried to harm both Oliver and Lilli, nearly killing them. But he had also saved them from Mintz and that savage raccoon.

It felt obvious to both this wasn't the time to talk about the past, or the future. After a few seconds, Baxter merely nodded. Thurl nodded back. Baxter turned and, as quickly as he could, limped off after his crew, his staff thunking along the ground.

"Save some for me, boys!" Baxter called out into the night. "We'll be grillin' up my momma's special rat-ka-bob's tonight! Maybe a side of rat-tat-touille!"

"I'm alright," Thurl said with a chuckle when the three cats crowded him to make sure he was unharmed. "Thank you all, but you needn't fuss over me. It is Oliver I'm concerned about. Something tells me the key in his vest is as real as the secret lock I told Mintz was hidden behind that 33."

"But Thurl," said Lilli, "Oliver doesn't have the key."

"Exactly," Thurl winked.

"Ah," said Kimball, a knowing smile spreading across his face. "That sign doesn't hide the keyhole, does it? But Thurl, what if we hadn't been here, and Mintz found out you were lying?"

"It was a risk I had to take," Thurl said. "A calculated risk, my boy. Your favorite kind."

Kimball nodded with a grin.

"When Mintz sent his rats for me, I realized just how desperate he was," Thurl went on. "It made me sad for him."

"Sad for *him*?" Elias and Lilli said at once.

"Holding in so much anger and sadness. It must be such a heavy burden. It led him to take desperate steps. It caused him to underestimate my Cats of the Castle." He paused as they all bowed their heads. "I allowed them to overtake me. Sensing he'd need a bargaining chip, I had no doubt they would bring me to Mintz, and that was where I'd find all of you. Just as I trusted you'd find a way to free me."

"Okay, just so I'm clear," said Elias, raising a paw, "that sign isn't the keyhole? There's nothing behind it, right?"

"Well, not entirely," Thurl winked. "There is something behind that glass. A night sensor for the security system."

"Uh oh," smiled Kimball. "So, when Mintz placed his palm over the sign, he triggered a silent alarm in the security office."

"Yes," said Thurl. "An alarm he wouldn't know is connected to the switchboard by a separate electrical system from Walt's private club, and therefore he would not have instructed his raccoon technician to gnaw through its wires."

"Which means a pack of security guards should come barreling through New Orleans Square any second now," Kimball said.

"Precisely," said Thurl. "Which is why it's an excellent time for us to be moving along. Let us go try to be of assistance to our Oliver, in the event Mintz catches up to him, before the guards catch up to Mintz."

Chapter Twelve

Oliver was hauling tail across the park to lead Mintz away from his friends. He was sprinting on all four paws, occasionally slowing to glance over his shoulder, making certain Mintz was indeed giving chase. When he reached Frontierland, Oliver stopped and waited for Mintz to catch up then bolted off again when the human appeared a few yards away. He made a hard right at the Golden Horseshoe and on toward the hub. He could hear Mintz panting behind him.

Oliver shot past the lavender-and-pink tent-shaped Royal Theatre and around the front of Sleeping Beauty Castle. His strategy was to lead Mintz in front of every security camera he could, in the hopes they'd been repaired. Since there was no way to know if the system was back on-line, he figured the more twists and turns he made, the better the chances of running into a roving security detail. At the very least they might find Louie and Pete. *Better than nothing*, he thought.

Oliver paused at the Partners statue to catch his breath. He leaned on the guard rail and peered up at the bronze visage of Walt and his beloved creation, Mickey.

"Don't worry, sir," Oliver said. "I'm not going to let him take over your park. I promise. I don't care what I have to do. I won't let either of you down." As he spoke, the white beam of Mintz's flashlight bobbed toward him in the distance. Oliver trotted to the middle of the hub, making sure Mintz saw him.

"Run all you like, cat! I won't rest until I have that key, and you're dangling from the monorail by your tail!"

"That's some serious anger your holding onto, Doc. This is Disney. You should let it go!" Oliver turned and took off again, rounding the castle toward Fantasyland. It spilled out between Alice in Wonderland and the Matterhorn.

Alice, Oliver thought to himself. He made a hard right, almost tripping over his own tail. He stopped at the edge of the attraction. Mintz came jogging toward him, panting and waving his flashlight over his head like a club. His round glasses were fogged up and his red scarf hung loosely around his nose and mouth.

"How about it, Sorrell? I think it's time you finally took that ride through Wonderland?"

Oliver ran around to the front, and there was the attraction in all its storybook glory. The top was a castle of beige bricks with squared towers. All around it were abnormally tall, feather-shaped leaves colored pink and teal. The bottom of the show building looked like an underground burrow with a dark tunnel that carried guests into the adventure. Above the cavernous façade, another curvy track swerved in and out of the castle along a rooftop.

Out in front of the ride, a large book with a picture of a yellow-haired girl in a blue dress stood atop a giant yellow mushroom. Oliver looked across the road at the Mad Tea Party. By day guests sat inside giant white tea cups with colorful accents, and the ride sent them twirling and whirling in circles. *Ugh*, Oliver thought. It seemed like a recipe for losing your breakfast. Now the cups, with their yellow and pink and blue and purple designs sat dormant on their giant turntable.

Oliver heard Mintz running up behind him just as a castle door swung open and an empty vehicle shaped like a pink caterpillar rolled out. It idled at the load area, awaiting guests to board, unconcerned about the time. Oliver squeezed through the short iron fence in front of the ride and climbed into the seat, ignoring the disapproving look on the caterpillar's face. Mintz was bent over on the street in front of the attraction, wheezing, trying to catch his breath. Oliver gave him a wave and patted his vest as he disappeared through the cave entrance.

Mintz clumsily swung one long leg over the railing, but he hooked his other knee, falling forward. He caught himself, somewhat, stumbling uncontrollably, nearly crashing into the wall. In a moment, another caterpillar appeared in the load area, this one green, but with the same smug expression. Mintz climbed inside. His long legs and knobby knees folded up, visible over the front. Mintz shook the sides of his caterpillar, angry it wouldn't move faster. He swerved slowly along the track, left then right then left again, his head starting to swim.

"This is ridiculous," Mintz hissed. He awkwardly stood up in the ride vehicle and swung one leg out over the side. He swiveled around, pulling his other leg up. His shoe caught the concrete and he nearly fell out altogether. Just as he found his balance, the head of the caterpillar turned sharply and bumped his backside. Mintz tumbled over again, barely putting his hands out to catch the guard rail, before falling face first on the concrete.

"Oh, this horrible ride," Mintz growled, more irritated than ever. "This horrible park. These infernal cats! I'll string up every one by the tail!" Mintz got to his feet, straightened his glasses which were hanging askew across his face, and smoothed the lapels of his coat. The cat would be deep inside the attraction by now. There was little sense in chasing after it. Mintz looked around for an idea. Behind him empty caterpillars continued to emerge from the exit. During operational hours, they would be unloading mesmerized guests returning from Wonderland. He turned his gaze to the roof, where another track zig-zagged overhead. Mintz pried open the exit door. He had an idea.

Inside the attraction, Oliver watched as cabinets, lamps, and other furniture swirled over his head. A door handle with a yellow face invited him to have a look around. A white rabbit in a red jacket and yellow waistcoat hopped by, apparently late for something. Alice, the yellow-haired girl from the book atop the mushroom, chased after him.

Oliver's caterpillar made a sharp turn and there was a rotund little man standing over him in a yellow shirt and little red cap. Suddenly he split into two silly twins. The caterpillar rolled on, encountering that white rabbit, now checking his pocket watch. Ollie continued through a garden of giant, singing flowers. Something about this strange glowing world full of fantastic sights made Oliver's tail twitch, like some crazy dream after too much tuna, he thought, and maybe a bite of catnip.

Oliver spied something almost familiar. A cat, hanging upside down with a giant grin as though it concealed a family's parakeet in its mouth. This unusual feline's fur was pink with purple stripes. Could there be another former Castle Cat living in exile? Before Oliver's eyes, the colorful cat's entire body disappeared, leaving two yellow eyes and wide smile. A second later, all traces of the cat vanished completely.

"What kind of crazy ride is this?" he wondered aloud. "It's so weird. I like it!"

Things continued to get stranger. An owl with an accordion neck. A large honking horn, surrounded by little baby horns. The pink cat reappeared pointing him further into the attraction. Oliver's caterpillar turned a corner and encountered a battalion of guards wearing playing cards for armor. Red hoods gave their heads the appearance of upside-down hearts. They marched in formation holding heart-tipped spears. The white rabbit appeared and announced the presence of the queen. There she stood, a robust woman with large cheeks and clown lips. She was holding some poor bird by its legs, swinging it like a golf club.

A strange little rolled-up rodent, similar to a hedgehog, served as her ball. The Queen of Hearts gave it a whack and sent the poor creature spiraling into a tree. When Oliver rounded the next bend, there was her majesty again, her arms raised, screaming in anger. The queen is quick, Oliver thought. Behind her stood more card soldiers, including one in a black hood wielding an intimidating axe. Her infuriated cries indicated she was angry with Oliver for ruining her game, and she demanded his head.

"What?" Oliver gasped. "I didn't do anything. You want a head, swing for the guy behind me. He's wearing glasses and scarf! He's the bad guy!"

As Oliver realized his pleas fell on the deaf ears of an animatronic queen, his caterpillar sped toward a swirling vortex of purple and black. Panicked, Oliver gripped hold of the safety bar. Just as it seemed he would be sucked into the swirling storm, the doors opened and he was thrust outside into the night. Oliver had forgotten the overhead track. Down below, the Mad Tea Party cups, which moments before had been quiet and still, were now spinning around their table without a single rider, while jovial calliope music filled the air. The colored lanterns that hung around it were now shining bright.

Once again, a ride that should have been dark was operating as if it were the middle of the day. Could this truly be the magic of the park? His caterpillar swerved along the outdoor track. Large leaves of pink, green, and blue grew tall on all sides. Oliver peered over the side to the street, hoping to see park security surrounding the attraction. Yet aside from the cups spinning and music piping through the breeze, there was not a single sign of life. HIs caterpillar turned back toward the castle. The doors burst open and for a split second Oliver saw glowing tea pots and cups of many colors bouncing and steaming ahead. He could hear fun party music playing inside. Oliver rolled through the doors, excited to see this scene, when something clamped down on the scruff of his neck and yanked him forcefully out. Oliver turned to see his own frightened face reflected in a pair of round glasses.

"So sorry, cat," said Mintz, holding Oliver in the air. "No merry unbirthday for you!"

Oliver began hissing and desperately swatting at Mintz. He was far enough away that his claws couldn't reach. Mintz wagged his gloved finger at him.

"No, no, no, you bad kitty," Mintz said. He began shaking Oliver up and down. "You brought this on yourself. Do you think I enjoy touching the bane of my allergenic existence? It's time someone de-cat-ified this theme park!"

"You...want...the...key?" Oliver said between shakes. "It's inside my vest. Go ahead, reach in and take it. I don't care anymore."

"Don't even think about scratching me," Mintz threatened, ceasing to shake him but tightening his grip to give Oliver a painful jolt.

"Wouldn't dream of it," Oliver winced. He held up his paws. "Look, claws in. I'm done fighting. The game is over. Just take it."

"There now," Mintz said, feeling victorious, "I prefer this attitude. Isn't it easier to simply give up when you're bested? You're a cat. I'm a human. A rather smart one at that. You never had a chance." He loosened his hold on Oliver's neck. Overcome with glee at his impending victory and the fortune that would follow, Mintz hastily slid his hand inside the cat's vest.

In fact, he jammed it in so forcefully, it made it all the easier for the open pin of the old tin sheriff's badge to poke right through his thick rubber glove and burrow deep into his index finger.

"Gaaaaah!" Mintz screamed. He yanked his hand back and forth, trying desperately to pull it out of the cat's vest. Despite his predicament, the sight made Oliver laugh uncontrollably, even as he was shaken like a rag doll. Finally, Mintz pulled his hand out, revealing the badge stuck in his finger.

"Ooh, that's gotta hurt," Oliver said, knowing it would only antagonize him. "You're going to want First Aid to take a look at that. Maybe a princess bandage might help."

"You nasty animal," Mintz growled between gnashed teeth. The pain was excruciating. His hand throbbed as the sharp pin penetrated deep into the meat of his finger. "You tricked me! Where is the key?"

"I never had it, Mintz," Oliver said. "It wasn't on Splash Mountain! I don't have a clue where Imagineering hid it. None of us does."

"You deceived me!" Mintz roared in an almost possessed voice.

"This grudge is going to destroy you, Sorrell," Oliver said. "Even if you find the key. Which, by the way, you're never going to. The Cats of the Castle will always be there to stop you, with or without me."

"Never!" Mintz spat. "I will find that key! I will tear that cotton candy castle down, brick by brick if I have to."

"Why?" asked Oliver. "You would deny every child a Disneyland just because you got in trouble?"

"Trouble?" Mintz sneered. "They banned me, for life!"

"You were never banned, Sorrell," Mintz yelled at him. "They were just trying to scare you. All you had to do was come back, return the dust, and say you were sorry. They would have let you back in."

"ENOUGH!" Mintz roared. He swung Oliver around in the air, shoving him against a tall pink fiberglass leaf. He twisted his hand and clamped his rubber-clad fingers around the cat's furry throat. They were both shocked to find the giant leaf gave way, bending backward the harder Mintz pressed Oliver against it.

"This is the end, cat," Mintz growled, pushing his coat sleeve up with his free hand, even with the gold star still protruding from his finger.

"Not...yet...," Oliver choked as the grip on his neck got tighter. The leaf bent further back with a groan. Oliver was looking straight up at the night sky. He swiped his claws at Mintz's face. He missed any skin but hooked the red scarf and yanked it away, revealing Mintz's pointy nose and quivering lip. It only took a moment after that.

"Ah-achoo!" Mintz immediately broke into another sneezing fit. "I...*achoo*...hate...*achoo*...cats!"

Whenever Mintz sneezed his whole body convulsed. As dark clouds were forming in the corners of his eyes, Oliver saw that as Mintz sneezed, the sleeve of his coat pulled further away, exposing his pale white flesh. Instinctively Oliver reached out and dug four claws deep into his skin, drawing stripes of ruby red blood. Mintz was mid-sneeze when the pain hit.

"*Ah-chaaaaaaaah!*" Mintz cried. His hand released Oliver's neck as he stumbled back. He reached for his arm which now had a searing pain rippling through it. Had there been even a second, Oliver would have felt relief at the loosening around his neck. However, the moment Mintz stopped pushing him against the flat leaf behind him, it sprang forward with incredible force, flinging the cat like a stone launched from a slingshot. Or, like a cat-apult. That leaf had been another forgotten "quick escape" installed at Walt's request. If he'd had time to think about it, Oliver might have made a mental note to add it to Kimball's map.

The young cat ordained to lead the Royal Order of Cats of the Castle found himself sailing helplessly, paws flailing, through the air. Over the whistling in his pointy ears, he could hear the cheery tunes of the Mad Tea Party and saw the colorful blur of party lanterns around him. Oliver had one last idea. He grabbed his sword and hooked it over the nearest light cable holding the lanterns. Gripping the end of the plastic blade, he pulled down and slid across the chord like a zip line. It seemed a good idea in the moment, right up to the part he found himself speeding toward a big blue lantern, unable to slow down. The light erupted in a shower of hot sparks and glass when he hit it. That was the last thing Oliver saw, sparks, and then everything went dark.

Mintz stood on the rooftop, his bleeding arm pulled against his chest, wrapped inside his coat. His other hand was going numb from the Sheriff badge lodged in his finger. Suddenly he was bathed in white light. He attempted to shield his face with his scarf but only succeeded in bumping the badge against his chest. The pain made his eyes cross behind his glasses. Mintz began to feel woozy.

"You up there," a voice called out. "Do not move! This is Disneyland Security! You are trespassing! The police are already at the gates so don't bother running. Sit down on the ground and place your hands over your head."

Mintz began to lift his hands when his stomach fluttered and his knees gave out. Just as he began to faint, Mintz made out the dark shapes of security guards running out of the attraction toward him. A few minutes later, Anaheim Police officers had revived him. A paramedic had extracted the pin from his finger and bandaged his arm. The police led Sorrel Mintz out of Fantasyland with his wrists behind his back in handcuffs. As Elias, Kimball, Lilli, and Thurl watched from hiding, security officer Pete Klemme and his partner Louie Prima returned from checking out a disturbance in New Orleans Square.

"What did you boys find?" asked Tony Forte, the night captain.

"Eh, mostly nothing," said Pete. "A knocked-over garbage can. Some broken glass somebody better sweep up."

"Tell him about the other thing," Louie said. "About animal control."

"Animal control?" Forte asked.

"Well, we might know who chewed the alarm wires," said Pete.

"It's a raccoon," added Louie. "Ugliest thing I've ever laid eyes on. He had his head stuck in one of the clay honey pots from the Pooh meet and greet. It was kinda funny, actually. He tried to scurry away with it stuck on his noggin. I wanted to record it for one of those shows where people send in funny home videos."

"Okay," said Forte, "I got it. So what did you do about it?"

"Well, that's a weird story too," said Pete. "We found this old tin washtub, all banged up. Some genius attached wheels to it. Not sure what it was doing there, but we trapped the raccoon underneath and set a trash can on top of it."

"Yeah," said Louie, nervously adjusting his belt, "that's when we called Anaheim Animal Control. They said they'll come take care of it."

"Good job, boys," Forte said. "Maybe we should create a special Rat & Raccoon Patrol."

"Nah," Pete smiled. He looked back over his shoulder. Lilli was certain he was staring right at the bushes where they were hiding. Slowly the tall guard looked back at his colleagues. "I'm pretty sure that's taken care of."

"What about that doctor?" Louie asked.

"We got him on two counts of trespassing, breaking and entering, destruction of private property," Forte answered. He held up the gold sherriff's pin, inside a clear plastic bag. "He had this tin star from Frontierland on him. It's not from any of the shops. Might be a collectible."

"You're kidding," said Louie, wide-eyed. "I haven't seen one like that since I was a kid. That should be on display somewhere. Wonder where he found it."

"Not sure," Forte shrugged. "We'll let the Disney Archive figure it out. Plus we saw him throw something off the top of the ride. So weird. It looked like a plush. Probably stolen from the Emporium or some other gift shop. Some of the other guys got a little better look and swore it looked like a cat wearing a vest, and a sword."

"I don't remember any Disney movies about cats with swords," said Louie. "Well, there was a cat in one of those movies about that ogre, you know, with the donkey."

"That wasn't Disney!" Pete snapped.

"Either way," Forte interrupted, "he could've been dangerous to our guests. He shot out one of the Mad Tea Party lights somehow. Looked like fireworks. This Mintz clearly hates this park. Guess the old guards really scared him as a kid. Somebody should've told him the BFL isn't real."

"What's a BFL?" Louie asked. "Bacon, French fries, and lettuce?"

"The banned-for-life list," Pete said.

"Anyway, he's going to be sitting in a jail cell for a while because of it," said Forte.

When all the humans were finally out of sight, the cats emerged from their hiding places.

"Oliver," Lilli called out, her paws cupped around her mouth.

"Yo, kid," Elias called. "Where are you?"

"I'm concerned about the exploding lantern," Kimball confided to Thurl.

"Yes," Thurl nodded softly. "So am I. Let's keep looking, and keep thinking positive thoughts."

"Hu-hu-hey," they heard a voice from the tea cups. All four cats ran that way, their eyes darting in every direction. It took a moment, but finally Kimball spotted it. A black arm with a white paw sticking up out of a cup with a swirly blue design. "C-c-ca-can somebody hu-help get out of this thing?"

Another arm appeared, and Oliver hoisted his head up and hung it over the side in exhaustion. Oliver was alive.

"Ollie!" Lilli screamed and ran to him, followed closely by Elias.

Even on the tips of their claws they could barely reach the top of the cup. Elias took hold of Oliver's paws and carefully pulled him over. They each hooked an arm under Oliver's shoulders and gently helped him to his feet. His fur was singed and he had bare pink patches over his body from the sparks of the exploding light, but there seemed to be no damage that wouldn't heal.

"You alright, kid?" Elias asked.

"I, uh," Oliver started, head bobbing from side to side, "I don't think I like that ride."

"Oliver, you're okay," said Kimball, who was helping Thurl hustle over. "Look what we found in the street!" Kimball held out a plastic handle with hardened blob of melted gray goo hanging from the end. It was his sword.

"T-t-told you it would come in handy," Oliver managed a smile.

"Yeah, well, good thing I gave it to you," Elias ribbed him. Oliver moaned. "Oh, sorry, kid."

Elias hoisted Oliver onto his own back and carried him. All of the Castle Cats began to slowly make their way to the castle.

"Where's Mu—Mu…" Oliver stuttered. "Where's Doctor Owl?"

"That bird's in a cage," Elias smirked. "You did good, Oliver."

When they made it back to the castle, Thurl and Lilli examined Oliver's wounds. All were indeed superficial. He would heal up fine in short time.

The cats rested all that night and late into the next day. Except Lilli, who spent much of the night in Oliver's doorway, making sure he was okay. Before retiring to his own bed that night, relieved the park was safe and proud of his Order, Thurl stared up at the picture of Mr. Disney and Mister Lincoln. He imagined even Walt might say "that'll work" knowing the Cats of the Castle had once again defeated a threat to the park. At least for another night.

Epilogue

The next night, when the park closed and all the guests had gone home or returned to their hotels, the Cats of the Castle went to work once again, fanning out through the park. Mintz and Scavenge were contained in their own respective cages, far away from Disneyland. The three rats were missing, but no one considered them a threat on their own. They wouldn't be returning.

Once the other cats left for their respective lands, and Lilli had given Oliver a good long hug, Thurl followed them out the secret door and across the stepping stones. He asked Oliver to walk with him. They ended up near the banks of the Rivers of America, quietly watching the moon's reflection on the water. In the reflection, the *Mark Twain*'s black smoke stacks disappeared in the dark water but the gold caps reflected magnificently like two royal crowns. Only a few ducks disturbed the serenity of the calm water as they caught a late-night snack below. It was a peaceful night.

"How are you feeling, son?" Thurl finally asked.

"I'm fine," Oliver shrugged. "Tired. Sore. Wishing I hadn't let Kimball cover my bald patches with a black marker. But otherwise, I'm fine."

"How are you feeling?" Thurl asked again.

Oliver took a minute. "Frustrated. Overwhelmed. Unprepared for anything."

"I am not surprised, but you shouldn't. I am so proud of you. Of all of you. You came together as a team. As a result, you saved the park."

"We didn't find the key."

"True, but you led Mintz to park security," said Thurl. "As I understand human laws, he'll only be in jail a few years, but the immediate threat is gone. More importantly, you sacrificed your safety to protect your friends, and me. That is courage. That's leadership. You even turned Baxter's heart around, at least for a moment. You may not feel ready for leadership, but true leaders rarely do, at first."

"That's another issue," Oliver said, embarrassed, trying to redirect. "What should we do about Baxter? Should I reach out to him?"

"That is not to be decided tonight. We'll take kitten steps with Baxter. He has shown that a Cat of the Castle still resides somewhere in his soul. But so does the creature that tossed you over a waterfall. Baxter is still dangerous. Let us simply celebrate the tiny victories for now, and see what time reveals."

They were both silent again. After a few minutes Thurl rose with a groan, leaning on his staff. Oliver helped him straighten up. They began to walk again.

"I was just doing what I had to do," Oliver said, almost absently, looking at the castle. "This is my home. I couldn't let Mintz take it away. Where would I go?"

"Nice try," Thurl chuckled. "I will accept that response for now, but we both know your own welfare was the last thing on your mind. Now Mintz, he only thought of himself. He had no idea of the repercussions of his plans. This place is much more than a theme park."

"You've said that before. What do you mean?"

"This world of man is full of darkness. Disneyland provides light. Without this park, the darkness would consume mankind. In time you will learn that Mr. Disney was more than just a man who made cartoons. Disneyland is not an amusement park. Disneyland is an engine of joy. Disneyland manufactures magic."

"You really believe that, don't you?" Oliver marveled, looking into the old cat's eyes.

"Oliver, you don't understand," Thurl stopped and looked directly at him. "It's not what I believe. It's the truth. There are things in this world that man does not see. Walt was able to see, with help."

"The fairies?"

"Among others. That's why he had to build this park, and build it his way. The world needed Disneyland. The world will always need Disneyland."

The words washed over Oliver. He didn't completely understand and yet it made perfect sense. He felt more connected to the park, and more responsible than ever. He could feel the energy that surrounded them. Oliver felt proud to be a part of it, but he also felt the weight of responsibility to protect it resting heavily on his shoulders.

"We probably should find that key," Oliver said after they walked a little farther. "I'd sleep better knowing where it was."

"Ah, yes, well about that," Thurl chuckled. "Funny thing. This morning, a senior Imagineer received a small note on his chair, strongly suggesting it was time to move the key."

"Seriously? Wait, how do you...did you tell? Did you know where it was?"

"The key will remain safe," Thurl said. "I trust it will find a new hiding place within the week. We needn't speak of it any more today."

"But if you did know all along.... I mean, why not just tell us? Why send us on an crazy adventure? Why send me to the Oracle?"

"My boy," Thurl chuckled, placing a gentle palm on his face, "I didn't send you to learn the truth about the key. I sent you to discover the truth about yourselves." He straightened his lopsided purple cap and turned to walk back to the castle.

Oliver thought about his words. It was true. He learned he was a leader. He had a legacy to uphold. They all did. The adventure made them a real team. Still, there was something else bugging him that he couldn't quite let go.

"I just have one more question."

"Of course you do," Thurl laughed. He stopped by the petrified tree. He slipped under the small guard rail and leaned against the old stump with a playful sigh. His eyes sparkled in the moonlight. "Very well."

"Even if Mintz had gotten to the key," Oliver began, "well, as I said, a key needs a keyhole, right? There was always one last hope—if Mintz couldn't find the lock, he couldn't use the key, right?"

"You know, I believe you're right," Thurl grinned. "Walt was a wise man. Just a few years after opening Disneyland he decided that the key presented too much danger to his creation. He couldn't destroy it, but he could render it powerless. Without the lock in which to turn it, the key was useless. So he did the next best thing. He hid the keyhole. And hid it in such a way, it would likely never be found."

"And you know where it is, don't you?" Oliver pressed playfully.

"Perhaps," Thurl answered sheepishly, stroking his white beard. "But I'm afraid, at least for now, I cannot say where." Thurl patted the old tree memorial with his paw. He let out a forced sigh and again slapped his paw against the side of the petrified stump, this time considerably louder, almost deliberately. "No, Oliver, I'm sorry. I just can't tell you where that lock is hidden."

The elder feline looked at his ward and winked. He grabbed his staff and shuffled off toward the castle, whistling while he walked.

"I'm pretty sure I just missed something," Oliver mumbled, watching Thurl hobble off.

"It's alright, Oliver," Thurl called back. "You'll probably never need to know. Lock and key are safely hidden, that's all that matters. Now, off you go. Protect your legacy."

"You know," Oliver laughed as he watched Thurl go, "I could be a much better leader with some of this information you're keeping to yourself."

"Yes, I suppose," Thurl said without looking back. He cracked a smile, knowing Oliver couldn't hear him anymore. "But who said you're the only leader?"

That same night Oliver returned to New Orleans Square. All was quiet, as it should be. At least on the French Quarter streets. A certain Colonial-style building with blue iron features and three dark archways stood empty, waiting for morning. But hidden behind its walls was another famous Disneyland attraction. One where raucous buccaneers pillaged and plundered and drank rum, all to a catchy tune. It should've been dormant until guests arrived the next day, but after all the unexplained activity of the past few days, Oliver couldn't help but wonder what might be going on inside. He left New Orleans Square to do a lap around Main Street, and hopefully bump into Lilli.

Of course, the queue for Pirates of the Caribbean was currently deserted and the ovens of the Blue Bayou restaurant inside had been cold for hours. But the music of a slow banjo plunked along on the air. The disembodied voice of a phantom pirate warned it was too late to alter course. The sea turned rough and a waterfall cast long boats into another time. A pirate ship launched cannonballs at an old Caribbean fort. Scallywag pirates dunked the town mayor in a well, trying to force the whereabouts of some notorious captain. Amid a steady stream of empty boats that floated along the canal, a single rider in a hooded gray cloak pulled up over their furry head, feet dangling gleefully above the bottom of the boat, was enjoying the piratical display.

The boat floated under a bridge and past one tubby pirate sitting on the dock, bragging about his treasure map and flaunting a large gold key. The rider's eyes went wide. No, that wasn't it. The shape wasn't right. A trio of pirates, accompanied by a smiling donkey, sang a lively shanty about the life of a pirate, or something. It was quite catchy.

Soon the port town was lit up in oranges and reds, as flames raged inside the buildings. The pirates had set fire to the town they'd just sacked. The lone passenger had no fear, watching it all with a bemused grin. The ride led the boat into a flooded prison where locked-up pirates attempted to entice a yellow dog with the cell keys hanging in its mouth. The stronghold looked to be in terrible shape. Rafters were split and beams were broken. Flames crackled beyond their tiny windows. Up ahead on either side of the canal, pirates exchanged gunfire while two barrels of powder hung precariously between them. One stray shot and *kaboom!* That's what the boss had said. Although it had never happened in 60 years. Just part of the story.

The boat passed under the dangling powder kegs and up ahead, someone was singing and boasting of his exploits. This was it. The rider waited until the eerie blue glow of the treasure room came into sight, just as it had been described. The pirate came into view, a red scarf around his head and black circles around his eyes, tipped back in a throne fit for a king. Along the canal wall was one stone jutting out, as if set there on purpose. The rider stood up on the seat and sprang effortlessly over the side of the boat, flipping in the air and landing on the pedestal. The rogue pirate captain didn't seem to notice or mind. He was deep in his own revelry.

The hooded rider scaled the stones in the wall to the treasure room. There were boxes and chests of treasure all around the pirate's feet and scattered about the room. But it was the big one over his left shoulder that mattered. On the face of it hung a heavy lock but upon close inspection, it was not fastened. The intruder reached out a hairy arm which also looked blue in the light but was actually covered in beige fur. The lock slid out of the latch easily. Inside, the chest was loaded with gold coins. Not the pretend kind found in the gift shop, either. These were solid gold, meant as an enticement, or at least a diversion to would-be thieves.

Not to be dissuaded from the task at hand, the small thief dug through the cool coins until the real treasure was discovered. Held high in the blue light it was astonishing, the handle indeed shaped like a D, encrusted with red rubies and rare blue diamonds. This key would be worth a fortune, for its composition and the power it possessed. Few human eyes had ever seen it, as even fewer knew it existed at all.

"He will be so happy," the bandit said softly, pulling back her hood. She stowed the key in a drawstring sack at her waist. She leapt up onto a shelf and swung hand-over-hand across the rafters, over the belt that carried boats back up, and dropped down, running into the gift shop. Outside she effortlessly scaled the iron rails of the buildings and made her way across the rooftops of New Orleans Square, into the trees of Adventureland. She paused only once at the edge of the Jungle Cruise. She gazed longingly at the quiet rainforest and sighed. Soon, she thought. She dashed over the shops along Main Street, U.S.A. without any chance of being detected. Up the hill and over the railroad tracks, just as the boss had advised to avoid being spotted, and soon she saw the gates. She slid under a turnstile and was out of the park with the key.

The little thief ran across the promenade, using her arms to pull herself along faster, until she reached the curb of Harbor Boulevard where an old white Volkswagen Bug sat idling. The door opened and she jumped in. She chattered wildly at the driver. The door shut and the car screeched away from the curb and drove off into the California night.

About the Author

Bart Scott is a podcaster, writer, husband, and dad in reverse order of importance. Sadly, this Bart Scott never played in the NFL. He lives in the suburbs of Chicago where he enjoys Chicago Blackhawks hockey, watching cartoons with his kids, and the pursuit of the perfect chili dog. As you may have guessed, he also loves all things Disney, especially the Disney theme parks.

More Books from Theme Park Press

Theme Park Press is the largest independent publisher of Disney, Disney-related, and general interest theme park books in the world, with dozens of new releases each year.

Our authors include Disney historians like Jim Korkis and Didier Ghez, Disney animators and artists like Mel Shaw and Eric Larson, and such Disney notables as Van France, Tom Nabbe, and Bill "Sully" Sullivan, as well as many promising first-time authors.

We're always looking for new talent.

In March 2016, we published our 100th title. For a complete catalog, including book descriptions and excerpts, please visit:

ThemeParkPress.com

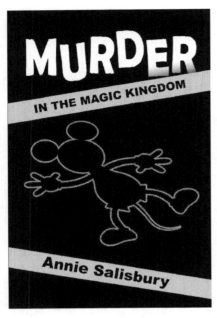

Who's Killing Cast Members?

When Imagineering apprentice Tommy Boyd is found face-down in the waters of the Jungle Cruise, the evidence points to mild-mannered Josh, a Cast Member in Fantasyland. But Josh didn't do it.

themeparkpress.com/books/murder-magic.htm

The Rosetta Stone of Disney Magic

Warning! There be secrets ahead. Disney secrets. Mickey doesn't want you to know how the magic is made, but Jim Korkis knows, and if you read Jim's book, you'll know, too. Put the kids to bed. Pull those curtains. Power down that iPhone. Let's keep this just between us...

themeparkpress.com/books/secret-stories-disney-world.htm

Stuff Even Mickey Doesn't Know

When a theme park has been around for 60 years, it hides a lot of secrets. Disneyland expert Gavin Doyle has swept aside the pixie dust and uncovered little-known stories about the happiest place on earth that will make you a master of the magic.

themeparkpress.com/books/disneyland-secrets.htm

Disney World for the 1%

The rich and famous experience Disney World differently from the rest of us: they're escorted by VIP Tour Guides, elite Cast Members who truly *do* hold the keys to the kingdom. Annie Salisbury was one of these Cast Members, in charge of making the very best magic for those who could afford it.

themeparkpress.com/books/ride-delegate.htm

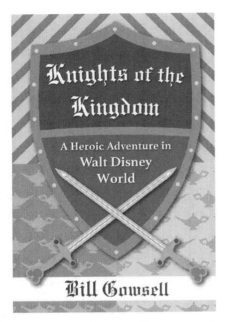

Mayhem in the Magic Kingdom

In 1938, Walt Disney smuggled Aladdin's magic lamp out of Europe and away from the Nazis. Much later, Roy Disney buried the lamp in Walt Disney World and threw away the key to its hidden vault. Now the key has been found. Evil gathers in the Magic Kingdom. The world hangs in the balance!

themeparkpress.com/books/knights-kingdom.htm

Teens Gone Wild... in Disneyland!

When Disneyland announces a contest with the prize an apartment in the Tower of Terror, a group of junior high school friends, the Disney Pros, embark on a scavenger hunt throughout the park, pursued by their villainous principal and a pair of psychotic classmates.

themeparkpress.com/books/disney-pros-unite.htm

Made in the USA
Middletown, DE
09 December 2018